MAGIC INC.

MAGIC INC.

THE EVERMORES CHRONICLES™ BOOK 1

MARTHA CARR

MICHAEL ANDERLE

Cover by Fantasy Book Design

A Michael Anderle Production

LMBPN Publishing
PMB 196, 2540 South Maryland Pkwy
Las Vegas, NV 89109

Version 1.00, October 2021
ebook ISBN: 978-1-68500-583-2
Print ISBN: 978-1-68500-584-9

THE MAGIC INC. TEAM

Thanks to our Beta Readers
Larry Omans, John Ashmore

Thanks to our JIT Readers

Dave Hicks
Zacc Pelter
Jackey Hankard-Brodie
Dorothy Lloyd
Diane L. Smith
Thomas Ogden

Editor

SkyHunter Editing Team

CHAPTER ONE

Kiri glared at the back of Trucker, the giant mole-rat, as it dug its way steadily through the dirt beneath the kemana. The creature was nearly as tall as Kiri and substantially larger. It advanced on four wide paws, the front ones digging the tunnel and the back ones compacting loose soil so they could get past. Dirt covered its short black fur, but the creature didn't seem to mind. Maybe that didn't matter when you were half-blind and spent your life underground.

"Can't you go faster?" Kiri asked. For what he'd paid, he felt like Trucker should've been digging quicker, speeding them through the dirt. The sooner they got there, the less risk that someone would beat him to his prize. Although in fairness, if no one else had managed to steal it in twenty-six thousand years, maybe Kiri didn't need to worry too much about the competition.

Trucker's only response was a noisy fart, a sound that filled the tunnel around Kiri as surely as the smell of it did.

"Dammit, Trucker, I told you already, quit that!"

The mole-rat kept digging.

Kiri sighed. He should've been at home in a place like this. His mother, a good old-fashioned Oriceran gnome, had tried over and over again to make him love their mountain home—from the steep natural valleys to the beautifully built dwarf holds to the tunnels and mountain-side houses that the gnomes lived in. Kiri had never liked those dingy spaces with their stink of dirt and too-close bodies. He'd wanted to get out and see the world. More than that, he'd wanted to own it.

Now the same desire that drove him from the home tunnels had dragged him back into the dirt and smell not only of other gnomes but of a mole-rat with gastric difficulties. Would his mother have been pleased to see him in the depths? Would she have laughed at the irony that he was back here? One thing was for sure. She would've been appalled at why he was underground.

Kiri lifted his flashlight and pointed it past Trucker at the dirt ahead in the futile hope that he might see an opening. The flashlight was a souvenir of a past job when a band of entrepreneurial elves had hired him to rob a bank vault on Earth. It was the only time Kiri had crossed the divide, taking a portal through to the other world tied to Oriceran.

That was a place worth visiting, with its bright flashing screens, wild music, and crazy fashions. Sure, some of that technology was coming through to Oriceran now, but not half as much as he would've liked. One day, when he'd made his fortune, Kiri was going to retire to Earth. He'd watch soap operas and eat pizza all day like he imagined an Earth king would do.

Trucker grunted and turned its pale, wrinkled head to look back at Kiri. Instead of dirt, a wall of iron ore that gleamed dully in the flashlight's beam now blocked the tunnel's end.

"That's not supposed to be there." Kiri scowled.

He spread the fingers of his free hand, triggering one of the spells his financial backers had provided. Normally, he wasn't smart enough to spot people's magical trails, but now they hung in the air all around him, some sparkling, others black and green, more magic than should be underground. Magic from this unique, hidden kemana and the power source hiding here. Magic that was about to make him very rich.

That thought raised Kiri's spirits. He smiled and pointed to the left, following the direction of one of the magical trails.

"That way, Trucker. You should find a way around the ore."

Trucker raised a shovel-like paw, farted, and set off again.

Kiri stood for a moment longer, looking at the magical trails. He also saw the outline of the cloaking spell his employers had given him to hide him from the powerful guards this place was supposed to have. Kiri was never one to turn down free magic, but he didn't think he would need the cloaking. If there was a place he couldn't sneak into, the universe hadn't shown him yet.

They carried on through the darkness. Trucker carved a path through the dirt while Kiri followed, dreaming about what he would do with the money he was being paid for this heist and trying not to worry about what his ruthless employers would do if he failed. Who needed a head anyway?

A *thud* of falling dirt and a grunt from Trucker brought Kiri back into the moment. At last, open air was visible at the end of the tunnel, and a soft glow of magical light. Kiri switched off the flashlight, and under cover of his cloaking spell, squeezed past Trucker to peer out into the kemana.

It was a spectacular space, a vast cavern with buildings carved into its walls and ceiling, their balconies, steps, and doors protruding at angles that utterly defied gravity. Between them, trees and bushes thrust out in ways he was sure they shouldn't. A thick carpet of roots crisscrossed the ground his hole emerged from. Light seemed to emerge from the air itself, gently illuminating everything it fell on.

According to Kiri's employer, this place had remained hidden since before the gates between Oriceran and Earth were last open. It must take a colossal amount of magic to do that and to make this place liveable, but this kemana didn't contain the giant crystal that powered every other one he'd been to. Instead, the tangle of roots thickened in the center of the cave, forming a tight knot where a brighter light shone.

This was it. Kiri hooked the flashlight onto his belt, rubbed his hands in anticipation, and simultaneously quashed the fear that threatened to rise through him. Fear was a terrible leader and not one he ever intended to follow. Sure, this was a step into the unknown. No, he had no idea who protected this place or what they could level against him. Still, he was a professional, and he'd prepared.

A heavy tapping on his shoulder made him jump and

spin with his fists raised. Trucker was squinting at him with what could have been a glare.

"Oh, yeah," Kiri said. It didn't matter if he spoke. As long as he didn't scream or shout, the cloaking spell should hide him. He pulled a pouch of cash from inside his jacket and handed it to Trucker. "There, happy now?"

Trucker took the pouch's string between his teeth, turned, gave one last noxious fart, and started digging again. He'd vanished within seconds, leaving only an empty tunnel behind him.

Time to get to it. Kiri hurried across the kemana, climbing over the thickest roots and jumping over gaps where the tangle disappeared into the ground. His cloaking spell was starting to flicker. That shouldn't be happening. Better to get this over and done with quickly, just in case.

In a house on the kemana's wall, Enfield of the Evermores turned from his stove with a steaming kettle in hand. Something had entered the kemana, a source of unfamiliar magic. He set the kettle down on the table and looked out the window. Sure enough, a gnome was crossing the kemana from a hole between the roots. The gnome's cloaking spell might hide him in the world above, but it couldn't conceal him from the ancient power of the Evermores, the power that protected this place.

Enfield touched two fingers to his throat and thought about the words he wanted to send. In an instant, magic transported them to other Evermores. Then Enfield stepped out of the window and dropped silently to the ground below.

In the center of the kemana, Kiri reached the tight cluster of roots from which light and magic glowed. He climbed up the heap, expecting to see a gap hiding the treasure, but instead, he found more tangled roots with light beaming through the narrow gaps between them. He thrust his hands in, wedging them between the roots, and started to pull them apart.

"You!" Enfield shouted. "Stop that right now!"

Kiri looked up in alarm. How had he been spotted? His spell was still up. Never mind. Get the treasure and get out. He still had time before this pesky guard reached him.

Moaning filled the air, a noise that came from the ground itself as much as from the living, twisting roots. The sound sent a shiver up Kiri's spine.

"Don't look back," he muttered, tugging the roots apart with ever more vigor. This wasn't fear he felt. It was excitement, anticipation, the thrill of the chase. Never fear. He wouldn't follow fear.

The roots parted to reveal a metal box from which the light and magic radiated. It was too simple to be the treasure itself, the sides perfectly smooth. Kiri pulled it out and looked for a catch or a button, something to open the lid.

He glanced up, looking to see how close the guard had got. Instead of running toward him as Kiri had expected, Enfield was running away.

"Why would he..." At last, Kiri let his fear guide him. He slammed a hand down on the top of the box to contain whatever had sent the guard running. It was too late. A crack had appeared around the container's upper edge. The lid flew off. Light and sound burst out, a wild rush of power that obliterated Kiri in an instant.

Enfield looked back. Where the gnome intruder had

stood, nothing but ashes drifted like black snow across the roots.

A creature emerged through that dark drift, a fluid shape made of light and sound. It shifted form every few seconds, becoming a blur of waving lines, a swarm of darting arrows, a hunched man robed in gray, a beast with claws and fangs. Enfield's whole life had centered on this thing, on guarding and containing it, but he'd never seen it. Now that he did, his mouth hung open in horror.

Other Evermores rushed out of the buildings on the walls and ceiling, dropping onto the root floor. Each of them raised a pair of fingers, pointed them at the beast, and readied their magic.

The creature howled, a sound like reality snapping in two, something that made no sense to living ears. Then it bounded across the kemana, shapeshifting with every step. Enfield grasped his courage and stood in its way, only to be flung aside with terrible ease. He crashed to the ground. The creature leaped into the hole through which Kiri had entered the cave and vanished from sight.

Winslow, one of the most senior Evermores, appeared at Enfield's side.

"That was valiant." Winslow helped Enfield to his feet. "I only wish it had been enough. If we don't recapture the monster soon, every single kemana is doomed."

"With all due respect, revered master, are the kemanas what matter most here?" Enfield bowed his head to Winslow, acknowledging the elder's millennia of experience. Beyond him, the gnome's ashes were still falling. "Every magical on Oriceran is in danger from that thing."

"The people and the kemanas, the two are linked, and

so are their fates." Winslow whistled, and the other Evermores gathered around. "We must immediately begin a search to follow the monster's trail and to contain it. Start in the deep forests, in the trees it is used to, and from there…" Winslow hesitated. It had been a long time since he'd seen the surface world. "Well, from there, we will see. The world is in danger. It is time for us to protect it."

CHAPTER TWO

Fran sat in her cubicle, eyes fixed on her monitor, running her gaze across line after line of code. The problem was in here somewhere. She had to work out what it was. Then the purple rabbit would pop out of its hole on command and Bunny Race 3000, the latest Bunnisiom app game, would be that little bit closer to completion.

Fran bobbed her head in time to the music from her podcast. Technically, she wasn't supposed to be listening to it at work, which was why she didn't have her headphones on. Instead, her magic bent the sound emerging from her phone and carried it directly to her ears without anyone else knowing.

Sure, her mom had told her not to use her magic in the open, but did it really matter? These days, humans knew about magicals, and she was hardly going to get locked up by the Silver Griffins for such a simple spell. Her mom hadn't wanted her to work in Silicon Valley either, which just went to show how much moms knew. At the grand old age of twenty-three, Fran was more than old enough to make these decisions for herself.

"Hey, Berryman, I'm talking to you!" A finger tapped on Fran's shoulder, and she spun in her seat so fast that she rotated a full three-sixty and had to turn again. David Wilson, her team leader, was looking down at her. He was wearing a shirt and tie, which meant that he'd been in a management meeting.

Fran thrust one hand behind her back and waved two figures through the air. The sound from her phone stopped, and she smiled up at Wilson.

"Hi, Dave! How was it? Did you tell them my ideas for the bunny? What did they think? They were impressed, right?"

"For crying out loud, Berryman, cool your rockets." Wilson shook his head. "Between the roller skates and the constant chatter, it's like working with a kid."

"But you told them my ideas?"

"I did."

"And?"

"They said no."

"But they're good ideas, Dave! They'll make the game more dynamic and reduce the risk of it bugging out. We could even use this as a chance to—"

"What part of 'no' don't you understand, Berryman?"

Fran scowled and crossed her arms. "Why not?"

"Because the design's locked in. Because the marketing's begun. Because they're happy with what they have. Pick a reason. They're all true."

"Let me meet them next time. I can convince them."

"No, you can't because the real reason they said no is that no one cares about the opinion of a junior debugger."

"That's not fair! I know more about programming than half those overstuffed suits. I've put my heart and soul into this game since I've been here."

"You've been here six weeks."

"Six weeks in which I've worked really hard."

"And yet." Wilson shrugged. "Get over it, Berryman, and get back to debugging."

Fran's scowl deepened. This wasn't how life was supposed to work. It certainly wasn't why she'd come to Silicon Valley. Whatever happened to inspiration and innovation and all the other things that Bunnisiom Inc. listed in their value statement?

"This is crap, Dave, and you know it."

Wilson pressed thumb and forefinger against his eyes. "Please don't make me write you up again. Your completion bonus is already gonna be shit."

"I don't care about my bonus. I care about what we make, unlike the stupid directors."

"Seriously, you know the rules, and this is going into your monthly evaluation."

"You know what, don't bother. I'm wasting my skills here anyway. I quit."

Fran shoved her phone into her pocket, grabbed her backpack and her roller skates from under the desk, and got out of her seat. Wilson stood staring at her.

"What?" she asked. "Are you gonna make me work my notice month?"

"You know this is a good job, right, Berryman? The pay, the medical cover, we even get decent leave."

"No, Dave, this is a nonsense job." Her voice rose, and other programmers peered over the walls of their cubicles to see what was going on. "We don't get to program properly, we don't get to be creative, and we still lose way more in crunch time than we gain in holidays. I'm done."

"Fine." Wilson held out his hand. "Pass."

Fran yanked her security pass on its lanyard over her head and slapped it into his hand, then stormed out of the room. She was halfway down the corridor before she realized that now she couldn't get out of the building.

At least, not by normal means.

Still furious, Fran strode into a bathroom. It was empty, but she headed into one of the stalls anyway, in case anyone came in. Once she'd safely bolted the door, she opened her backpack, stuffed her skates in, and took out a mirror.

On its front, the mirror seemed fairly ordinary, a silvery disk the size of her hand. The frame was a little odd, with wires soldered onto the sides and a couple of crystals glued onto the top, but that could've been decoration. Combining bits of technology and nature was popular among a certain sort of artists and designers, a trend recently labeled Neo-Age.

The mirror would've fit in well among the cheap goods in tourist traps and head shops across Silicon Valley. However, while those other objects were for show, this was for real. Fran knew that for sure because she'd made it.

She turned the mirror over and examined the tangle of wires, circuits, and magical runes on its back. She'd started disabling the mirror when not using it after that mess where it had accidentally triggered, and rustroaches had gotten into the office. She should probably add an on-off switch when she had some spare time.

She might have that time now after she'd impulsively quit her dream job.

No. This wasn't a dream. It was a waking nightmare of frustration and pointless activity. Her dream job was running her own business, inventing and producing devices that would make a real difference to people's lives, not another app game designed to hook people to their phones all day. Maybe now was the time to make that dream come true.

She slid a couple of detached wires into their slots on the back of the mirror, then turned it over. A soft magical glow filled the glass. Fran touched a finger to that light, and it rippled like the surface of a pool.

As the motion subsided, she saw a landscape viewed from the air. It was part of Oriceran, Earth's magical twin world, the two connected by magical gates. This was her home stretch of Oriceran, a coastline across the waters from where the Light Elves lived. Off the coast, clouds swirled darkly around the towers of Trevilsom Prison, the island jail that held the worst magicals. That wasn't what interested her.

She spread her fingers and light flowed from them, catching the sensors on the sides of the mirror and focusing the spell. The view zoomed in, closing on the coastline and the urban sprawl there. A dense collection of ingenuity and industry trapped between two steep stretches of hills, Silicon Valley's magical mirror world: Mana Valley.

The magic that Fran's mom had taught her was useful,

these enhanced spells that other witches and wizards didn't seem to have. When she was younger, Fran would've traded them all in for the ordinary spells other witches used to be able to work with more than light and sound. As she'd grown older, she'd come to appreciate them and to see how she could achieve things that others couldn't when she set her mind to it.

Still, it wasn't the spells themselves that Fran took real pleasure in. It was when she combined them with her other skills. It was moments like this.

The view shifted at dizzying speed, hurtling in toward the streets of Mana Valley. Buildings and people shot past as she zoomed in ever closer to her destination, then stopped under the trees in the park outside her apartment building. Perfect.

Fran stood, slung her backpack over her shoulder, and snapped her fingers. There was a flash of light, and she was standing in the park. In her hand, the mirror briefly showed her a Silicon Valley bathroom before she touched the mirror again and the image rippled away, replaced by her reflection.

It was a moment's work to disable the mirror again, then Fran slipped it back into her pack. Some people might've considered it an unnecessary gadget. Why have that when you could take a portal back and forth between Earth and Oriceran? But the mirror was safe, it was reliable, it was easy to control, and above all, it could work for people who couldn't summon portals. There had to be a market for a thing like that.

Perhaps that would be her new business. Fran considered the possibility as she headed for the door of the apartment building. She had so many ideas. The problem wouldn't be coming up with something to produce. It would be keeping herself from getting distracted by the rest.

As she opened the door, a crow swept down out of the trees and settled on Fran's shoulder. It eyed her, the doorway, then her again.

"Yes, I have some seeds for you." Fran smiled. "Come on in. I figure we both deserve a treat."

CHAPTER THREE

Nightmare creatures swirled around the Darkness Between Dreams, things of teeth and claws and monstrous hunger, insincerity and insecurity, and moments of terrible shame. They were the stuff dread was made of, and the Darkness Between Dreams loved every one of them.

"I know, my pets," it said, tentacles rippling out to caress the creatures as they passed. "This isn't the place for you. Too little prey. Too few minds to latch onto. No warm bodies to chase."

The creatures howled at the swirling wasteland around them, where skeletal trees loomed over acid rivers and rot rained down from a scab red sky. It was the world they'd been born into, one they most perfectly fitted, the world that the Darkness Between Dreams ruled. It was their everything, and it was nowhere near enough.

"Soon," the Darkness Between Dreams promised. "I'll find a way. I'll crack open the precious shell of magic protecting Earth and Oriceran. You'll come streaming out, a tidal wave of dark glory, and we'll seize a new hunting ground. Then when we've stripped that one dry, just like that, we'll move on again."

It sighed. "But first, I have to make a crack in that shell, a gap that will let more than me through. Until then..." It shrugged, a gesture that turned into a rippling wave of its tentacles. "Until then, I must leave you."

Five tentacles rose and scratched a magical symbol in the air. The deep red of the air parted, and a clear light shone through. The nightmare creatures reared back from it, howling in distress.

"This is why I must go through alone," the Darkness Between Dreams said. "To make somewhere safe for you. I'll be back, my pretties. I promise."

The Darkness Between Dreams stepped into the light, through a rift in the wall of its reality, and emerged into an office. It was a large, expensively decorated space, with one large desk of red hardwood, a firmly upholstered chair, and a pair of abstract paintings on the walls. The windows in the far wall looked out from twenty floors up across the sprawling, irregular mess of Mana Valley.

"Oh yes," the Darkness Between Dreams muttered, its fleshy lips framing a grin of pointed teeth. "Soon, I'll make a home for my people."

The portal closed with a sound like tearing fabric, cutting off the sounds of howling, and the Darkness Between Dreams stood alone. It picked up the skin suit that hung over the back of a chair and squeezed its writhing body down to fit inside, the tips of tentacles wriggling into the fingers and toes. A *snap* of magic sealed the skin suit shut, and the Darkness Between Dreams became something else entirely: Howard Phillips, tech entrepreneur, wizard, and CEO.

A wardrobe was built into the back of the office, its doors designed to blend in seamlessly. It didn't exactly hide what was there. It simply drew no attention to it. Phillips walked over, opened the doors, and began to dress in front of the mirrors inside.

He was a tall man to make more space for tentacles while matching these people's beauty standards. There was enough gray in his dark hair to lend him an extra gravitas. Phillips was particularly proud of the shape he'd chosen for his chin.

His outfit was also perfectly tailored: sharply cut suit, crisp white shirt, slender tie, leather-soled shoes. His pocket square was a subtly soothing blue-gray, not one of the ostentatious colors too many of the new executives were wearing. As for casual-dressed leadership, that was the past, and Phillips was most definitely the future. The terrible, dark, screaming future.

Fully dressed, he returned to his seat and pressed a button on the intercom.

"Julia, could you and Handar come in, please?"

The door opened, and two magicals walked straight in. That was one of the things that Phillips liked about the people he'd hired. They knew to be ready the moment he called.

Julia Lacy was a witch, short and slender with blond hair tied back from an expression of frightening alertness. She wore a suit almost as well cut as Phillips', but with a silver necklace gleaming at the open neck of her blouse. In her hand was the weapon of every great personal assistant, a tablet open to her boss's schedule.

The contrast with Handar Ennis couldn't have been more striking. Handar was six-foot-eight, a hulking brute of a Kilomea whose muscles strained the bounds of plausibility, not only the seams of his suit. He'd sharpened his tusks to deadly points and his expression to a frown that deterred anyone from approaching without permission.

Among his many natural bulges was one more, the shape of a hefty pistol strapped under his shoulder, ready for action at an instant's notice. Phillips had never seen him use it, but he didn't doubt for a minute that every shot would kill.

"Boss." Handar nodded and coarse fur rasped against the back of his collar.

"You wanted to see us, Mr. Phillips?" Julia asked.

"Close the door, please," Phillips said, and Handar obeyed. "I want to talk to you about our long-term goals as a company."

"You mean this year's targets or the five-year strategy?" Lacy tapped on the tablet with a perfectly manicured finger.

"I mean bigger than that."

A tentacle emerged from Phillips' sleeve to set two polished black stones down on his desk. To their credit, neither of his employees flinched, unlike the first time he'd revealed to each of them who he really was.

"My staff on the other side are growing impatient, but when I try to bring them through, this is all I get." The tentacle retreated, and he ran a finger over the stones, remembering the fine nightmare beasts they'd been before the magical crossing did this to them. "It's not enough for me to visit this reality. If I'm going to conquer it, I need my followers, my army, and all the magical power I have there. I need more than this."

He tugged on the skin of his neck, which stretched like elastic and snapped back into place.

"You want us to explore cross-dimensional transit techniques?" Julia asked. "Portals, transportation spells, potential technological solutions?"

"No. I don't want to build a ladder to cross the wall that stands in my way. I want to tear that wall down." Phillips slammed his hand into the desk, making the stones bounce. "I want to rip this reality open and let nightmares loose."

If he had any doubts about the loyalty of his lieutenants, they vanished at that moment. Both of them understood his goals, and both understood that there was far more to gain by working for him than from opposing him. Sooner or later, something magical would conquer this wretched place. Better to be on the side of the conquerors than to die standing against them.

"We'll need to start work on the project plan." Julia's fingertips danced across the screen as she made notes. "Consider potential approaches, resources to acquire, objectives along the way. We can't determine our critical path yet."

"This is why I like you, Julia." Phillips smiled, and she blushed. "You have a gift for management. In the new world, I will give you a realm of your own to run."

"Thank you, Mr. Phillips."

"What do you want right now, boss?" Handar growled.

"That's why I like you, Handar," Phillips said. "Your directness. I've sensed something unusual in the magic between worlds. Someone has created a device that allows safer passage between Earth and Oriceran, a better way to do what portals do."

"You think it could help to break down the barriers?" Julia asked.

"Perhaps, in time, but that's not what interests me now. I think I could use it to visit the World In Between."

"Is that a good idea, boss?" Handar asked. "You're tough, I get it, but that place..."

"Is a nightmare?" Phillips grinned at his little joke, and his employees dutifully laughed. "Don't worry. I won't be traveling there without precautions, if at all. What I'm interested in is what we can call out."

There was a moment of quiet while he let them work this one out for themselves. What could anyone do with a gate to a netherworld where living and dead alike became trapped, a place haunted by all those who found themselves there, able to see both Earth and Oriceran but to communicate with neither, eternally preserved and eternally frustrated?

For once, Handar was the first to find the answer.

"An army," the bodyguard said. "Living and dead, half of 'em angry and insane. Only able to go anywhere 'cause you say so."

"Exactly. A powerful tool to progress our plans and a test of what we can achieve with this device. But first, we have to acquire it."

"Where is it? I'll send the boys around."

"I don't know. All I've seen are broken glimpses of the

idea it represents. Some sort of mirror that acts as a portal. Find that, and we're on our path toward victory."

Julia and Handar stood. They'd learned to tell from the tone of their boss's voice when a conversation was over.

"We're on it, Mr. Phillips," Julia said.

"Good." Phillips waved dismissively. "Now go get to work. If you need me, I'll be looking over the financials. A world-conquering business doesn't run itself."

CHAPTER FOUR

Fran skated around the kitchen in time to an old Weird Al Yankovic song. She liked the stuff that Young Al was doing since the magical accident that had restored his youth, but she preferred the classics. Some people said that *River Deep, Mountain High* was a song for the ages, or *Smells Like Teen Spirit,* but as far as Fran was concerned, you couldn't beat *Amish Paradise.*

There were a few problems with skating around the kitchen. Number one was the size of the kitchen, which barely had space for Fran to fall over in. Number two was the crow, which kept hopping down to the floor for the birdseed Fran had spilled so she had to keep half an eye out to avoid running over it.

Number three was the number of gadgets that Fran and her roommate Josie had installed, which meant that breakage was almost inevitable if Fran fell, for example, while trying to avoid killing a feather-brained crow. Still, what was life without the fun parts? Where was the fun in making a smoothie if you didn't sing and skate while you peeled the fruit?

Fran dropped a banana into the blender as she skated past, then opened the fridge. She grabbed a tub of strawberries, but she was moving a little too fast. Her fingers only caught the edge of the tub, and it started to fall.

Momentum kept her from skating straight back, so instead, she reached out with her magic. A sound wave shook the tub back, keeping it upright long enough for Fran to turn and catch it. Only a couple of berries fell out and ended up crushed beneath her skates.

The front door opened, and Josie walked in. She was wearing dress pants and a blouse and had neatly tied back her dark hair.

"Ooh, did you have another interview?" Fran asked. "You look super professional! I would hire you in an instant."

"No interviews any more. I got that job offer from Philgard Technologies, remember?"

"Oh yes!" Fran slapped her hand against her forehead, leaving a smear of juice that ran down her nose. "How could I forget? My best friend is working for the biggest tech company in Mana Valley!"

"You could forget because you're a delightful lunatic who would forget her head if nature hadn't nailed it on." Josie sat to take off her shoes. "They're not the biggest. Not quite. Top five."

"It's still amazing." Fran squeezed the juice from most of an orange into the blender, only spattering a little of it over the counter. "You'll be working with Howard Phillips. *The* Howard Phillips."

She pointed at the wall screen across the room, and it flickered into life. A snap of her fingers, a spark of magic, and an Internet search executed, revealing Phillips' *Oriceran Review* "Man of the Year" cover, with the tech billionaire looking stylishly relaxed on the front steps of his mountainside mansion.

"I won't be working with Phillips. I'll be working fifty-seven layers of managers below him as a lowly coder." Josie looked at the ceiling for a moment while she did some quick calculations. "All right, more like eleven layers of managers, but still, it's a lot."

She slid her shoes into the magitech box they'd adapted the previous summer, which immediately started cleaning them. Then she slid on her slippers, walked over to the kitchen, and sighed as she saw the mess.

"You know you've got berries caught in your skates, right?"

Fran looked down. "Oh yeah! I should clean that up." She noticed Josie's expression and finally took in the sticky state of the kitchen. "I should clear this up too, right?"

"Absolutely. But finish making the smoothies first. I really want one. And remember to put the lid on the blender this time."

"The stains are totally gone from the ceiling, you know."

"That doesn't mean we should make new ones."

Fran finished making the smoothies and poured them into glasses, then dropped the sticky blender bowl into the sink. There was a flash of magic, and the juice and pulp vanished off its insides. Then Fran hit a button beside the sink, and a robot cleaner rolled out of one of the cupboards.

"You know that Hoovernator can't clean the countertops, right?" Josie asked.

"He's done it before."

"Technically, yes, but he broke the microwave in the process and broke himself when he fell on the floor. This time, you need to clean them yourself."

"Poor Hoovernator, everyone underestimates your abilities." Fran patted the appliance, and the googly eyes she'd stuck to its front rolled back and forth. "I believe in you, Hoovernator. One day, you'll clean our whole house."

"House seems a bit grand," Josie said as she made her way to the couch, smoothie in hand. "I believe that what we live in technically qualifies as a shoebox, even if our rents would buy a palace elsewhere."

Having wiped down the kitchen, Fran rolled over to sit down beside her friend. In the kitchen, the crow hopped onto Hoovernator's back and rode back and forth, its eyes open for any signs of birdseed.

As Fran sat, a gentle voice emerged from the couch.

"Activate lounging mode?" it asked.

"Ooh, yes please!" Fran replied.

A cushioned panel slid from under the couch and floated out until she could put her feet up on it, then it shifted from magical to mechanical mechanisms and rods locked the cushion in place.

"That's more like it." Fran crossed her legs.

"Wait for it…" Josie said.

There was a crunch, a flash of failing magic, and the cushion fell. Fran's feet hit the floor.

"I told you when you bought it, I spent last summer working for a smart sofa company," Josie said. "The tech's not ready for market yet."

"But it's on the market!" Fran exclaimed.

"And now it's on the floor."

Fran sipped her smoothie and felt her spirits revive. "One day we'll have a house of our own. Just you, me, and Hoovernator."

"And your crow friends."

"And your boyfriends."

"I wouldn't say that anyone fits that label yet."

"What about Adam?"

"Adam's fine, and he's fun for now, but I don't think he's boyfriend material."

"I worry about you. If you keep using them up and discarding their worn-out husks, you'll never find love."

"You worry about me?" Josie laughed and patted her friend's shoulder. "When was the last time you had a date?"

"I'm too busy for that, what with work and everything."

"Yet here you are, skating around the apartment in the middle of the afternoon. Which brings me to the question I've wanted to ask..."

Josie looked at her friend with concern but didn't say it out loud. In the kitchen, the crow angrily squawked as Hoovernator sucked up a stray sunflower seed.

Fran sighed, curled her legs up under herself, and took a long drink from her smoothie, but eventually, she had to answer the unspoken question.

"I quit," she mumbled.

"Oh, sweetie." Josie brushed back a strand of her friend's hair. "What happened this time?"

"Same thing that always happens. They want me to do boring, pointless tasks, and they won't listen to my ideas. It was driving me crazy."

"I get it, I really do, but if you want the sort of job where you get to do the cool, creative coding, you have to pay your dues first. Be the bug hunter, the code monkey, the slogger in the trenches. You're brilliant, talented, and creative, but no one is going to notice that if you don't stick around long enough to show them."

"What if I make a job for myself?"

Josie raised an eyebrow. "What do you mean?"

"I thought I could start my own company. Instead of trying to get a job with Howard Phillips, I'll become the next Howard Phillips." Fran pointed at the magazine cover still shining down from the screen. "In five years, that could be our mansion. Imagine Hoovernator cleaning those steps."

"Hm." Josie looked down at her glass, eyes narrowing in thought.

"You don't think I can do it?" Fran asked quietly. She'd been wondering about that herself since the idea first struck. She might be a dreamer, but she was realistic enough to know that running a business took focus, discipline, and organization. Those weren't exactly her strong suits. Maybe this was going to be one of those times when Josie laid a harsh truth on her, like their second week in kindergarten, when Josie had told her that her skirt had stuck in her underwear.

When Josie looked up, she was smiling. "I think it'll be tough, but I think it's a great idea. You've got so much energy. You could make something amazing if you can build the right team around you."

"Yay!" Fran flung her arms around her friend, and in the process flung smoothie across the couch. "Do you want to be the first part of that team?"

"A week ago, I would've said yes, but I can't miss out on this chance to work at Philgard. Don't worry, though. I'll be here to support you every step of the way."

"Brilliant." Fran leaped from her seat, a thousand thoughts flashing through her mind at once. She would need an office, and a name for the business and a plan, and some accounts, and she still hadn't decided what she was going to make and...

First, she needed to clean the smoothie off the couch.

"I've got this." Josie nodded at the stain. "You go down to the skate park."

"But I—"

"No buts. You've got that look in your eyes that says your mind's a total jumble. Go skate it out, start planning your big dream, and I'll clean this up. You can grab me a donut on the way home to say thank you."

"You're the best." Fran kissed her friend on the top of the head, then skated to the door. The crow flapped over to join her. "See you later, Hoovernator. I'm off to found the next Microsoft."

CHAPTER FIVE

The skate park was a short way north of Fran's apartment, on a patch of low ground in the shadow of two shiny new wizards' towers. The towers were a familiar Mana Valley mix of Oriceran traditional and Earth modern, combining balconies, arches, and sharply pointed turrets with sections of glass wall and polished chrome. This was the Valley: part magic, part technology, with enough money and power to raise in six months the sort of building that would once have taken decades to complete.

That money was part of why places like the skate park were so rare and so precious to Fran and the others who spent their time skating back and forth across its surfaces of concrete and magically shaped stone. She loved the Valley's technology and the big businesses that made it possible. Still, they tended to trample over whatever lay in their path, buying up all the ground, turning it into tower blocks, test labs, and factories.

Sure, the more progressive companies also provided some space for play and relaxation, but those were corporate enclaves, only accessible to those who worked there. The skate park, though, was a patch of land whose eccentric owner had refused to sell it to the high price bidders and had instead carved out a niche where anyone with wheels could come out to play. Fran loved that.

She drifted gently around the track at the edge of the park, half watching the people practicing on the half- and quarter-pipes in the center. Oricerans with a taste for Earth culture had taken to skating with enthusiasm but little concern for sticking with its forms. There were Earth-style skateboards, of course, as well as boots and blades, but there were odder possibilities as well.

Boards with extra sets of wheels that bent in the middle or that were accelerated by magic. Skates that used balls in place of wheels for travel in any direction. Miniature skateboards for gnomes and Willens. Strengthened boards for Kilomea. Troll skates that changed size with the feet of their wearers.

Fran's mind wasn't only on the park. She was thinking about the future, about her business, about what she could create. Copies of her mirror seemed like one possibility, an easy way to get started, but there were problems with that. For one, it relied on her light magic to trigger the spells, and she wasn't sure if she could make that work for everyone. For another, her mother kept telling her that she shouldn't show that magic in public, and it would be hard to sell a product if she couldn't prove that it worked.

Maybe there was something else that she could do with the principles embodied in the mirror. Or a way she could discreetly invest the technology with her magic so that no one else needed the same spells or to see her cast them.

Was that a possibility? Perhaps, if she rearranged the wiring and invested in a more expensive sort of crystal, like the ones starting to come out of the southern dwarf mines. She could use the crystals as a kind of battery for her power, put some light into it, and…

An Arpak on rollerblades snatched her attention away again as he flung his wings wide, rolled off the top of a half-pipe, and glided in a smooth upside-down curve to land on the far side. His wheels hit the curve so that he came straight down for another loop. It wasn't an innovative move by the standards of the Arpak skaters, who loved their flashy wing tricks, but its perfect execution was lovely to see.

Ahead of Fran, another skater also had his attention grabbed by the Arpak. A gnome, wearing a safety helmet and more pads and guards than Fran even knew existed, turned to gape in amazement at the flying skate trick. Unfortunately for the gnome, the distraction was more than his skating skills could handle. He veered left, rolled off the track, and fell into a construction hole, arms madly waving.

Fran rushed over. The gnome lay in a puddle of rainwater, spluttering and twisting, but his skates uselessly spun as he pressed them against the side, trying to push himself upright.

"Hey there." Fran reached out for him. "Would you like a hand?"

The gnome grasped her hand and Fran pulled him up the hole until he could lay his other hand on the edge and haul himself, dripping, onto flat ground.

"Thank you so much." He shook the mud off his arms and legs.

"New to this?"

"Is it that obvious?" The gnome sighed and took off his goggles and helmet, releasing a mess of tousled white hair. There was a resigned smile on his wrinkled face.

"I get so bored at home, and you kids make this look so easy, I thought it might be fun to give it a try. Bruised myself blue around the apartment before I got these." He patted his assorted protective pads. "I thought now I could give it a go safely. Yet, somehow, I almost ended up drowning myself."

He spat out mud, then pulled out a large spotted handkerchief and wiped more dirt from his face.

"It takes time to learn a new skill," Fran said. "Keep practicing, and you'll get there. Just maybe pay more attention next time."

"Fair." The gnome laughed and held out his hand. "Bartholomew Trumbling at your service, but you can call me Bart."

"Fran Berryman. Great to meet you, Bart. Would you like to skate together for a bit? I can give you some tips."

"That would be marvelous, but I don't want to be a burden. A young person like yourself probably has better things to do than show me skills I'm too old for."

"If you were too old, you wouldn't be here." Fran helped Bart to his feet. "Let's do a couple of loops. See how you're doing on those wheels."

They skated slowly around the park, Fran guiding Bart to improve his direction and control.

"What made you think to come skating?" she asked

once she thought he had enough control to talk while skating straight. "Not many people take it up at your age."

"And you said I wasn't too old!" Bart laughed. "But I suppose I am for some things. I used to be an accountant, still have all the skills for it, but I hit retirement age, and the company wanted to bring in fresh blood. They gave me a nice commemorative watch and pension packet, and a pretty send-off speech that made clear they didn't need to see me ever again. I know you're supposed to look forward to retirement, to enjoy the time to relax, but honestly, it's not for me. I need to be active, so I decided to take up a new hobby, and here I am."

"But why skating? You could've gotten into knitting or local history or magic tricks or anything."

"There's this other gnome in my building, name of Kiri. We'd chat in the hallway when he was on his way out with his skateboard. He's not as young as you, so it was a bit less intimidating."

"You'll get the hang of it." Fran pointed at Bart's feet. "Look, you're already doing better."

"I suppose so. But enough about me. What do you do, Fran?"

"I run my own business." She felt so proud saying it but immediately knew she had to backtrack. "Or I'm going to. I work in tech, but I quit my job today, and I'm going to set up a magitech business of my own."

"A startup, eh? How exciting! What are you going to make?"

Fran blushed. She knew that should be the one thing she had a clear answer to, but it was still eluding her.

"I'm not sure," she admitted. "I've got an idea for something to do with mirrors and travel, but there's an issue with the power source."

"You should meet Kiri then. He's got some big ideas about hunting down a supreme energy source, says it's out there in Oriceran."

"A supreme energy source."

"Sounds dramatic, doesn't it?"

"Could you introduce me to him?"

"Sure. Although I've not seen him for a few days, probably off on another of his adventures. Give me your contact details, and I'll mention you to him when he gets back."

"Thanks."

They skated on, Fran's mind starting to wander. That talk about an energy source had given her an idea. People always needed power to fuel their technology, whether it was magical or not.

She'd done a good job of powering the magical mirror. If she could do something like that, but usable for other devices, that could be useful to many people. If it were helpful to many people, then a lot of people would pay for it...

With a croaking cry, a crow landed on her shoulder. She wasn't sure if it was the same one she'd fed earlier. The creatures seemed to like her, but it was friendly enough. It sat on her shoulder, feathers fluttering as they did slow circles of the track.

Some sort of power source. If she could make that and the gadgets to show it off, surely she was in business.

"It was great meeting you, Bart," she said. "I've got to go. Inspiration calls!"

CHAPTER SIX

Fran sat in the corner of the Blazing Bean coffee shop, typing on her laptop. Her ideas for the business now stretched to dozens of pages of assorted notes, from the information on batteries that she'd pulled off the web to the two pages of name ideas. Next to her, a half-finished cappuccino had gone cold in its cup, and she hadn't touched her third cookie. She'd never been so focused on anything in her life.

"Here you go." Someone set a fresh coffee down on the table.

Fran blinked in surprise and looked away from her screen to see a barista smiling down at her. He appeared to be a wizard, or possibly one of the mundane humans who were starting to come over to Oriceran. He was tall and slim, with a wide smile and blue eyes sparkling from behind a pair of round glasses. As she looked at him, he ran a hand through his shaggy blond hair.

"I'm sorry, I think there's a mistake," Fran said. "I didn't order that."

"I know," the barista said, picking up her cold cup. "But you looked like you needed a fresh one. After the first four hours, the foam starts to lose its froth."

"Four hours?" Fran glanced at the time on her screen. He was right. How had she been sitting there so long without even realizing it?

She rolled her neck, easing out the stiffness that she hadn't noticed until now, and looked around the room. The Blazing Bean, with its bright furnishings and comic art decorations, stood out among the rest of the local coffee shops, with their soothingly bland style tailored to harassed executives and informal business meetings. Because of that, it drew a livelier crowd, skaters and rockers and experimenters with fringe magic, most of them under thirty. There was always music playing and a lively level of chatter filling the place.

Except that, right now, it was quiet, only a couple of other customers sitting at a table by the window. Outside, it was dark.

"Is it too late?" Fran asked, finally registering how late those four hours made it. "Do you need me to leave so you can close?"

"You're all right for now," the barista said. "We stay open for the late-night crowd, cake cravers, and Silver Griffins looking for a coffee to see them through their patrol."

"That's good to know. I'm setting up my own business. I might need places to work late."

"Your own business? Cool. What do you do?"

"Magitech." Fran said the word with pride.

The barista raised an eyebrow. "You know that's, like, ninety percent of what everyone does around here, right?"

"So I'm in the right town." Fran grinned.

"What I mean is, what sort of magitech?"

"Something with batteries, I think. Or mirrors." Fran frowned. "I'll be honest, I've had, like, eighteen ideas since I came in here, and I'm still trying to choose between them."

The barista laughed. "Well, which one are you most excited about?"

Fran thought for a long moment before she answered.

"All of them."

He laughed again. It was a nice laugh, the sort that said he was laughing with her, not at her.

"Well, if you want someone to bounce your ideas off, I'll be around. Magitech isn't my specialty, but I hear a lot of talk in here, so maybe I can help you pick what to make."

"Thanks, um…" Fran squinted at his name badge. "…Cameron."

"Call me Cam."

"I'm Fran."

"Enjoy your coffee, Fran." He headed back toward the counter, whistling as he went.

"Wait!" Fran called after him. "Don't I need to pay for the coffee?"

"That one's on me."

Fran smiled. Everyone seemed so friendly today. It was a great omen for what was to come.

She got back to work, making sure to drink her coffee this time. She would need the caffeine to carry her through a long day and late night of thinking. A few more people came in, all to get takeout, including some of the Silver

Griffins Cam had talked about. The magical investigators wore their official amulets openly on silver chains and their wands prominently on their hips. In a town full of magic, money, and ambition, there was plenty of opportunity for trouble, and their job was to deter it before it started, not only clear up after the event.

As the Silver Griffins were leaving, a crow fluttered in over their heads and came to land on Fran's table. It cocked its head to one side and cawed.

"Sorry, I don't have anything for you right now," Fran said. "Unless you like cookie crumbs?" She pushed the empty plate toward the crow, which ignored it, and hopped over to sit beside her screen. "I'm not sure you should be in here. Lots of places don't allow pets or familiars."

The crow ruffled its feathers and shook its head in defiance of what rules anyone might set. Behind the counter, Cam was intent on some work of his own, his face lit by the screen of a small laptop.

"Tell you what, I'll check if you can stay, and if that's all right, I'll get you some seed cake," Fran said. "How does that sound?"

The crow hopped down onto the seat beside her and prodded her leg with its beak, hurrying her on her way.

Cam looked up as Fran approached the counter.

"More coffee?" he asked.

"Please. And I'll pay this time."

"That's usually how this works." He started up the grinder.

"Do you have a policy on animals in this place?"

"I don't think so. I mean, we might have practical problems if someone brought in their pet giraffe or shifted into an elephant, but there's nothing saying they can't come in."

"Including crows?"

"That's a weirdly specific example." He looked over at her table, and the crow waved a wing at him. "Friend of yours?"

"Kind of. All crows seem to like me, or at least the ones I meet."

"That's nice. You must have a trustworthy aura."

Fran laughed. "Is that your magic, working with auras?"

Cameron shook his head. "No magic on me. I'm a dud."

"A dud?"

A loud *hiss* cut off the conversation as he used a steamer to foam her milk. When it finished, he turned to the counter and slowly poured the milk into the coffee, forming a flower pattern with the foam.

"Dud's a word some people use for when witches and wizards have kids without powers," he said. "I guess it might not happen over here, but it's a thing occasionally on Earth."

"Dud. Huh, I guess it makes sense."

"Probably not a word to repeat. A lot of people don't like it, say it's hurtful."

"You don't?"

Cam shrugged. "It's harder for words to hurt you if you own them. Besides, being a dud has freed me."

"Really?" Fran turned her gaze to the cakes behind the counter. She wanted to listen to Cam, but her stomach was reminding her that she'd missed dinner and several hours more since then.

"My family are a big deal in the magical world back on

Earth. Lots of Silver Griffins, some of them really senior. If I'd had powers, they would've expected me to do the same thing, but without magic..." He shrugged and offered her a lopsided smile. "The worlds are my oyster." He followed Fran's gaze to the cakes. "You want something else with your coffee?"

"Yes, please. Your biggest slice of chocolate fudge cake. Oh, and something with seeds in for my friend."

"Will lemon and poppy seeds do?"

"Perfect." She licked her lips as she watched him slide the cakes onto a plate. "Aren't your family disappointed in you? I mean, the fact that you're not a magical."

"Oh yes. I mean, some of them pretend not to be, say it's great that I'm doing a Ph.D., that mundane academia is as valuable as the magical kind, but they obviously don't believe it. The rest don't even pretend. Family dinners can get pretty awkward. Ironically, that's why I'm here. Less judgment for not being magical in a world where magic feels mundane."

"If you're doing a Ph.D., why are you working in a coffee shop?"

"Not a lot of money in history."

"There should be. History's fascinating. All those knights and dinosaurs and, um..."

"Didn't pay much attention in history class, huh?"

"No, but it sounds fascinating."

Cam smiled. "Not as fascinating as what you're doing. Did you pick a project yet?"

"Batteries," Fran declared with confidence. "Then I can make all the other things too, powered by them. A perfect balance of synergy and diversity."

"Sounds like a corporate motto."

"Thank you!" Fran frowned, sensing his barely suppressed laughter. "Wait, isn't that a good thing?"

"For the business you're going into, I think it might be perfect. But I hope you don't mind if I laugh at the business speak and tech industry habits once in a while. It's the only way to stay sane around here."

Fran thought about her experiences in the industry—the crowded cubicles, the unrealistic targets, the slogans, and repeated rebranding. She started laughing too.

"I think I might need someone like you to make sure I don't lose sight of that."

"You're on. You keep coming here for coffee, and I'll keep you from getting lost in the corporate jargon." He stuck out a hand, and they shook. "Now, here's your coffee and cake. You'd better get back to work. The world of magical batteries isn't going to synergize and diversify itself."

CHAPTER SEVEN

Fran crouched on the top of a parking garage, looking out across San Francisco. It was three in the morning, and the city was like a sea of stars, a scatter of bright lights running down to the bay. Mana Valley had some splendid sights, but there was real beauty to be seen on Earth too.

She'd considered staying in Mana Valley for this first test of her new technology but decided it was better to do it here. Fewer flying magicals to see what she was up to or to get in the way of her flight path.

She finished taping a layer of aluminum foil to the underside of the rug that she'd picked up from Worn Threads, a carpet shop back in Mana Valley. Between the enchanted foil reflector and the carpet itself was a layer of wires and runes written on tissue paper, a sort of improvised magical circuit board. An old phone, converted into a navigational computer, carried the software she'd written to control the enchantments.

At the back and powering it all was Mark One of her new crystal magic battery. It had come a long way in the two days since she'd talked with Bart and Cam, and she was pleased with the progress she'd made. Now came the time to put it to the test.

Fran strapped on her backpack, picked up the control computer, and planted her feet firmly on the carpet. It was tempting to call upon her magic, but that would be cheating. She'd used it to build the technology, but that technology needed to work by itself.

"Almost forgot!" She pulled a miniature bottle of champagne from the side of her backpack, a gift from Josie to christen this first creation. "I name this carpet, um…" She looked around for inspiration. "The USS Streetlamp."

She knew it was traditional to break a champagne bottle against the side of a new ship, but that seemed like a waste. Instead, she popped the cork from the bottle, downed half the champagne, and flung the bottle down on the pavement. It shattered with a pleasing *crash,* and Fran hit the launch button on her controller.

The USS Streetlamp trembled, and the tassels at its edges rippled as if blowing in a breeze. Then it started to take off. Slowly, the carpet lifted into the air, carried on magical currents reshaped by sound waves. With a low *hum,* it drifted away from the car park and out across the city.

"Yes!" Fran exclaimed. "It works." The carpet veered wildly to one side, and she fell flat, face pressed into the woven threads. "No!"

The carpet shot wildly back and forth through the sky. Fran clung on tight with one hand while with the other she grappled with the controller, trying to alter her flight path.

San Francisco shot past underneath as the carpet accelerated and the wind flapped her hair around.

"No, no, no!" she screamed, slapping the controller. "Follow the program. Follow the program!"

The carpet raced across the rooftops, twisting and turning as it went. It was all Fran could do to keep from screaming.

"Retardo!" a voice called, far calmer than Fran.

The carpet slammed to a halt, still hovering above the city. Fran looked around to see a witch floating into view, wand in hand and a Silver Griffin amulet around her neck.

"Hi," Fran said. "Thanks for stopping me. This thing is getting out of control."

"So I see." The Silver Griffin peered at the carpet. "Did you make this thing fly, ma'am?"

"Oh, yes," Fran said proudly. Nobody ever called her ma'am. "Isn't it cool!"

"I've never seen anything like it." The Griffin leaned in closer and sniffed. "Have you been drinking?"

"Just a little champagne to celebrate the launch."

"Launch?"

"Of the Streetlamp."

"You launched a streetlamp?"

"This is the Streetlamp."

"No, ma'am, that's clearly a carpet." The Silver Griffin waved her wand and restraints appeared around Fran's wrists. "I'm taking you in for driving a magical vehicle under the influence of alcohol and possibly something more. Anything you say can be—"

"But I wasn't—"

"A word of advice ma'am: before you incriminate yourself, at least let me read you your rights."

Fran sat in a cell at the Silver Griffins' waystation. They'd unfastened her hands but taken her bag and phone, and now she didn't know what to do with herself. She drummed her fingers against the side of the cot that was one of the cell's two pieces of furniture, then got down on the floor and tried to do push-ups, like criminals on TV. It turned out that push-ups were hard, and anyway, Fran wasn't sure if she counted as a criminal yet. That might depend on whether she could post bail.

They'd given her a single phone call, like on a cop show, and that had been kind of exciting. Less exciting had been leaving a message on her mom's answering machine, all the while worrying about what her mom would say. Mom liked to keep her head down, liked her daughter to do the same, and Fran had taken her head right up above the streets of San Fran, only to come back down in handcuffs.

In the corridor outside the cell, two Silver Griffins were talking.

"Did you hear?" one of them asked. "There's been another brown-out in one of the kemanas."

"Which one?"

"Which one do you think?"

The other Griffin snorted. "Probably just stoned wizards messing with the crystal again."

"No way. There's a pattern here, all these weird events

over the past week. Brownouts and energy surges. Something's going wrong."

"You sound like old Jenkins, down in the lab. He says this is magic but not magic, that something else is disrupting the flow."

"It's not man-made. I'll tell you that much."

"I'm not so sure. Supervillains have pulled some pretty weird things in their time."

"Does that count as man-made?"

"Well, it's not natural, is it?"

"Coming through." A third voice cut across the conversation. "I need to get to that cell."

There was a *clunk* of keys in a heavy lock, and the door swung open. Fran looked up from the floor to see her mom standing next to another witch.

"You have ten minutes," the witch said, then closed the door, leaving Fran and her mom alone.

Irene Berryman looked down at her daughter with one eyebrow raised.

"What are you doing on the floor, Francesca?" she asked.

"Push-ups." Fran blushed. "Thanks for coming, Mom."

"I was hardly going to leave you here, was I?" Irene shook her head and smiled wearily, then sat on the edge of the cot. "They tell me you were drunk and flying some sort of carpet contraption?"

"I wasn't drunk! And it's not a contraption. It's a prototype powered by another prototype."

"A prototype."

"For my new business."

"New business." Irene pressed a hand to her eyes. "How

many times do I have to tell you, Francesca, you can't go drawing attention to yourself like this."

"I'm sorry, *mother,* but that won't do." Fran got to her feet. "I'm an entrepreneur now. I have to draw attention so I can find investors and market my products and other things that business people do."

"Things that business people do?"

"Yes, things they do." Fran sagged. "Look, I'm new to this. I can give you better answers soon, but it's only been two days, and I'm doing really well for two days. I mean, did you see the carpet?"

Irene shook her head. "The Griffins had dismantled it before I got here."

"Dismantled it?" Fran glared at the locked door as if she could show the witches and wizards beyond it just how angry she was. "That was my only prototype."

Irene patted the cot. "Could you sit down for a minute? We need to talk."

Fran sighed and flung herself down next to her mom. It was good to have someone there, but this wasn't quite what she'd expected. She'd thought that there would be a swift handing over of bail and she would be out. Instead…

"Do you remember what an Evermore is?" Irene asked.

"People from those fairy tales you told me when I was small," Fran said. "Early cousins of the witches and wizards, a bit like Neanderthals to Homo sapiens."

"Not a comparison I would choose, but it sort of works." Irene patted her daughter on the head. "You were always so smart. What else can you remember?"

"Their magic was simpler, like a prototype of the magic

we have now, bending particles of light and sound to do their bidding. Like our magic."

"Exactly like our magic."

"Mom, I don't mean to be rude, but I'm under arrest. Is this really the time for fairy tales?"

Irene drew a deep breath.

"I've been meaning to talk to you about this for a while, but I could never find the right time." Her fingers twisted together, and she picked at the chewed edge of a nail. "Those stories weren't fairy tales. The Evermores are real, they're secret, and we're both Evermores."

"No, we're not, we're..." As she said it, Fran realized how stupid she'd been. Now that her mom said it out loud, the connection was obvious and explained the unusual powers they shared. "Why didn't you tell me sooner?"

"Because the Evermores are a carefully hidden secret. The only reason I was allowed to leave the community was that I promised not to tell anyone else about them. When you were a child, there was no way you could keep a thing like that secret, then you grew up, and I never knew when the right time was to tell you."

"So why are you telling me now? Why couldn't I keep thinking that I was a witch?"

"Because of this." Irene waved a hand at the cell around them. "The Silver Griffins noticed that there was something odd about your carpet creation, and now they've spotted a discrepancy in my ID. They won't let me bail you out."

"That's not fair!"

"I know, Francesca, and I'm doing my best to fix it.

When I do, you're going to have to keep your head down. Do you understand?"

Fran shook her head.

"No, Mom. This was your secret, one you promised to keep, but I never made that promise. I don't plan on telling anyone, but I'm not going to hide away because of how I was born."

"You could be putting yourself in danger."

"If that's what it takes to live a life I can be proud of, then that's what I'll do."

Irene opened her mouth as if to say something, then closed it again. Her expression softened.

"You're right," she said. "I'm sorry. I'll do what I can to get you out. I just don't know what that is yet."

"Don't worry about it, mom." Fran hugged her mother. "You get out of here before they arrest you for a fake ID."

"But you…"

"I'll work something out." Fran grinned. "When people interview me for my entrepreneur of the year award, today will make a great origin story."

CHAPTER EIGHT

If Gruffbar Steelstrike had one complaint about the Silver Griffins' San Francisco waystation, it was the terrible coffee. Acrid, bitter, mouth-scouring stuff that was barely tolerable however many sugars he tipped in. He was seriously considering donating a proper coffee maker to the Griffins to make his time waiting in reception more bearable.

If he had a second complaint, the Griffins weren't providing him with work, contrary to all expectations. This should've been the perfect place for a dwarf lawyer to pick up cases, helping out magicals who had fallen foul of the Griffins or their own mistakes. Instead, for the past week, the San Fran Griffins had spent ninety percent of their time chasing magic failures at nearby kemanas. Sure, it sounded like the beginnings of a crisis, but couldn't they do their job of picking up magical criminals too?

"Don't you have anything for me, Al?" Gruffbar asked, looking hopefully at the Griffin behind reception.

"Sorry, Gruffbar." Al shook his head. "You know how it goes."

"I know." Gruffbar leaned back in his plastic seat and stared at the clock. Nearly dawn. Maybe he should go back to the office, in case any clients came in. Except that he didn't have an office here, not like he'd had in the old days back in LA. Of course, in the old days he'd mostly worked for criminals and magical monsters, and now he was trying to go straight. It had taken decades to get to this point, but would he really give up his integrity for the sake of a desk and a comfy seat?

Maybe, if it came with decent coffee.

"You should go over to Mana Valley," Al said. "You know the Griffins have a special license to police that place? Only place on Oriceran they've got authority. There'd be plenty of work for a magical lawyer with your experience."

"I like it over here," Gruffbar said. "Plenty of industry. You can taste the smoke in the air."

"Plenty of industry there too, just with spells."

"I guess."

A witch emerged from the door beside reception. She looked tense, chewing on a nail and clutching her handbag close. She'd tied her hair back, and she wore just enough makeup to look very ordinary, by human standards.

"Just you?" Al looked up something on his computer.

"Just me." The witch hurried across reception. "I have to go."

"Wait a minute, Ms. Berryman, could you…"

It was too late. The witch was gone.

"Problem?" Gruffbar asked. It was a good idea to make

nice with the station staff, and it was good practice at making himself care about people.

"Not a big one." Al shrugged. "I was supposed to delay her with paperwork."

"Suspicious character but no grounds to hold her?"

Al nodded.

Gruffbar laughed. "How many times have I seen that trick?"

A thoughtful expression crossed Al's face. "This might mean that there's a job for you."

Gruffbar jumped to his feet. "Really?"

"Maybe." Al picked up his phone. "Give me a minute. I'll see what I can do."

Fran sat on the edge of the cot, her head in her hands. It turned out that she wasn't as good at getting out of jail as she thought. She could come up with a hundred ideas for new inventions, two hundred ways to write a line of code, but she knew nothing about how to make bail or pick the lock on a cell door. It had only been fifteen minutes since her mom left, and she already wanted her back.

The cell door opened and a Griffin peered in.

"You're still short on legal representation, right?" he asked.

Fran nodded.

"Great." The Griffin grinned. "I've got you some short legal representation."

He pulled the door wide, revealing a dwarf with a dark,

neatly trimmed beard, dressed in biker leathers and carrying a briefcase. The dwarf rolled his eyes.

"Seriously, Al," he said. "A height joke?"

The Griffin shrugged. "Sorry, couldn't resist. I'll leave the two of you to it."

Al closed the door, leaving Fran and the dwarf alone.

"Who are you?" she asked.

"Gruffbar Steelstrike, lawyer." Gruffbar held out his hand, and Fran shook. He had a firm grip and tough hands as if he used them for more than paperwork. "You want representation?"

"Absolutely!" Fran said excitedly, but then her face fell. "Except I'm not sure I can afford it. I quit my job, and spent my spare money on components for my carpet, and rent's due in a week, and…"

"How much have you got in your pocket?"

Fran rummaged around in her jeans, then held out a handful of crumpled notes and loose coins. "Three dollars and fifty-seven cents."

"By a remarkable coincidence, that's my fee for a case like this."

"Really?" Fran stared at him, incredulous. She wasn't sure she wanted the sort of lawyer who came that cheap, but maybe he was better than nothing.

Gruffbar held out his hand.

"Look, I need some cases like yours to establish my practice here, and I've got nothing else to do tonight. So hand me your pocket change, we'll establish attorney-client privilege, and I can get started on your case."

That made as much sense as Fran needed. She handed him the cash.

"Now," Gruffbar said, "tell me what happened."

Fran explained about her prototype, the carpet ride, and her arrest, skipping over the parts about Evermores and her unusual powers. She even had the restraint not to ramble on about how she was setting up a business, exciting as that was. Gruffbar made notes on his phone. Occasionally, he stroked his beard. At the end, he thrust his phone back into his pocket and pulled out a cigar.

"Mind if I smoke? It helps me think."

Fran wrinkled her nose. "Could you save it until we're outside?"

"I suppose." Gruffbar closed his eyes and sniffed the cigar. "I'm running out anyway. I should save this one until I can afford some more."

He stuck the cigar back into his pocket, then glanced again at the notes on his phone.

"You said that the Griffins smelled the alcohol on your breath. Did they test you with a Breathalyzer?"

"No."

"Any sort of intoxication testing spell?"

"I don't think so."

Gruffbar made a note. "And they've confiscated your vehicle?"

"Not only confiscated it, dismantled it! Days of work, hours of magic, some very delicate spells, and I'll have to start all over again."

"Do you think they could rebuild it?"

"Definitely not. Only I know how it works." Of course, there were parts of the flying carpet that relied on Evermore magic, powers the Griffins simply didn't have, but Fran had told her mom she wouldn't talk about that.

"Let's get this straight." Gruffbar grinned. "You're here on a charge of being drunk in charge of a magical vehicle. The Griffins have no proof that you were drunk when they arrested you. They have no vehicle you were piloting. Even if they put the parts of that vehicle back together, they couldn't make it fly."

"When you put it like that, you're right."

"So out of your drunk driving charge, they can't prove the drunkenness or the driving?"

Fran laughed. "Oh my days, you are, like, the greatest lawyer ever!"

She flung her arms around Gruffbar, who stood stiffly with his arms by his sides.

"Ms. Berryman, they made this so easy that I've barely earned the three dollars and fifty-seven cents." Gruffbar banged on the door of the cell. "Hey, numbskulls, come and let my client go!"

Al held the door of the waystation open for Fran and Gruffbar.

"Again, Ms. Berryman, I can only apologize," he said. "We'll contact you as soon as we've gathered up all of your components."

"And compensation for the damage to her device." Gruffbar frowned sternly.

"I'm sorry, Gruffbar, but I can't authorize that."

"That's Mr. Steelstrike while we're both on duty, and I suggest that you find someone who can authorize it. Otherwise, we'll see you in court."

"Seriously, Gruffbar?" Al sighed. "After I helped you out?"

"Don't take it personally, kid." Gruffbar patted him on the arm. "This is how the system works. Someone has to keep you Griffins honest. The donuts are on me tomorrow night."

"Fine." Al laughed and shook his head. "Make sure you bring some proper coffee too. The stuff they give us here is filth."

Fran and Gruffbar walked out into the street, leaving Al behind. The sun was rising over San Francisco, the start of a fine spring day.

"By my beard, but this lot are amateurs," Gruffbar said. "The Griffins I used to know in LA would put them all to shame."

He walked over to a large, old-fashioned bike, midnight black with gleaming silver fittings, and strapped his brief-case onto the side.

"Is that yours?" Fran looked admiringly at the bike. "It's lovely."

"Harley Davidson Deluxe," Gruffbar said. "Take care of a machine like this, and it'll take care of you forever." He unhooked a helmet from the handlebars. "You got a lift home?"

Fran took the mirror out of her bag. "It's not as impres-sive as yours, but it'll do the job."

"Good. Now, you remember what I said?"

"Same thing as my mom, that I should keep my head down."

"Your mom sounds like a smart lady. Any time you have a run-in with the law, right or wrong, it's good to lay low for a while after. No point causing trouble while they might be watching you. If you do run into trouble, you have my number now."

"I'll make sure to keep three dollars and fifty-seven cents handy."

"Call me the moment they contact you about those components. They'll try to make you sign paperwork disclaiming responsibility for what they did. Bring me along, and I promise, you'll walk away with more than you pay me."

"Great. I can use the money to start my business."

Gruffbar jumped up onto his bike. "Tech entrepreneur, huh?" He looked her up and down. "Who would've guessed?"

Then he started up the engine and roared away.

Fran fitted the wires in place on the back of her mirror. It was time to head home.

CHAPTER NINE

Winslow rolled his head from side to side, joints clicking as old aches shifted. Evermore magic had preserved him for over twenty-six millennia, but it couldn't entirely stop the progression of time. Even a body preserved by the most powerful magic would show some wear and tear after this long.

He felt his age particularly strongly as he walked through the unfamiliar kemana. It was so unlike the traditional one where he'd stood guard over the Source. Instead of carved stone houses and ancient trees freshening the air there were concrete buildings and neon lights, casting stark shadows across the angular edges of alleyways.

Magicals bustled back and forth—dwarves, elves, gnomes, and above all Willens, all dressed in clothes that looked strange to Winslow. But then, the clothes he'd acquired before leaving his kemana looked also odd to him.

The soft-soled shoes had bright ticks on the sides. The trousers were a heavy, faded blue fabric, and the stretchy tunic with short sleeves and no buttons had a meaningless message printed on the front. He'd long ago grown out of trying to cling to the past, but still, the modern world was a weird place.

In the center of the kemana, a gigantic crystal glowed aquatic blue. Its light shone through the windows of shops, restaurants, and bars, sparkling off sequined clothes and the shining edges of cocktail glasses. Magical lights sparkled, and spells danced in the air. There was a party atmosphere to the place that was a far cry from Winslow's life.

It was good to see that the power of the place was still holding, the crystal radiating magical energy that replenished the magicals who came here. Still, how long could that power hold? With the Source gone from its place in the deep, the network would begin to fade, and if the Source itself found its way to one of the other kemanas, the havoc it could wreak was simply unknowable.

A shudder ran down Winslow's spine at that thought. No time to stop and contemplate the wonders of the world. He had a duty to fulfill.

As he was approaching a bar in the corner of the square, the crystal's light flickered. Winslow turned to look at it in concern as other magicals ignored the kemana's power faltering. Idiots, didn't they understand what was at stake here? Of course, they didn't. They were all too young, centuries at most. Such timescales didn't give you the perspective needed for real maturity.

The flickering stopped, and the crystal shone bright again. Not breaking yet, but fading. All the more reason to act now, to prevent a breakdown instead of having to repair something terribly broken.

Winslow hurried into the bar. It was more old-fashioned than the rest but in the inauthentic way of retro bars, pieced together from secondhand furnishings and replicas. Griff had probably chosen it to make him feel comfortable, and he appreciated the effort, but he would've preferred something authentically modern. Nothing anybody made here could ever be old enough for him.

"Beer, please," Winslow said to the barman.

"Sure. What sort would you like?"

Winslow smiled. He'd learned better than to try to bluff his way when he didn't need to.

"Surprise me."

"Okay." The barman laughed. "Don't often get that sort of adventurousness from a wizard your age."

"What can I say? Life's an adventure worth enjoying." He wouldn't correct the barman on his assumption. Wizard was as good a disguise as any.

Winslow looked around the bar. Sure enough, his contact was sitting at a table in the corner, on one of the tall stools designed for smaller magicals. The Willen gave Winslow a small nod, then took a sip of his drink.

"Here you go." The barman slid a glass across the bar to Winslow, who pulled a plastic card from his pocket and used it to pay. That was something he liked about this age: he didn't have to understand the currency. These thin strips of plastic sorted it out for themselves. He picked up the glass, walked over to the Willen's table, and sat across from him.

"Good to see you, Griff," he said.

"And you, Winslow. Been a long time."

"I suppose." It seemed like no time to Winslow, thirty

years at most, but those years had taken their toll on Griff. The wrinkles of his face had grown deeper, and his whiskers were starting to droop. A pair of spectacles perched on his rat-like nose, and he squinted through them as he peered at Winslow.

"You haven't aged a day, have you?" the Willen asked.

"I think this one's new." Winslow plucked out one of his gray hairs. They both laughed. "Our current situation is going to give me more if I don't solve it soon. What have you heard about the creature?"

Griff pulled a notebook from a pocket inside his vest, flipped through a few pages, then ran a claw down his notes.

"Excuse this, memory's not what it was, though my contacts are still as good. Now, where was... Ah, yes, here we go.

"Your energy creature has been seen in a few places in the underground. It caused a blackout in a magical survivalist compound under Texas and a destructive burst of growth in a Tolderai forest under LA. Disruptions at several kemanas, though its behavior's been strange there. It hovers around the edges, gets noticed, and hurries away again."

"Hm." Winslow drummed his fingers against the table. "So it's not attacked anyone yet?"

"Not that I've heard. Is that going to happen?"

"Eventually." Winslow sighed. "But it's so long since this thing has been loose, predicting its behavior is challenging."

"By challenging, you mean a total nightmare?"

"No, but I can see how it might seem that way to someone so short-lived."

Griff snorted, making his whole snout vibrate.

"If you start on the young species, old species lectures, I'm going to double my fee. It might've been thirty years, but I still remember how annoying you can be."

"All right, I'll behave." Winslow sipped his beer. It was good, much better than beer used to be. There was an intensity to the flavor and a mellow note running through it.

When he'd been young, a very long time ago, most beers had been watery, bitter, or both. Living long enough to see the world change was as wonderful as it was frustrating. "What else can you tell me?"

"Not much. It's hard to track a creature when it looks different every time, doubly so when I have to keep my inquiries secret."

"Your discretion is appreciated."

"I'd hope so. My people go to great lengths to meet your particular needs."

Particular. That was a word Winslow liked and one that suited him. Eccentric and precise, definitive and isolated, a critical particle in a far larger universe. How better to define the Evermores?

"Here are the times and locations of the sightings." Griff tore a sheet of paper from his pad and slid it across the table. "All in North America so far, which helps with the search. There's a pattern of sorts, an uneven spiral to where this thing's traveling. I don't know exactly where it's headed, and I guess that it doesn't either, but maybe you know something I don't."

Griff's eyes narrowed as he watched Winslow's reaction, but twenty-six thousand years was a long time to practice a poker face.

"Thank you, it's appreciated." Winslow read the paper, folded it in half, and put it in his pocket. He had a few ideas about where all of this was going, but he would need a map to work out what was most likely. "How are your people doing?"

"Making the most of our opportunities." The Willen grinned. "There are far more of them, now that we don't have to stay hidden from the humans. Although that brings its risks as well."

"Secrecy can be a blessing, and it can be a curse."

"You'd know better than me, old man." Griff laughed, and the laugh turned into a cough. "Not many creatures I get to call old anymore, but you qualify."

Winslow frowned. "Are you unwell?"

"Nothing that'll stop me doing my job." Griff brushed the back of a paw across his mouth, then downed the last of his drink. "That's better. Now, I need to get going once we've dealt with the matter of payment..."

"Here." Winslow slid a handful of silver buttons across the table. "I put in a few extra, as thanks for your future work."

"So you did." Griff picked them up, then hid them quickly in the folds of his skin. "I'll let you know what our future work leads to."

"I can trust you to keep my secrets?"

"Haven't we always?" Griff frowned. "Don't question our integrity."

The Willen dropped to the floor, and without another word, scurried off into the shadows.

Winslow watched the darkness into which Griff had disappeared. Had he caused some offense there? It hardly mattered. In a few more decades, he would be dealing with another Willen entirely. The network would remain, and that was all that counted.

He drank some more of his beer and gazed out the window of the bar at the kemana crystal, watchful for any faltering in its blue-green glow. In his mind's eye, a creature spiraled through the darkness beneath America, on a mission of its own.

CHAPTER TEN

Fran sat in her bedroom, posters for action movies and novelty bands staring down at her from the walls. A soft unicorn toy stared at her over the top of her monitor, its sparkly horn drooping over a rainbow smile.

"Who could get lonely when I have you for company?" Fran patted the unicorn on the head. "And who could get bored when there's work to do? Not me, for sure. You know I'm my own CEO now? Well, CEOs don't get bored. They get the job done."

The stuffed unicorn smiled back at her but kept its insights into corporate culture to itself. That was already an improvement on any manager Fran had worked with before.

She turned her attention back to the screen. The biggest problem with the flying carpet had been in the control software, so that was what she needed to refine now. Getting a program to interface correctly with a set of spells could be tricky, even when the program had magic wound into it, and debugging was twice as complicated when she was debugging spells as well as code, but she could do this.

With swift movements of her fingers, Fran started typing out a new take on the same old code from a week before, trying a different approach this time. Bits of Linux code and spell glyphs spilled out across the screen.

She reached for her cup with the grinning bear on it. The cup was cold, and there were only dregs of coffee left. Better make another one. She'd written a whole six lines of code. That earned her a coffee break, right?

Wearing giant bunny slippers, Fran padded through into the kitchen and switched on the hot drinks machine. It had settings for coffee, tea, and a new gnome drink called squirtle, made from a special sort of enlivening berries. Fran pressed the squirtle button, but the machine started growling and chugging and leaking steam, so she canceled that and went for coffee instead.

Modifying the machine had been a great idea, but it meant that it needed more maintenance, and she shouldn't get distracted by that now. Once she'd found her first investors, she would get a whole new coffee machine for her office, one with settings for hot chocolate and herbal tea and whatever the fashionable gnomes were drinking this month.

Coffee in hand, Fran walked back into her bedroom. With her attention on her cup and her monitor, she didn't look at her seat, but a loud meow alerted her to its occupant a moment before she would've sat on him.

"Hi there, Smokey." She smiled at the gray and black mottled cat. "Have you come to help me with my software?"

Smokey meowed again and pointed at the keyboard with his paw.

"I'm not sure what you're saying, buddy, but you can't keep my seat. I need to sit there."

Fran set her cup down and picked up the cat, who let out a snort of protest, and set him down on the beanbag next to her. He pushed at the beanbag with his paws. Then, apparently satisfied, he curled up around himself.

"You'd never see anyone if this building had proper air con, would you?" Fran glanced at the window. She hadn't meant to leave it that wide open, but she wasn't surprised. It was one of the little things in life that she often misremembered.

That sort of thing was why she hated tests. It was hard to remember all the little details. She patted Smokey on his head, and the cat purred contentedly. "Don't your owners worry about where you go during the day?"

The cat shook his head, almost as if he understood the question, and settled deeper into the depression he'd made in the beanbag. He still looked up at Fran, or perhaps past her.

"Is this what you're after?" She took the unicorn down off the top of the monitor. "Something shiny to hunt?"

She set the toy down on the floor next to Smokey, who reached out to bat it with a paw, then looked back up.

"Well, it's there if you want it." Fran turned back to her monitor. "Now I need to get on with some work."

She started typing straight away, not looking at her previous work but getting down an idea she'd had in the kitchen. It was important to do that. Ideas she didn't write down immediately all too often got lost, flying away like a balloon on a windy day.

After twenty minutes, she sat back with a satisfied sigh.

"Snack time." She looked down at Smokey. "You want something too?"

"Meow."

"I'll take that as a yes."

It was amazing how he was always looking up when she looked down at him, but cats had a knack for that sort of thing, didn't they? Waking up at the slightest movement, alert and watching for what happened next.

The bunny slippers flopped across the floor as Fran headed back into the kitchen. There was a slice of carrot cake in the fridge, alongside some chicken stew from the previous night. She fished a few pieces of chicken out of the stew onto a plate, then headed back into her room, cake in one hand and chicken in the other.

This time Smokey wasn't just in her chair. He was on the desk, one paw raised as if he was about to swat at the screen.

"Smokey!" She shooed him onto the floor. "Please tell me you haven't been on the keyboard."

She looked at the last lines on the screen, but there wasn't the rows of nonsense she had feared. No harm done.

"Here."

She set the plate of chicken down on the floor. Smokey immediately bent his head over the plate and gobbled it up while Fran ate her cake. It was tempting to hop on social media while she was snacking, but she needed to stay productive, so instead she scrolled back up her programming window and read back through the code.

"That's weird," she said after a moment.

The sound of plate licking stopped as Smokey looked up at her, whiskers twitching.

"Nothing to do with you." Fran leaned over to stroke his head. "Just a line of code I don't remember writing. I must've been in the zone."

Smokey meowed again, padded across the room, and leaped up onto the windowsill.

"Had enough of me now that I've fed you, huh?" Fran said. "I can't blame you. Sitting in here has to be a lot less exciting than running around out there."

She watched the cat jump out onto the fire escape and disappear. It seemed silly to be jealous of a pet when she was the one with an apartment and a fridge and a vacuum cleaner with googly eyes, but she wanted to be enjoying the sunshine. Maybe she could take a quick skating break…

From the corner of the room, her skates seemed to gaze back longingly at her. But above them was a sheet of paper and on it a message in Josie's handwriting, every letter written in extra-large marker.

Skating didn't build Microsoft.

Fran sighed and turned back to her screen. Josie was right, and Fran had been right to ask her for that reminder, a request made in a moment when her willpower was strong. She needed to stay focused if she was going to run her own company.

The code glared at her from the screen, lines of green text against a black background.

"That's weird too." She re-read one of the lines. It

wasn't quite like she'd meant it to be, and for a moment she thought she'd slipped while typing. Now that she considered it, that change could make the code better. Some subconscious part of her mind was smarter than she realized.

She wiggled her fingers, then scrolled down the screen, ready to get back to work.

An alert popped up in the corner of the monitor. She should probably switch those off. Too many potential distractions when every app was screaming for attention. Then she noticed what it was, a diary reminder about a magical invention competition taking place that afternoon in a local maker space.

She'd added it to her calendar in a moment of hopefulness a month before, knowing that work would get in the way of attending but feeling as though she should at least remember the community of technological creativity out there in Mana Valley. Now, though, she set her schedule, and events like this could be a useful tool, a way of raising her profile and networking with other tech entrepreneurs. Attendance was practically compulsory.

She saved her code, switched off her computer, closed and locked the window. If she headed out now, she could get in a quick skate before the competition to clear her head and shift her from coding to a physical creation headspace. There would be time for programming later, but only one chance to attend this event.

With a small twinge of guilt, she set aside the note from Josie, picked up her skates and backpack, and headed out the door.

CHAPTER ELEVEN

Handar Ennis sat in the corner of a bar on High Cosmologist Street, a large glass of cola in front of him. Handar enjoyed a good drink as much as the next muscular thug, but it was important to keep his mind in the game while he was on duty. If his contacts wanted to drink, that was on them.

"It's some sort of mirror," he said. "One that acts as a portal."

"That's all you've got?" One of his agents, an elf with a scar on his cheek and a perpetual sneer, raised a disdainful eyebrow.

"If I had more, I wouldn't need to use you lot," Handar growled.

The people around the table were a motley assortment, which was how Handar liked it. A pair of twins, witch and wizard, with silver-blond hair and matching twitches. A gnome with two fingers missing and a gambling addiction that kept her forever in Handar's debt. The elf, far too aloof for someone with so many bad habits.

Just a sample of the talent pool that Handar had built up in Mana Valley and across the divide in Silicon Valley, people with big needs and small scruples, but with the skills and contacts to find things that were missing, or to carry out jobs that others might balk at.

"What sort of mirror?" the twins asked in unsettling unison.

"I don't know."

"How big is it?"

"I don't know."

"Why do you want it?"

"That's none of your damn business."

"It's not him who wants it," the gnome pointed out before sipping her vodka. "It's Phillips."

"This had nothing to do with Mr. Phillips or anyone at his organization," Handar said. "If you try to tell anyone that it does, you won't be telling anyone anything much longer."

"But you're part of his organization," the wizard said.

His witch twin slapped him across the back of the head. "Idiot. I'll explain it later."

The twins rose from their seats, their movements identical, back to acting in smooth synchronicity.

"Remember, there's a bonus for whoever finds it first," Handar said. "And a bigger bonus if you bring it to me."

The elf stood. "That bonus will be mine."

He and the twins hurried across the bar and out the door. The gnome paused long enough to finish her drink, then wiped the back of her hand across her mouth.

"These are on you, right?" she asked, raising her glass. Hander nodded. "Great, then I'll have one for the road."

Handar nodded again. A few drinks were nothing next to what Mr. Phillips paid him and what else was at stake. Besides, the gnome was very good at what she did.

Julia Lacy sat in a small room in the Philgard offices with a summoning circle sketched on the floor around her. Candles dribbled, and incense drifted through the air as she chanted the verses of a long and complicated spell. Her grimoire was open in front of her, and she paid attention to its contents, making sure to get every last accent and flick of her wand correct. Some spells were delicate, some were dangerous, and some were both. It was important to get them right.

A final hand movement completed the spell. In the gloom around her, something shifted, swirled, and became a hovering spirit with ragged edges, like a Victorian picture of a ghost. Two more appeared behind it, a chill filling the air around them, eyes glittering like ice.

"What have you summoned us for?" the spirits asked.

"By hex and by blade, I bind you." Julia ran a knife across the back of her hand. She barely felt the pain as a small trickle of blood spilled onto the glyphs she'd drawn. "You are mine to command."

"Yes, mistress." The lead spirit bowed its head. "But do not pretend that it's your power that binds us. You could do nothing without—"

"Do not say it," one of the others hissed. "Do not bring him here."

Julia smiled. It was pleasing to know that even the

darkest creatures feared her employer. It filled her with a rush of pride at having risen so far in his service. It also made moments like this so much easier to negotiate.

"You are bound, and that is what matters," she said. "You will seek something for me. A magical mirror, one that can act as a portal between worlds."

The lead spirit hissed derisively.

"Such items are common, down the stretch of the years. You summon us for something like this?"

"This mirror is new, it is powerful, and it is of interest to the one I serve. But all that matters is that I command you." Julia squeezed her fingers together, and the spirits screeched in pain. "Do you understand?"

"Yes, mistress," the spirits hissed and bowed their heads.

"Then get to it."

When they had gone, she switched on the light and blew out the candles. Then she gathered up her materials, wiped away the frost where the spirits had hovered, and scuffed out the chalk marks on the floor. She didn't need to be precise, this room existed to cast magic in, but she didn't want anyone accidentally replicating what she had done.

Then she glanced at her watch. Nearly eleven o'clock. She should remind Mr. Phillips about his conference call with the circuit suppliers.

This was why she enjoyed being a PA. Every day brought something new.

The shopkeeper looked up as the bell over his door rang. He didn't get a huge number of customers in a shop selling custom mirrors, so he liked to pay attention to each one.

"Hi there," he said. "Can I ask what you're looking for?"

The gnome didn't look at him but around at the samples on display.

"I'm looking for a mirror," she said.

"Then you've come to the right place." The shopkeeper stepped out from behind his counter. "What sort of mirror are you after?"

"I'm not sure." The gnome waved a hand that was missing two fingers, and magic flowed across the nearest mirror. It looked like a spell for detecting magical fields.

"We can arrange enchantments," the shopkeeper said. "A spell that acts as a zoom setting, for example, so you can get the details of your makeup right."

She wasn't wearing a lot of makeup, but you never knew. Lots of people made less effort when they were out shopping.

"I'd like to look through your stock," the gnome said. "See if there's anything I like."

"That's not quite how it works," the shopkeeper said with a small laugh, one carefully crafted to humor rather than to condescend. "Each mirror we sell is custom crafted to individual specifications. There's no point in you looking through what we have when we can make something unique to you."

"I disagree." The gnome waved. "Show me all of them."

A haze fell across the shopkeeper's mind. Of course, he wanted to help this customer more than any other he'd met. He locked the door, set the shop sign to closed, and headed for the back room.

"You can start here," he said. "I'll fetch the others out."

Across the divide between worlds, in the lobby of a Silicon Valley office block, a security guard stepped from behind his desk.

"Can I help you?" he asked the white-haired couple in loose black clothes who were staring at the mirrored back wall. After five minutes of standing there, saying and doing nothing, they were starting to creep him out.

One of the pair turned to face him. She was younger than he'd expected. Now that he saw the other one's face, they were very similar looking, probably brother and sister rather than a couple.

"We are evaluating your mirror," the woman said. "Every inch of it."

"Uh-huh." The guard smiled. "Maybe you could take a picture and evaluate it from somewhere else?"

The woman raised a wand and sparks shone around its tip. "That will not do."

"Oh, you're magicals!" The guard laughed. "Guess that explains it. Seriously, you can't stand around here all day."

"We can."

"No, you can't." Her sharp tone had annoyed the guard, and now he was feeling less helpful. "This is private property, and I'm asking you to leave."

The white-haired man raised his hand and flicked a

wand. The guard was flung back across the room. Visitors stopped and stared.

"That was stupid," the wizard's sister snapped. "Now we'll have to leave."

"We're done here anyway." The brother waved his wand again. The phones of spectators burst into flames as they tried to photograph the pair. "This isn't it."

"Very well." The witch opened a portal, and they stepped through it, on to their next lead.

In a Silicon Valley middle school, kids ran screaming out of the bathroom.

"What's the matter?" the vice principal asked, catching one of them as they ran past.

"Ghosts!" the girl wailed. "The bathroom's haunted."

The vice principal shook her head. She believed in many things, including feng shui and the healing power of crystals, but haunted bathrooms weren't on the list. If this was another prank by the boys from the nearby high school, she was going to be deeply unimpressed.

She pushed the bathroom door open and stepped inside, then stopped in her tracks. Shapes were hurtling through the air, ragged, fraying forms, translucent bodies dressed in robes like gray fog. They flew in and out of the mirrors, hissing as they went.

"Not this one," one of them said.

"Or this," said the second.

"Or this," said the third.

The first spirit stopped in front of the vice principal

and ran an icy finger down her cheek. She stared, frozen by fear.

"Do you have a mirror?" the spirit asked.

The vice principal gave a tiny nod. With trembling fingers, she took the mirror out of the tray of equipment she had been returning to the science room.

"Not this either." The spirit peered at the mirror. Then it looked up at the vice principal, and its eyes were like crystals of ice. "You're warm. Would you like to be very, very cold?"

The vice principal screamed, dropped her tray, and ran out of the bathroom.

CHAPTER TWELVE

The maker space was a huge basement under an old department store in an area neglected during Mana Valley's growth. This was part of the old town, which had once catered to miners in the hills. It had been too slow to adjust when tech companies coming to use the dug-up resources overtook the miners. The businesses still working there were smaller, less flashy, and looking for additional ways to pay the bills, like hiring out their basements to creative collectives.

Fran was surprised by how many people had turned up for the competition. Normally, the basement was only occupied by five or six people, each working on their small projects, going up to a dozen on weekends. Today there were scores of them, some standing at the folding tables with their heaps of scavenged components, others standing around the outside, an excited crowd of spectators. Fran handed over her entrance fee and went to the last unoccupied table.

"Hi." She waved at the Willen in a flannel shirt at the

next table. "I'm Fran."

"I'm Singar." The Willen twitched her nose. "You should give up now, because I'm going to crush this."

Fran laughed. "I love your confidence!"

"You probably love glitter and bath bombs and unicorns too, right?" Singar asked, looking Fran up and down, taking in her jeans with the embroidered flowers and her sequined t-shirt.

"How did you know?"

"Wild guess." Singar shook her head and turned back to examining the components on her table.

"Good luck," Fran said brightly.

"Sure, whatever."

At the front of the room, an elf stood on a plastic crate.

"All right, it's time," she called. "Rules are the same as last time. You can use any tools you've brought, as well as the ones that are here, and magic is allowed, but no components we didn't provide. You can use anything on your table or from the storage bins." She pointed at shelves of plastic boxes at the back of the room.

"Anything else is off limits and will get you booted out. Judges will be going around while you work, asking questions. To make it more exciting than before, this time it's a knockout. If we think you're going too slow or your idea's too derivative, we'll ask you to stop. Last inventor standing wins half the cash pot, and the rest goes into running this place. Any questions?"

When no one asked anything, she waved her hand at a digital clock on the opposite wall, and it changed to show a four-hour countdown. "Today's theme is communication. Ready, set, go!"

The clock started and the creators set to work.

Fran looked across the pieces she'd been given. There were a couple of old phones, circuit boards, wires, mechanical components, runic paper, crystals... It was an eclectic assortment, which only made it harder to know where to begin. There were dozens of things she could imagine some of these pieces making to help people communicate. Which would stand out? And which could she prototype in only a few hours?

Her head was still in a coding place, so something with that, using the phones.

"Ooh, I know!" She clapped excitedly. Some of the spectators near her laughed and leaned in to see what she would do. At the next table, Singar shook her head and carried on screwing mechanical parts together.

Fran pulled a roll-out keyboard from her backpack and connected it to one of the phones. The software system was pre-cracked, set up so that the creators could lay their programs over it. Some people might've used that to try a system for voice calls or a translation unit, but Fran had something else entirely in mind. She rapidly typed out some familiar strings of code and new bits around them.

After an hour, one of the judges came over to see what was happening. He nodded approvingly at Singar, who had assembled a large box full of gears but looked less impressed when he turned to Fran.

"I don't see much sign of invention," he said.

Fran looked up from her screen. "I'm laying down the groundwork," she said. "I promise, it'll look way more interesting soon."

"Hm." The judge made a note on his tablet. "I'll let it

slide this time, but remember, this is a knockout, and I'm not seeing much yet to keep you in."

Once he had gone, Fran hurriedly finished her software and chucked in a couple of spells, remembering to pull out a wand to maintain the illusion that she was an ordinary witch. Then she turned to the wires and circuit boards. This part was going to be trickier, and not only because the last few days had been so code-heavy that she was practically programming in her sleep. The technology of it wasn't something people normally used.

She took a cable and plugged it into the phone at one end, then into a crystal set in a circuit board at the other. There wasn't a second crystal set up like that, so she had to improvise the other end of the line, using her magic to embed a piece of quartz into the phone. By the time the second hour was up, she had barely even started building the components around the crystal.

This time, the judge at her table was the elf who had told them the rules.

"What is it?" she asked, looking at what Fran had produced.

"Smoke signals." Fran tapped the phone, and a strand of smoke flowed from a small heated plate. As it rose, magic from the crystal next to it rearranged the smoke into dots and ashes, like a string of Morse code.

"Cute," the judge said. "But I've seen it on at least two steampunk western shows."

"There's going to be more," Fran said. "I promise. This is a step along the way." She held up her phone so the elf could read her code. "See?"

Past the elf, other judges turned several would-be

inventors away from their tables. The knockout was in effect.

"I don't get it," the elf admitted. "But I'm intrigued. You can stay in." She glanced at Singar, who was adding hinges to the fingers of a mannequin's hands. "Same for you. Whatever that is, I want to see more."

By the end of the third hour, more than half the inventors in the room had been knocked out or given up, unable to complete their projects with the time and resources they had. Fran wasn't sure that she could do it either, but she was determined to keep going. It was so much fun trying to cobble a project together like this.

"All right, enough secrecy," the elf judge said as she stood in front of Singar's table. "What's it going to be?"

"A sign language box," Singar said. "Magically powered but computer-controlled. It'll help people practice sign languages."

Singar tugged on a wire, and the jointed hands on top of the box waved. Some of the spectators cheered.

"Nice." The elf smiled. "Keep it up."

She came over to Fran's table.

"What's this about?"

"Do I have to say?" Fran asked. "I wanted it to be a surprise."

"No more surprises. Prove you should remain in the competition."

"Okay. I think you'll like it." Fran took a fresh orange from her pocket. "It's a scent transmitter."

She held her orange above one of the crystals and gave it a small squeeze. At the other end of the table, smoke dribbled from the hot plate and was transformed by the other crystal. The elf sniffed the smoke.

"Citrusy," she said. "Though a little burned. Cool idea, and it might just work. Keep it up."

The competition shrank as the last hour passed, with stressed inventors flinging their tools down in exasperation or the judges asking them to stop. As Fran made her final frantic adjustments, tweaking the code and the magic, repositioning the hotplate, there were only five of them left.

"Time's up," the elf announced. The crowd cheered and the makers set down their tools. "Show me what you've got."

First up was a translation machine, which got polite applause because it was so well-made, but everyone saw that the judges weren't excited. There were similar responses to the next two inventions, one that reminded the user of the word on the tip of their tongue, another stopping sound from interrupting quiet conversations. They were well-crafted and impressive for four hours of work, but everyone's attention was on Fran's end of the room.

At last, the judges came to Singar, who demonstrated the skills of her sign language device. It carried out a brief conversation with one of the judges, fake hands moving with dexterity and precision.

"Very nice," the elf judge said. "And now our last contender..."

"Who has something that smells?" Fran asked.

Someone in the audience passed her a bottle of

lavender perfume. Fran put a small dot onto a tissue and held it next to a crystal.

"I know it doesn't seem so impressive here," she said, "but imagine if you could share a smell over hundreds of miles or include smells in streaming shows. The scent of fresh cake while you watch a baker or forest freshness on a nature show."

The judges leaned in to smell the lavender smoke from the other crystal, then came over and smelled the original perfume.

"Not bad for a prototype," one of them said.

The judges gathered in a huddle while the audience chattered excitedly among themselves.

"Your invention is brilliant," Fran said, smiling at Singar.

"Yours is ridiculous," Singar replied as she stowed a small screwdriver away in the folds of her skin.

The judges separated and the elf went to stand on her box at the front of the room.

"It was a tough decision," she said. "Singar Twitchtail's device is impressive in its practicality, execution, and social utility. It's a useful creation well-made, overcoming a range of challenges. On that basis, we're offering a special second-place award, a year's free membership to the maker space. Congratulations, Sin!"

The crowd applauded, and the Willen went over to shake hands with the judges, but as she went back to her table, she glared daggers at Fran.

"This place is about wild imaginations and crazy invention, so on that basis, congratulations to today's winner: Fran Berryman and her smellophone!"

CHAPTER THIRTEEN

Fran whizzed around the track at the edge of the skate park, her personal victory lap. She was the champion inventor, the top creator of all rushed creators, the queen of smellophones. Her business was going to be a triumph. She spun as she rolled around the track, singing a song about her success. It was surprisingly hard to rhyme anything with "smell," but she was up to the challenge.

A familiar figure was making slower progress around the track, dressed in a helmet and an excess of padding, his movements careful and sometimes halting, but at least upright and on the track. Fran slowed as she approached him.

"Hey there, Bart!" she called.

The gnome looked around, waved, almost lost his balance, flailed his arms briefly, and found his footing again. He slowed further so he could talk while skating.

"Hello, Fran," he said, once he'd finished steadying himself. "How's the startup going?"

"Still just starting, but I guess that's how it works, right?"

"Oh yes. There's a long stretch of not getting far before you take off. As long as you can pay your employees, you'll be fine."

"I don't have any employees yet, only me and the stuffed unicorn on my computer."

"I don't imagine the unicorn needs much pay."

"Just sparkles and rainbows, and those come cheaper than you'd think. I had a great day today, though."

"Oh really, how's that?"

Fran told him about the competition at the maker space and all the people who'd come to talk to her afterward. Four hours of inventing had left her without much brain-power left to socialize. Still, it had been great to be acknowledged like that and to see so many people interested in collaborating with her. If it turned out that any of them had money to fund a business, she might be sorted.

"Can you show me this smellophone?" Bart asked.

"Sure."

Fran moved to the side of the track, sat, and rummaged through her bag. Bart half lowered himself and half fell onto the ground next to her.

"Here it is." Fran waved one of the crystals in Bart's face and pressed the other into a wildflower growing by the side of the track.

"My, that is clever," Bart said after a deep sniff. "There could be money in a thing like that."

"Maybe, but it's not the main thing I'm working on. I'm still trying to rebuild my flying carpet prototype, so I can test my battery again."

"Power over power seems like a good way to build a business."

"I don't suppose you've seen your neighbor again?"

"Kiri?" Bart shook his head. "He's disappeared off the map. Wouldn't be surprised if the Griffins are hot on his heels. He always struck me as living outside the law." He sighed. "Maybe that's what I should do, take up a career of crime. It would keep me busy, at least."

"You're too nice for that."

Bart started unfastening his pads.

"I think I've finished for the day, but did you say something about a flying carpet?"

"That's what I'm working on right now, to test the battery."

"Then I might have someone else who'd like to meet you if you've got the time. Might even lead to a sponsorship deal of sorts."

"Brilliant!" Fran leaped to her feet. "I need all the finance I can get."

They made their way through the Mana Valley evening, Bart walking and Fran skating beside him. It was getting dark, shops and offices closing while coffee shops and bars put out their brightest signs. She was surprised when Bart stopped in front of a shop, a big building in the old district with "Worn Threads" written above the door.

"I know this place," Fran said. "I bought the carpet for my prototype here."

"Perfect." Bart pushed the door open. "Raulo, Gail, it's me!"

The last time around, Fran had rushed in and out on a wild wave of excitement about her invention, paying very little attention to the place. Now she took her time to look around.

Worn Threads was a cavernous space that looked like it had once been a factory or warehouse. There were huge rolls of carpet piled up against the walls and samples on tables down the length of the room. In one corner were plastic floor coverings and patterns for wooden floors. In another were racks of skateboards and wheels.

"They sell boards here?" She was surprised.

"Raulo's idea," Bart said. "Before that, it was comic books, and before that old vinyl records. He always has to have some novelty to keep him entertained and to try to draw in younger customers."

A wizard and a witch appeared through a door behind the counter. Both were in their fifties, short and on the round side, with big smiles. He had dark, curly hair while hers was long and dyed blue.

"Bart!" The witch hugged the white-haired gnome. "What brings you around?"

"Fran, this is Gail and her husband Raulo," Bart said. "Guys, this is Fran, and she used one of your carpets to fly."

Raulo laughed. "They don't often do that. Must have been quite a trick."

"It was! I invented a flying carpet from scratch. It uses a special sort of circuit board, with dwarven runes in a containment field, a little bit like those elevators they use on building sites…"

Fran started explaining the technology, arms waving through the air, carried away in the excitement of what she did. It took five minutes before she noticed the glazed expressions on the others' faces.

"Um, did you understand any of that?" she asked.

"I understood flying carpet," Raulo said. "And I see the gleam in Bart's eye. We used to work together, and I know what it looks like when he spies a financial opportunity."

"What can I say, once an accountant, always an accountant." Bart wandered down the shop, looking at the samples on their tables and racks. "These pieces, you must need to get rid of them sometimes, when they've had too much customer handling, or you stop stocking a type of carpet, right?"

"That's right," Gail said as they followed Bart down the shop. "But I don't think we can sell them."

"That's not what I'm suggesting." Bart held up one of the larger samples. "These are the perfect size for flying on, right, Fran?"

"Oh yes!" she said. "Especially if they're thin or worn."

"So, why don't you give them to Fran in return for a bit of free advertising? She adds the phrase 'Carpets supplied by Worn Threads' to the publicity for her prototype. Maybe some people hear about it, maybe they don't, but all you've lost is the carpets you were ditching anyway."

"Honestly, I don't even need the adverts," Gail said. "Just glad to see someone put these old bits to use. It seems such a shame to throw them out." She turned to Fran. "Do you want some now?"

"That would be awesome! The Silver Griffins still have the rug I bought."

"The Griffins? Why?"

Leaving Raulo and Bart to catch up, Fran followed Gail to the back of the store, explaining about her arrest as they went. Gail opened a door, and they walked down a set of stairs into a dark and echoing space, brushing aside spider-webs. At the bottom, Gail flipped a switch, and neon lights came on, illuminating a basement as big as the shop above.

"Wow!" Fran looked around the dusty space. "What are those?"

She pointed at a row of heavy, rusted machines along the back wall.

"They were left here by the original owners, a company that manufactured mirrors." Gail went to a corner and started picking pieces of abandoned carpet out of a pile. "You said thinner carpets were better, right?"

"Uh-huh. Less weight to lift." Fran walked over to the machines and ran a hand over one of them. It was so hefty, so unsophisticated, and somehow so beautiful in its solidity. "Is this why the building's so big, for making mirrors?"

"Oh yes. It used to be the biggest mirror workshop on Oriceran. Mostly dwarf run, of course, an offshoot of a mining clan. Then other manufacturers sprang up, technology changed, the clan shifted more toward the gem trade, and they gave up on this. It's a shame. They made the most spectacular mirrors."

Gail tugged at the edge of a sheet that hung across one of the walls. It fell to the ground in a billow of dust, revealing a mirror eight feet high and thirty wide, with an elaborate gold-painted frame.

"Wow!" Fran smiled at her mirror self. "That's so cool. It makes the room seem twice as big."

"Oh, it's quite big enough. We lend the space to skaters sometimes to test out our boards." Gail nodded at the skates hanging off Fran's backpack. "If you ever want to come down here and practice when the weather's lousy outside, you're more than welcome."

"Thanks."

"Here are your carpets." Gail handed Fran an armful of samples. "Will that be enough for what you need?"

"More than enough. Are you sure this is okay?"

"Am I sure?" Gail laughed and pointed at the mound of discarded carpet samples. "I'm glad not to have to take them to the dump. Now come on up, and you can tell me more about this flying carpet. I might as well know what I'm sponsoring."

CHAPTER FOURTEEN

Josie sat at her workbench, tapping her wand against her thigh and contemplating the parts spread out in front of her. She felt a little guilty, staying in the office so late. If she didn't go home, there was no guarantee that Fran would remember to eat dinner, never mind going to bed at a sensible time.

Still, working late could create a good first impression, and Josie wanted to fit in. Besides, the things she got to work on here were so cool. How many people could say they had hold of the new Philgard Manaphone Seven when the Six had only recently hit the shops?

She put the phone pieces back together, raised her wand, and cast a small water summoning spell. Sure enough, the water ran out of another phone, dialed into this one, at the far end of the room. Her manager was right, though. The spell wasn't quite coming out the same. The water dribbled rather than flowed, and it looked more than a little dirty. Something was messing with the magical signal.

Josie took the phone apart again and looked at the parts. If she could work this out, that would be a big win for her team, which was supposed to be fixing magical glitches identified by the quality assurance team. The problem was, she wasn't used to working on technology this sophisticated, and she seemed to be missing something. No matter how many times she disassembled and reassembled it, she couldn't find the fault.

The test labs were mostly empty this late in the day, so the sound of high heels *clacking* against the floor echoed all around. Josie looked up to see a witch walking down the lab. She wore a blue pencil skirt and a fitted blouse, her blond hair tied tightly back, a style Josie had seen dozens of times among corporate PAs. It took her a moment to realize who it was: Julia Lacy, Howard Phillips' own feared and respected right hand.

Josie leaped out of her seat and started hastily gathering pieces of the phone together.

"Are you on the quality improvement team?" Julia asked.

"Yep." Josie nodded frantically. "Uh-huh. Quality. Absolutely."

She sounded like Fran, barely coherent in the face of authority. She had to pull herself together.

"They said that you've got the Seven down here for testing."

"Yes, absolutely, we do."

"Mr. Phillips wants to show it to some investors in Japan. Fetch it for me."

"Um..." Josie looked down at the pieces of the phone. "That might take a few minutes."

Julia looked at the parts, and for a moment Josie thought she might be in trouble. To her surprise, the PA smiled and gave a sharp nod.

"Of course. You can't find the problem without looking at the components."

"Exactly."

"But they come in pairs for testing, right?"

"Yes, but..." Josie pointed down the lab at the other phone, from which dirty water was still slowly dribbling. There was confetti plastered to its screen from an earlier spell.

Now Julia frowned. "Did no one tell you that we needed the phones this evening? I sent the memo two weeks ago."

"I wasn't here two weeks ago. If there was a memo, no one showed me. Sorry."

Julia shook her head. "Just what we need, Green dropping the ball again. Well, how long will it take you to reassemble the phone?"

"Five minutes?"

"Get on with it then." Julia took a seat, arms folded, and stared at the pile of parts.

Hastily, Josie started putting the phone back together. It was hard to concentrate with the PA to the company's owner watching her every move, judging her for what she did, but she drew deep, calming breaths and forced herself to focus. She'd taken this phone apart and put it back together eight times already. What was one more?

"You said that you're new?" Julia asked.

"That's right. Started this week."

"You can already disassemble and reassemble the Seven?"

Josie shrugged. "It's the job, right? They wouldn't have hired me if I couldn't do these things."

"You'd be surprised." A hint of bitterness slipped into Julia's words. "We've had more than a few idiots wind up here when the HR managers got lazy." She rubbed her temples. "Forget I said that. Just tired."

"That's understandable. Everybody works so hard here."

"They should, yet you, new technician, are the only one in the lab this evening."

Josie looked around. Julia was right. Everybody else had gone. When did that happen? "I guess I'm enjoying myself."

"Or trying too hard to impress."

Josie blushed. "I wouldn't say too hard..."

"Relax." Julia laughed. "Everybody does it at first, although most don't make themselves as useful as you have. Don't push yourself too hard right now. There'll be more than enough extra hours when we get near a product launch."

Josie pressed the last processor into place, double-checked the alignment of the runes down the side of the screen, and snapped the casing back into position.

"All done."

Julia took the phone, turned it over in her hand, then tapped the screen with a neatly manicured nail.

"Perfect." She got out of her seat and headed down the lab. Halfway to the exit, she turned. "What's your name, new technician?"

"Josie. Josie Bullworth."

"Excellent work, Josie Bullworth. I'll make sure that Mr. Phillips hears about it. Now clean the crap off that other phone and go get some sleep."

Josie hurried down the lab and grabbed the other phone. She peeled off the confetti, dismissed the still-running water spell, and dried the casing with a towel. Then she sagged against the workbench, the tension of the past ten minutes finally catching up with her.

She had faced Howard Phillips' PA, and she'd survived the ordeal. Not only survived it. Phillips was going to hear about how she had helped. How cool was that? Still, the fear of disgracing herself had been very real, and as the feeling wore off, so did the adrenaline holding her up. Julia was right. She needed to go home and get some sleep, not worry about fixing a phone this late at night.

Except that dirty water covered the phone she held now. She should check inside, in case any had got in. If it had and components deteriorated because of her sloppiness, she could be in a world of trouble.

Using her wand and a miniature screwdriver, she carefully opened the phone and peered at its insides. No water damage and no signs of confetti, but something else caught her eye. One of the magical crystals was misaligned. That couldn't possibly have happened during her testing, which meant that someone else had reassembled it wrong. And if this phone had been set up wrong, maybe that was what was interfering with the spells, not the sending phone but the receiving one.

She realigned the crystal, cleaned a couple of other components, and put the whole thing back together, smiling to herself. It was a shame she didn't have the other phone anymore so she could test this. It would've been a real feather in her cap to go to her manager in the morning with the problem solved. Perhaps if she came in early and tested it then? That would only work if the other phone were back. Did she dare ask Julia for it?

Josie drew a deep breath. She always encouraged Fran to do the right thing for her career, and now it was her turn. She pulled her work phone out and wrote a short email to Julia. She reminded her of who she was, explained that she'd potentially fixed a problem, and asked if, unless Mr. Phillips still needed the phone of course, she could pick the Manaphone Seven up from Julia in the morning.

She hesitated a long moment after typing all of that, daunted by her daring in asking a favor from someone so important. Then she hit "Send."

Five minutes later, in the elevator down to the lobby, she received a reply:

Well done on the fix, new tech. I'll be in from 7:00 a.m., come for the phone any time after that. J.

Josie punched the air. She'd taken a risk, it had paid off, and now the chief's PA was telling her well done. This was the best job ever!

With a *ding*, the elevator doors opened, and she stepped out on the first floor. In the middle of the lobby, a huge Kilomea in a crisp suit talked to a gnome with two fingers missing off her hand. Riding high on her success, Josie waved and greeted them as she passed, but they fell silent. Never mind. She'd been spending too much time around Fran and needed the reminder that not everyone was super friendly.

As she stepped out of the front doors, something shifted in the shadows. For a moment, a shape made of fog seemed to drift there, then it was gone. Josie shrugged. This place was a little odd, but what workplace wasn't?

As she strode down the street, she pulled out her phone and called Fran.

"Hey roomie, you haven't eaten yet, have you? Well, it's your lucky day. I'm celebrating my new job. Do you want me to pick up pizza or dumplings?"

CHAPTER FIFTEEN

It was a brisk day in San Francisco, with a strong wind blowing in off the sea. Fran wondered if that was because of magic. She'd heard they were testing air elementals to manage the weather here now. Or maybe it was simply one of those things, a dramatic day for her to finish some melodramatic business: her first run-in with the Silver Griffins.

Gruffbar the dwarf was standing outside the Griffins' waystation, a briefcase in one hand and a box of donuts in the other.

"Sorry I'm late," Fran said. "I was working late, then my roommate came home, and we were celebrating a big win for her, and I got distracted, and I was too full of dumplings, so I couldn't sleep, and—"

"Enough," Gruffbar said. "My advice, as your lawyer, is you should never be late for court, the feds, or the Griffins."

"What about the police?"

"Depends. Sometimes it's a useful power play." He gestured toward the door. "Let's go in. Al's expecting us."

Inside the building, at least a dozen magicals filled reception, all vying for the attention of the duty Griffins.

"Something's wrong with my magic," a witch said, holding out her hands. "See? No sparkle. And I'm due to shoot a product video this morning."

"Maybe you're sick?" a Griffin suggested.

"How dare you! I am not sick. My body is a temple, and I'm very careful about who prays there…"

Next to her, a dwarf was waving her pickax at another Griffin.

"I tell you, the enchantment has never failed," the dwarf said. "Someone has stolen my great-great-grandfather's ancestral mining ax."

"And replaced it with a replica that's the same in every exact detail, except that it's not enchanted?"

"Yes."

"Wow. That's either the weirdest crime of the century or your great-great-grandfather's enchantment stopped working. Which one do you think it could be?"

"Coming through," Gruffbar said, pushing people aside. "Al, where are you?"

Al, the desk wizard from Fran's previous visit, emerged from the back of the waystation.

"This way, guys." He ushered them through.

"By my beard, but it's busy here today," Gruffbar said as they followed Al down a corridor. "What's going on?"

"We don't know," Al said. "Lots of magic on the fritz, but when that happens, it's usually a symptom of something bigger."

"Ooh, like in *Killer Wizards Two*, when Dr. Dominator

makes all the light magic fail so he can take over the world."

"Yes, this job is exactly like the movies." Al shook his head.

"I knew it!"

They walked into a small, windowless room with a cluster of sensors in one corner and four folding chairs around a flimsy table.

"This looks suspiciously like an interrogation room." Gruffbar looked around. "What's going on?"

"Nothing, I swear!" Al held up his hands. "It's just that we're really busy right now, so all the other rooms are in use. Unless you want to go talk in the cells?"

"This will do." Gruffbar sat, and Fran took the chair next to him. He laid his briefcase on the table, then the box of donuts, and tapped the top of the box. "So, Al, do you deserve these?"

Al sighed. "I probably shouldn't accept them right now, too much like a bribe. But I do have what you came for."

He waved his wand, and a panel slid back in the wall, revealing Fran's carpet and the components that had made it fly.

"Brilliant!" She took a shopping bag out of her backpack and started filling it with parts.

"You should check that it's all there first," Gruffbar said.

"Honestly, it was kind of experimental. I'm not sure I even remember what all the parts were."

"Next time, don't say things like that in front of the Silver Griffins." Gruffbar shook his head. "Now, Al, compensation..."

"I don't know." Al pulled some paperwork across the desk. "Should we even have to pay for the labor costs of repairing this thing when your client doesn't know how she made it?"

"That only makes it more valuable. You've broken a unique and invaluable prototype."

"This is Silicon Valley. Everything's a unique and invaluable prototype."

"You want to test this in court?"

"Not really, and fortunately neither do my superiors."

"Hardly surprising, given the lack of evidence for her arrest."

"No need to rub it in. Here." Al slid a pile of papers across the table. "You'll need to sign the bottom one to say I've given your property back, but you'll want to check the top sheet first. It's a waiver for other costs, in exchange for—"

"A thousand bucks!" Fran yelped in excitement. "That's awesome. Give me a pen."

"Hold on." Gruffbar snatched the papers away. "I've seen this before. If they're straight up offering a grand, then the brass has authorized three but are hoping not to pay it. Right?"

Al sighed, pulled out another sheet, and slid it across the table.

"Better." Gruffbar read the paper carefully, then gave it to Fran. "You can sign that one. And the release form." He took a pen out of his briefcase. "Here. Never trust the other side's pens."

"Seriously, Gruffbar, you think we'd use trick ink?"

"I'm protecting my client. On that topic, she'll be taking payment in cash."

"You think we'd stop a check?"

"Like I said, protecting her interests."

"Fine, but it'll take a few minutes." Al walked out of the room.

"That was brilliant!" Fran said as she handed back Gruffbar's pen. "How did you know they could pay more?"

"I'm a lawyer, not a Silver Griffin, but I used to spend a lot of time around them. They're like any other bureaucracy, and bureaucracies never pay out more than they have to." He nodded at the bag full of carpet and components. "What now for all this?"

"I'll use it to build a new prototype. I need something to show off the battery technology I'm working on."

"Magitech?"

"Exactly!"

"I prefer pure technology myself. There's nothing more pleasing than a well-built machine."

"I know, right? But you can make even better machines when you add spells, and that's what I'm going to do here. Batteries powered by a special sort of magic so that magitech devices can do even more.

"It's just a startup right now, and by a startup I mean it's just me, but there's real potential in it. Imagine if your phone could last a week without charging and open portals for you. Or if a touch of magic could start your car. Or if you could fly home from work on a carpet, sure that it would stay safely in the sky, far above the traffic. Wouldn't that be awesome?"

"You've got some solid ideas, kid, but there's more to a business than concepts. A mine isn't just diamonds. It's pit props and shovel work."

"Oh, I'm not planning on mining, though I guess we will need minerals, and you could maybe use diamonds for part of the device, though that would probably make it too expensive."

"It was a metaphor." Gruffbar stroked his beard, which was the shortest she'd ever seen on a dwarf, short enough for him to pass as a short human if he needed to. "Think it over."

The door opened, and Al walked back in. He held out an envelope full of banknotes.

"Good thing for you we keep this handy for emergency expenses." He held the envelope out toward Fran.

"Wait." Gruffbar took the envelope, removed the cash, and weighed it in his hand. Then he nodded and stuck it back in the envelope. "Three grand exactly. We're good."

They walked back out through the waystation, leaving Al to help with the crowd of disgruntled magicals, and stepped into the street. The wind had died down, leaving a drift of thin clouds like streamers in the sky.

"Here you go." Fran took three hundred dollars from the envelope and handed it to Gruffbar. "Ten percent, as agreed."

"It's certainly a step up from three dollars and fifty-seven cents." Gruffbar put the cash in his leather jacket and zipped the pocket shut.

"Your metaphor, the pit props were people, right, ones who can hold the business up while I dig for the diamonds of ideas?"

"I knew you'd get it."

"I wish I could afford to hire you more often. You'd make a great pit prop."

"I'd expect a compliment like that to come from a dwarf, but I'll take it from a human." A thoughtful expression crossed Gruffbar's face. "Are you serious about hiring me?"

"Oh yes, but this is all the company funds I have." She waved the envelope. "Ooh, and five hundred dollars from a maker contest. How long would that cover your wages for?"

"Not long, but still... There are a lot of bad things in my past, things I'm not proud of, and I see you here trying to build something good. It seems like fate's given me a second chance. I'd like to take it."

"What sort of chance?"

"Instead of wages, I'll work with you on a profit share basis. Not your first employee, but the second member of your management committee."

"Who's the first?"

"You."

"Oh, yes!" Fran beamed. "Wow, a lawyer and a management committee. This is turning into a proper company."

"I hope so. At least with two of us, it stands a better chance." Gruffbar held out his hand. "We can sort out the contract later, but a dwarf's handshake is his bond, so here it is: if you want me, I'm in. What do you say?"

Fran grabbed his hand and shook it vigorously. "I say let's get to work."

CHAPTER SIXTEEN

Fran skated wearily down the sidewalk toward her apartment block. It had been a long day. First the trip to the Silver Griffins waystation, then an afternoon talking about legal and business issues with Gruffbar.

She still didn't understand half the things he'd explained, first patiently, then with increasing frustration as the light of understanding failed to dawn in her eyes. But hey, this was why she wanted him as part of the business, to understand the things she couldn't. And to get her out of trouble if any more of her prototypes drew the authorities' attention.

Dusk was falling as she gently rolled up to the front of the building. A movement caught her eye, a black and gray shape lurking outside the corner of the building.

"Hey, Smokey!" she called, waving at the cat.

Normally, Smokey was happy to receive any attention from the local magicals, but today seemed to be different. He ducked back out of view. Fran frowned. Was something the matter?

She shifted her backpack and skated down to the corner. There was a small green space next to the apartment block, a patch of grass with a bench and a small tree. A furry tail disappeared into the bushes at the far end, leaving behind a scatter of papers. Fran quickly switched from her skates to her sneakers, then walked over.

"Hey, Smokey?" she called out. "Are you okay, buddy? You still around here somewhere?"

She picked up one of the papers. They were all the same: fliers advertising something called Paws and Claws.

"The support group for non-bipedal magicals," Fran read. "Tired of being pushed around by the two-legs? Sick of not finding a seat to suit you? Had enough of being forced to conform? Come make the change you want to see."

At the bottom of the flier were an address and a time for a meeting that evening.

Fran looked down at her legs. She had two of them, but she also had an overwhelming sense of curiosity. And while this might not be anything to do with Smokey, it was quite a coincidence that she'd found the fliers while chasing after him. Had she unwittingly been feeding a magical cat?

She pulled up a map app on her phone, and still carrying her backpack and her skates, followed its directions to the address on the flier. The place was in a large, rounded hill riddled with gnome and Willen burrows, which had once been the headquarters of a trading cartel but were now mostly cute apartments for magicals below a certain height. The ground floor was shops, half of them empty, and a couple of meeting rooms. It was one of those meeting rooms that the flier directed Fran to.

Despite her curiosity, she didn't want to intrude on someone else's meeting, so she decided not to head straight in. She would wait until the meeting had gotten started, then peek inside to see what sort of people attended and what they were talking about. No need to cause a fuss or for anyone to even know she was there.

She paced back and forth impatiently around the far side of the hill, spinning the wheels on her skates with one finger and trying to think about her prototypes. For once, all attempts at distraction failed.

Fifteen minutes after the meeting was due to start, she decided she could safely head in. The burrow's lobby was a round room with a magical light fitting, a set of mailboxes against one wall, and a rope ladder running up from the center. The meeting room for Paws and Claws was at the far side. Fran crept over to it, finding to her surprise and relief that the door of the room was open, saving her from having to try to open it quietly. She peered around the door frame.

The room was a fairly ordinary one, with a couple of potted plants, a screen on one wall, and a whiteboard on the one facing it. There was a circle of seats, but not the sort she would normally have expected to see. Instead of folding chairs, there were beanbags, cushions, backless stools, perches, and even a couple of blankets. It made sense if none of the attendees had the right shape of bodies to use human seating. The problem was, there were no attendees.

Actually, that wasn't quite true. Someone occupied one

of the cushions. Smokey sat alone, his tail curled up around him, glaring at the floor. Fran looked around, expecting to at least see the meeting's organizer, but there was only the cat. She felt sorry for him, sitting there all alone, and was about to make her presence known when something unexpected happened. Smokey shifted.

One minute, a cat was sitting on the cushion, staring angrily at the world. The next, his body started twisting, legs growing, spine straightening. There were some *pops* and *crunches,* some expanding flesh, and a hairy dwarf sat where Smokey had been.

"You're not a cat!" Fran exclaimed. She strode into the room and pointed accusingly at the dwarf. "You're a shifter, and you've been getting pet time under pretenses."

The dwarf snatched a pair of jogging pants out from under the cushion and hastily pulled them on.

"I am too a cat," he said. "Just a cat who turns into a dwarf sometimes."

"Were your parents cats?"

"No. Were your parents programmers?"

"Well, no."

"So we don't need to be what our parents were. I'm a shifter, I'm a dwarf, and I am most definitely a cat."

Fran thought about her mother and her Evermore background. She'd never defined herself in Evermore terms and didn't plan to start doing it now. Why should she expect any different from him?

"What's your name?" she asked.

"Smokey. You know that."

"Yes, but what's your real name, your dwarf name?"

"I go by Smokey."

"Oh, okay. Sorry." Fran blushed, realizing that she had no idea how to deal with a situation like this. There wasn't a lot of guidance for what to do when you found out that a pet was a shifter, but calling someone by their chosen name seemed like basic good manners.

"I thought that shifters turned into bigger animals. Wolves, leopards, lions, that sort of thing."

"Well, some of us don't," Smokey snapped. "What are you doing here anyway? You've got two legs. This group isn't for you."

"It doesn't seem to be for anyone." Fran clapped a hand over her mouth, then mumbled through her fingers. "Sorry, I shouldn't have said that. It was, like, totally rude."

"It was, but I'll let you off this time since you fed me that chicken the other day. But this space isn't for you, so please go before you put off any latecomers."

The jogging pants fell to the floor as he shifted back into his cat form.

"Do you think that anyone else is coming?" Fran peered out into the building's lobby. No one was there. She didn't expect a reply, seeing as Smokey wasn't a dwarf anymore.

"They should be turning up," he said, and to her surprise, his voice was still deep and dwarf-like. "I put up plenty of fliers."

"Maybe you should've tried Internet advertising."

"Of course I did. I'm not an idiot. I'd hardly make a living working on computers if I didn't think of them for things like this."

"Sorry, didn't mean to be rude again."

"Seems to happen to you a lot."

He was glaring at her while she tried not to laugh. It

was hard to keep the chuckles in when looking at someone who shifted into a household cat. The whole thing was so at odds with shifters and their dramatic reputation.

"Do you have some more fliers?" she asked. "Maybe I could go stick them up somewhere for you."

Smokey sighed. "No, it's too late. I should give up."

He wandered over to the doorway where she stood and brushed up against her leg. On instinct, she reached down to pat his head, and he purred.

"Is this weird now?" she asked.

"Course not. You're a person. I'm a cat. This is how we interact."

"Wait, if you can shift into a dwarf any time you want, how come you eat cat food and drink water from bowls on the floor? And don't deny it because I've seen you do it." An alarming thought crossed her mind, and she jerked her hand back from him. "Is this... Is this a kink?"

"What? No! Don't be such a pervert." Smokey shook his head, and his whiskers trembled. "What is it with witches and wizards? Anything slightly odd happens, and you think it must be about sex."

"I don't! I usually think it's about inventing."

"Whatever. We've finished here. I should tidy up and take the keys back to the building manager."

Fran helped Smokey put the assorted seats away, then locked the room and returned the keys. Together, they walked back through the night toward the apartment building.

"Would you mind keeping quiet about this?" Smokey asked. "I've got a certain image to maintain, relationships around the neighborhood. I don't want to ruin them over nothing."

"Sure, I get it." Fran hesitated. "All right, I don't get it, but if you want me to keep quiet, I can. I'd shake on it, but..."

They stopped, and Smokey raised a paw. Fran leaned down to shake it.

"You're not bad, Fran Berryman," Smokey said. "For a biped."

CHAPTER SEVENTEEN

Summoned by Julia Lacy, bound by magic to obey, three dark spirits flew through the darkness of the Mana Valley night, looking for a magical mirror.

"This is absurd," the first spirit hissed as they hovered above the rooftops. "Like hunting for a specific drop of blood in an abattoir."

"It would have been easier in the old days," the second spirit said. "When mirrors were rare and precious. Now every house has them, not only one but two, three, four, dozens. Mirrors in bathrooms and bedrooms. Mirrors as decorations. Portable mirrors that they carry in their purses. How are we supposed to find the right one?"

"It is a magical mirror," the third spirit said. "That narrows our possibilities."

"Not here, it doesn't." The first spirit sniffed ostentatiously, though it had no nose or smell receptors to judge a scent by. "The whole place reeks of magic. They use it in their work, their leisure, their machines. Magic imbues everything from pencils to parking lots. Magic and mirrors, everywhere."

"Magic here used to be grand," the second spirit said. "Used for great works: summoning armies, opening portals, turning enemies to dust. Now it is everyday, mundane, diminished. Who can tell which mirrors are magical when magic hangs in the air around everything?"

"Do you have a point?" the third spirit asked.

"That the world used to be better."

"That this is a waste of our time."

"Will making those points mean that we don't have to do this task? Will complaining about them get it done any sooner?"

"Perhaps, if we can find a way to break the spell…"

The third spirit sneered. "That would take us years. This task…" Its insubstantial body rippled in the ghostly equivalent of a shrug. "Days. Weeks. Months at most. What is that compared with the length of our existence?"

The others hovered in the air, silently seething, unable to muster a response that could counter what their companion had said.

"Well then," the third spirit said. "Let's get this done. Take any mirror that has magic in it. We'll work out which is the right one later."

Fran eased the apartment door open and stepped inside. It wasn't late-late, but she wasn't exactly home early either. Josie had been working so hard lately that she needed whatever rest she could get. Fran wasn't going to interfere with that.

The light had been left on in the living room but turned down low. That made Fran smile. Josie was smart enough to know that Fran in the dark was a liability to her sleep, likely to kick over furniture and curse at herself in the darkness. She would've made a terrible ninja. The light meant that Fran could get to bed without waking half the neighborhood.

She took off her shoes and crept in socks across the living room, then put her bag and skates down in her room. The light in the bathroom buzzed when she pulled the cord, illuminating the place with a bright white light. She closed the door, found her toothbrush, and quietly closed the cabinet above the sink.

As the cabinet closed, her face came into view, reflected in the mirror there. She blinked and stared at herself, sleepy and caught off guard. Josie wasn't the only one who had been working hard, or at least keeping long hours so she could tell herself she was working. Now those hours were visible in Fran's reflection. Her unbrushed hair was escaping from her ponytail, and she thought she could see the beginnings of bags under her eyes.

"No way," she mumbled around her toothbrush. "I'm not that old yet."

She'd installed an enchantment on the mirror when they first moved in. The small spell let her zoom in or out or change the angle of the reflection. It could even redirect light to illuminate her face better and show her how it would look in different conditions. That one spell made all the difference in fixing her makeup. She used it now to zoom in on her eyes.

"Oh no." She tugged at the skin under her eye. "It's all dark and puffy. Are those wrinkles? I think those are wrinkles."

If Josie had been awake, she would've told Fran that it was nothing and that she was being ridiculous. If Fran herself had been less tired, the effect would've seemed like nothing. Now, exhausted and alone in the unforgiving light of the bathroom, she felt like she was facing a major crisis.

The air shimmered. The spell zoomed back out and then in again. Fran frowned and tapped the side of the mirror. It wasn't supposed to do that without her telling it to.

The light shifted, the mirror using one of its other tricks. Something was clearly interfering with the enchantment. Fran set her toothbrush down on the side of the sink and ran her fingers across the mirror, feeling the magic. Something else was there, something that she hadn't put in.

Fran sighed. Sensibly, she should deal with the problem in the morning, but once she spotted a broken device, she found it hard not to leap in and fix it. Plus this should be an easy one to solve. Take the mirror down, recast the spell, and put it back in place. She pulled a screwdriver out of her pocket and opened the cabinet door.

A ghostly face, pale and indistinct, surrounded by a ragged gray hood, stared out at her.

Fran yelped in alarm. Without thinking, she dropped the screwdriver and flung a blast of light magic at the shadowy shape. It hissed and lashed out. Though its hand was ghostly enough to pass through the wall, it was still solid enough to knock Fran back across the room. She crashed into the bathtub and tumbled over into it, knocking the shower controls as she went. Warm water sprayed down on her.

The ghost wrapped its hands around the mirror cabinet door. There was a hard cracking sound as it ripped the door off its hinges.

"No, you don't!" Fran sent a bright bolt of light straight at the spirit's eyes. It might not be solid like she was, but it still needed to see, and it screeched in pain as the bright light briefly blinded it.

Fran scrambled out of the bath and flung another blast of light at the spirit. It twisted the mirror around, reflecting the light back at Fran, who closed her eyes to avoid being blinded.

When she opened her eyes again, the spirit was by the bathroom window, about to make its escape. It was clutching Fran's bathroom mirror. Its hands had become solid where they gripped the edges of the mirror. A thin layer of frost was creeping out from those fingers.

Fran grabbed the pipe running up to the showerhead and summoned a wave of sound. It shook the showerhead so hard that it swung up to point at the spirit as Fran yanked on the shower controls, turning the heat all the way up. Steaming hot water hit the spirit's icy hand. It hissed in alarm, and the hand became insubstantial. The mirror slid from fingers that weren't solid enough to hold it and fell to the floor.

"I've got plenty more just like that." Fran pointed her hands straight at the spirit and summoned dancing points of light. If she was going to bluff, best to make it a big one. "Try me."

The spirit hissed again. The heat had hurt, and it was frustrated by this unexpected opposition. Was it worth taking this mirror? Only an idiot would hide a portal to another world in a bathroom cabinet. Instead of grabbing for the mirror again, it turned incorporeal and drifted out through the wall, off to look for other mirrors.

Fran hauled herself out of the bath and turned off the shower. There was a knock at the bathroom door.

"Fran?" Josie said softly from the other side of the door. "Are you okay in there?"

"I'm fine." Fran picked up the mirror. There was a crack right across the middle. "But I think we might need to do some repairs."

She opened the door. Josie looked in at the broken mirror and the water all over the floor.

"Sorry for waking you up," Fran said sheepishly. "Would you believe that I was fighting off a ghost who wanted to steal from our bathroom?"

Josie laughed. "That's such a stupid story that I don't think anyone would make it up."

"I'll tidy all this up. You go back to bed."

"That's okay. I'm awake now. I might as well help by mopping."

"It's my mess."

"I think you'll find that it's the ghost's mess. Besides, you've done enough for tonight. If not for you, the supernatural world might've stolen our toothpaste."

CHAPTER EIGHTEEN

Fran and Josie walked down the street, a bathroom mirror hanging in the air between them, levitated by Josie's magic.

"I like that we have shopping malls here now," Fran said. "It makes it so much easier when you need something. No running off to a dwarf artisan to get a new mirror made or finding pixies to cobble your shoes. Just pop down to the mall, look for the right shop, and you're set."

"You spent half your childhood on Earth," Josie said. "Surely shopping malls can't still have novelty value?"

Fran shrugged. "I guess I'm easily pleased."

"Wait, does that mean that I'm friends with you because you'll accept just anyone? Am I secretly a terrible person, but you'll tolerate anyone, and that's why we ended up together?"

"Oh yes." Fran nodded seriously. "With your tidiness, your intelligence, your kindness. So many terrible traits. You're a regular monster, Josie Bullworth. The sort they make horror films about."

"I always did want to make it onto the big screen. I

figured it would be for a biopic about my life as a world-changing tech guru, but horror monster will do."

They paused at a set of traffic lights, where red, amber, and green salamanders lit up to signal who should stay and who should go. A mixture of riding beasts, magical vehicles, and dwarf-built steam wagons waited for their turn to move. There were even a couple of electric-powered cars that must've been portaled across from Earth.

"When I make my first million I'm buying a Tesla," Fran said. "Then I'm going to install a magical relay in the roof so I can shoot bolts of lightning and pretend they're lightning blasts. It seems like the Tesla thing to do."

Josie opened her mouth, closed it, then opened it again. "I don't even know how to respond to that. You do you."

The pedestrian lights turned green, and they crossed the road behind a pair of trolls. Bells tinkled on the bars of a Willen's steam-powered tricycle as they walked past.

On the far side of the crossing, a coffee shop caught Fran's eye. The Blazing Bean, where she'd gone to work earlier in the week.

"Why don't we go for coffee and cake before we head home?" she asked.

"You know that we have coffee at home, right?"

"Yes, but we have to make that coffee. This is coffee that someone else will make for us. That makes it better. And we don't have cake."

"We have three different types of cake. You buy them, have a slice, put them in the fridge, and forget."

"So you don't want to stop for coffee and cake?"

"I didn't say that."

The Blazing Bean was full of the sort of crowd that

came with a late Saturday morning. Fewer of the suited executives who filled the local coffee shops during the week, more couples taking a break from shopping, or parents trying to keep their kids happy with hot chocolate and cookies.

It still had some of the crowd that spent their evenings there, the guys with skateboards, girls who'd been up all night with their ears still ringing from loud gigs, magicals leafing through books of unusual spells. For Saturday daytime, this wasn't their space anymore. The shopping crowds would take whatever coffee shop they could get.

"Ooh, table free!" Fran pointed at where a couple of Arpaks were getting up. "You grab it. I'll get our drinks."

Josie hurried across the room, towing the levitating mirror behind her, and grabbed the table seconds before a group of young elves, who frowned and went back to their stools by the window. Fran joined the back of the queue at the counter.

There were a lot of people in line, but it was moving quickly, the baristas hustling to get everybody served. Cups and plates shot past above their heads as they rushed to get orders fulfilled. It took a steady hand with a spell to do that without spilling anything, but someone had a gift.

Fran barely had time to evaluate the available cakes before she reached the front of the queue.

"Hi there." Cam smiled at her from behind the till and pushed his glasses up his nose. "Good to see you again, Fran."

"You too." She smiled and pointed as a couple of cardboard cups of coffee floated out of the air and settled down in front of him. "I thought you couldn't do magic?"

"That's not me. We have plenty of magicals on the staff here though, usually people who are doing this to pay the bills while they try to sell their big idea or get a startup funded."

Fran frowned. She hadn't even considered getting a job while she tried to start her company. Was that something she should do? Then, if she did, would she have time to develop the business?

Cam leaned forward and gestured for her to do the same.

"Between you and me," he whispered conspiratorially, "some of these guys have been working here 'temporarily' for years. If I were you, I'd concentrate on the big business idea and leave the coffees to the professionals." He winked. "Speaking of which, what can I get you?"

Fran ordered coffees and two big slices of cake, one chocolate, and the other blueberry. At the other register, crystalline magicals were ordering something that looked like a pile of pebbles topped with tiny gemstones. She wondered what it tasted like to someone made of minerals and whether chocolate cake would taste as unpleasant to them as dirt would to her.

"Is it like this all day?" she asked while Cam prepared her order.

"Pretty much," he said. "It gets even worse at lunchtime. Never come in here on a Saturday if you want to work. You won't get quiet, and I won't be able to bring you extra coffees when they get cold."

"You mean standards are slipping?" Fran tutted. "What is the world coming to?"

"To a very busy place." Cam handed her a tray of coffee

and cake. The cake slices were the largest she'd seen. "Now excuse me, but I have to serve the next customer."

He flashed her a final smile, then turned to take a dwarf family's order.

Fran made her way through the crowded coffee shop. Her eyes were so fixed on the coffee cups, afraid that they might spill over, that she almost bumped into the blond witch who was turning away from Josie's table. The witch glared at Fran, then stalked away.

"Who's that?" Fran asked as she set the tray down.

"Someone from work," Josie said. "She's far more friendly than I thought she would be. I didn't expect someone in her position to remember me, never mind stop to chat."

The witch hadn't seemed all that friendly to Fran, but that was only going by a second of glaring. Perhaps she was lovely when someone hadn't almost walked into her.

"More importantly," said Josie, "who's the cute guy behind the counter?"

"Cam?" Fran glanced back at the barista, who looked increasingly harassed as he tried to take orders from a group of overexcited trolls. They kept changing size and clambering over each other, pointing at cakes and changing their minds. She hadn't thought about it much, but he was pretty cute, with the big smile and the shaggy blond hair. "I met him when I was working here the other night."

"That's the free coffee guy?" Josie leaned forward and peered across the coffee shop, scrutinizing Cam. "Well, that makes sense. A girl could do a lot worse."

"What about Adam?"

"Not for me, for you, dummy. He's clearly into you."

"He is?"

"Honestly, Fran, it's no wonder you're always single." Josie shook her head. "He did this big smile for you, leaned in close to chat, gave you that coffee the other night."

"Service staff have to be friendly. That's how they get tips." Fran slapped her hand to her mouth. "Oh my God, I totally forgot to tip!"

"Come back later. You can give him something special then." Josie winked.

"Seriously, we've met twice, briefly, while he was working."

"He was checking you out as you walked away from the counter."

"He was probably making sure that I didn't chuck my coffees over everyone else."

"Suit yourself." Josie leaned back and shrugged. "It means more options for the rest of us. Now, which of these slices of cake is mine? These extremely large slices of cake that definitely weren't cut specially for you by the cute guy."

"Whichever one you want. As long as it's the chocolate one."

"That's fine. I'm not in a blueberry mood." Josie took a bite from the chocolate cake. "Oh wow, that is amazing. I don't care if that guy loves you or hates you. We're coming back here. Now tell me, how's the startup going?"

"I'm still trying to work out what I could make to showcase the batteries. I usually wake up with a ton of new ideas, but this morning I was thinking about that spirit from last night."

"Ew. Super creepy, that thing being in our bathroom, but maybe that could give you some ideas too. Like, I don't know, a haunting detector or a burglar alarm."

"Huh." Fran took a sip of her coffee. An idea was starting to form in her head. "I did have trouble dealing with it. Maybe..."

She grabbed a napkin, pulled a pen from her pocket, and started scribbling notes. Across the table from her, Josie sat eating her cake, smiling as she watched her friend at work. There was never a dull moment with Fran.

CHAPTER NINETEEN

Fran tightened the final screw on the cabinet door, then carefully swung it shut. Her face looked back at her, and she smiled. She didn't look half as tired during the day, fueled up on coffee and cake, the wrinkles and bags far less noticeable. Panic over.

She tapped the mirror to zoom in and double-check, but nothing happened. Of course, the mirror with the enchantment on it was sitting cracked in the corner of the bathroom. This was a mundane mirror, or at least it was so far.

She raised her hand, ready to cast an enchantment on the mirror again, but hesitated. What if the magic was the thing that had attracted the chilling spirit? She didn't want to be faced with that again. Maybe a normal mirror would be good enough, for now at least.

The broken mirror looked up at her from the corner of the room. The crack across the middle sliced her image in half. She had intended to throw it out, but now that she thought about it, maybe she could put it to use. After all, she'd built her portal device around a mirror, so other mirror enchantments might be useful too, in unexpected ways.

"Taking that to the dump?" Josie asked as Fran emerged with the broken mirror.

"Not yet." Fran leaned it against the wall inside her room. "I think it might be useful."

"A broken mirror?"

"An exciting component for magical technology."

Josie laughed. "Suit yourself. Off skating?"

Fran hadn't noticed that she was picking up her skates, but now that she'd done so, it seemed a shame not to.

"It'll help clear my head while I think through some ideas."

"Cool." Josie picked up the book from her lap, a modern translation of an ancient Elven epic. "Have fun out there."

"Will do."

A few minutes later, Fran was skating down the street, on her way to the skate park. A crow fluttered down from its perch in a nearby tree and flew along next to her, occasionally cawing conversationally.

"I guess you're right," Fran said. "Or at least, you might be if I could understand what you were saying."

As she arrived at the skate park, a familiar person was skating in slow loops around the outer edge. By now, Bart's protective gear looked increasingly battered with scrapes on the knee and elbow pads and even a couple of knocks on the helmet. Still, he didn't seem deterred, even though his progress was still slow.

His persistence was admirable. Fran hoped she could

bring the same attitude to her business that he brought to skating, perhaps with more competence to support it.

He slowed as she approached the track and came over to say hello.

"I'm doing better, don't you think?" he asked.

"Absolutely!" Fran beamed. She didn't have to say how little he'd improved, and she wanted to encourage him. It was hard not to feel upbeat around Bart and his determined positivity.

"How's your day going?" He sat on a bench and rested his hands on his knees.

"Pretty good." Fran sat beside him, and the crow settled on her shoulder. "I've got an idea for the next thing I could make."

"And what is it?"

"A containment unit to hold rogue magicals."

"Wow. That's certainly a change of direction from flying carpets."

"Not really. The underlying principles to how it will need to draw on power resources are the same, which is what matters most for the batteries. The unit I have in mind is a step up in scale, but that means it will work better as a proof of concept because it will show the endurance of the power source. And a containment unit lets me reach out to some larger customers."

"Like governments?"

"Exactly! The Silver Griffins, the feds, local police forces, all sorts of people need to contain rogue magicals these days, so why not give them a way to do it? I'd be helping to keep the world safe, as well as showing off what my technology can do."

"How big is this magical cage going to be?"

"It might not be a cage. I'm thinking more like a box of light or a mystical field or something that uses sound waves to contain bodies in a particular area."

"I didn't mean a literal cage. I just meant, you know, like keeping animals in a cage at the zoo."

"Ooh, that's a good idea! Zookeepers might want to use this as well. They could use it to trap elephants and giraffes and giant mountain lizards."

"It's going to be big enough for an elephant?"

"I think so. I want it to be able to hold large magicals so it's useful for whatever the owners are doing."

"Sounds like it could be challenging to get right. Large magicals can have a lot of strength, not to mention supernatural power."

"Ah, that's the clever bit..." Fran rummaged through her pockets. "Or at least, one of the clever bits..."

After going through the pockets of her jeans, shirt, and hoodie, she finally found what she was looking for in a side pocket of her backpack. The crow, recognizing a paper napkin as connected to food, leaned in closer, ready to peck at the piece of paper, but Fran shooed the bird back.

"This is it." She unfolded the napkin for Bart to see. She'd scribbled words, equations, spell fragments, and design diagrams all around the Blazing Bean logo, some of them drawn so small that Fran had to squint to remind herself of what they were.

Bart took the napkin, peered at it, turned it around, turned it over, turned it back again, stared at it with a look of intense concentration, and shrugged.

"My experience in business was about the accounts," he

said, "not the design side. Perhaps you could explain it to me? And perhaps go slowly, using short words?"

"Um…"

"Think of it this way: if you want to attract investors, you're going to have to be able to pitch your idea clearly and succinctly. So let me play the role of one of those investors, and tell me what it is I'm investing in."

Fran drew a deep breath and got to her feet as if speaking to a room full of executives. Why not? It would be good practice for this idea or another one in the future.

"This is the Berryman Mark One Cage-omatic. Name pending approval. It is a magical containment unit that combines magic and electricity to hold its occupants, which can be substantial in size."

"How substantial?"

"I don't know yet."

"Then pretend that you do." Bart grinned. "Trust me, confidence sells, and if you were wrong, you can always tell them later that you've refined the design."

"OK, cool. In that case, it's big enough to hold a magical elephant."

"African or Indian elephant?"

"African."

"Good confidence. Keep going."

Fran smiled wide. She was getting into this now. She always enjoyed talking about her ideas, and this was a chance to show one off.

"The Cage-omatic is built on a feedback principle. It taps into the energy of the contained magical to reinforce the unit. The strength of the captive reinforces the strength of the structure, meaning that the more powerful the magical inside it, the more powerful the Cage-omatic will be. This helps preserve energy for powering the unit while ensuring that it always works to the standard needed."

"I see." Bart stroked his chin. "What happens when you have to open the unit to tend to the magical inside? Surely that would provide a weak point?"

"Not with the Cage-omatic. Its internal AI not only manages the field strength but also tends to the needs of the magical inside, based upon its assessment of the magical. This reduces the effort of managing containment while ensuring more humane imprisonment. The Cage-omatic isn't only about the safety of those using it. It's about treating prisoners right."

"Nicely done. Was that more pretending you knew the answer?"

Fran shook her head.

"I was already planning for the feedback and the AI. I might have expanded on it a bit, but it's all good. I can add those things to the design."

Bart held the napkin out toward her.

"This is impressive stuff, Fran, both your ideas and how you present them. You'll need to refine things, of course, but you'll get there."

"Would you be able to keep on helping? You know business, but it's a mystery to me. I could do with someone more experienced to get advice from."

"Of course. Happy to help, and it'll keep me from getting bored without risking my life on these all the time." He spun the wheels of one of his skates. "You'll need a name, though."

"You don't like Cage-omatic?"

"A name for your business."

"Oh!" Fran contemplated her options. "How about Mana Wave Industries? I was thinking of a sound wave, but I want people to know that we're working with magic, not just technology."

"Mana Wave." Bart nodded. "I like it, and I'll be happy to keep offering my consulting services, for my usual fee."

"Fee?" Fran blanched. She hadn't thought about the fact that Bart might charge for his help, but then he was an experienced executive, so it made sense. If only she had the money to afford him.

Bart chuckled. "My fee is that you keep picking me up when I fall over. Speaking of which…" He got carefully to his feet. "We should get out there on the track. I don't know about you, but I came here to skate."

CHAPTER TWENTY

The Blazing Bean was a lot less busy first thing on Monday morning than before lunch on Saturday. Fran had wondered if she should have the first meeting for Mana Wave's team at her apartment, but there wasn't a lot of space there. Besides, this way she could buy coffee and cake for her colleagues to say thank you. And if Cam happened to be behind the counter, that would be nice too, but it wasn't why she was there. That would be silly.

Definitely not.

"Good morning, Fran." Cam brightly smiled as she approached the counter. "Cappuccino?"

"Yes, please." Fran smiled back equally brightly. "I've got a meeting. Got to be alert."

"Good for you. And cake?"

"Not yet."

She took her coffee, grabbed a seat by the window, and got her laptop out. A few minutes later, Bart appeared.

"Let me get this," Fran said, intercepting him before he could get to the counter. "After all, you're here to help me."

"That's very kind of you. I'll have a tea, please."

In a roar of engine noise, a black motorcycle pulled up outside. It looked like the team was all there.

"Tea, please," Fran said to Cam. "And..." She tried to work out what Gruffbar would want. "A black coffee."

By the time the dwarf lawyer came in, she was returning to her table with the drinks and a plate of cookies.

"For you," she said, pointing at his drink.

"Good guess." Gruffbar took the coffee and slung himself down in a seat. He put his bike helmet on the floor and pulled a laptop from his backpack.

"Bart, this is Gruffbar, my lawyer," Fran said. "Gruffbar, this is Bart. He's...my mentor, I guess?"

"I like the sound of that." Bart shook Gruffbar's hand. "Pleasure to meet you."

"And you." Gruffbar glanced at his watch. "I've managed to pick up a bit of court work, so I need to get out of here by noon. Shall we get started?"

"Absolutely." Fran tapped a cookie against the table. "I call the first meeting of the board of Mana Wave Industries to order."

"I'm on the board?" Bart asked, confused.

"Well, no, that's just Gruffbar and me, but I assume that boards have consultants in sometimes."

"Well, it's an honor to be here, consulting or not. What's the first item of business?"

Gruffbar pulled out a thick wad of papers.

"Documents for the legal foundation of the company," he said. "Not exciting, not fun, but it needs to happen."

For the next hour, he guided Fran through the documents that he'd assembled, explaining everything down to the smallest clause. She signed each one as instructed, with Bart acting as a witness. The sheer weight of paperwork made everything feel more real and a lot more serious.

"No getting out of this now," Bart said as he added his signature with a flourish.

"There's always a way out, as long as you've got a good lawyer." Gruffbar tidied the stack of documents that they'd gone through so far. "Of course, whether it's worth taking that way out depends on..." His voice trailed off as he stared toward the entrance to the coffee shop. "By my beard."

Fran looked around. An elf was standing in the doorway of the coffee shop. She was tall and slim, with long blond hair running down her back. She wore a pencil skirt and blouse, made from shimmering elven silk, and the sort of heels that Fran could barely have stood upright in, never mind used to walk around. She seemed to glow with an internal light. It was hard to be sure, but she might have been the most beautiful woman that Fran had ever seen, and she was staring straight at Gruffbar.

"You," the elf said. Her voice was as controlled as her face, not a hint of emotion showing, but her hand tightened a little around her handbag as if she was on the verge of forming a fist.

"Elethin." Gruffbar nodded to her. "What brings you here?"

His voice was low, his hand shifting to something inside the leather jacket slung over the back of his chair. Fran kept looking from him to the elf and back, unsure what was going on but certain that it couldn't all be good.

"I just came across from Trevilsom." She walked over to their table. Her heels *clacked* against the floor with each step, a sound so sharp it seemed to stab the air. "I finally finished my prison sentence."

"I thought you cut a deal, that they gave you some sort of community service."

"Oh, they did." She stopped within arm's reach of Gruffbar and stood staring down at him. She was smiling and speaking sweetly, but the smile didn't reach her eyes. "Then they decided that they couldn't allow that. The court case had been too public, the crimes I was involved with at Nuada Industries too severe. Apparently, someone wrote them a report that drew attention to these problems, someone very well informed on the law."

Gruffbar shrugged. "My part in that case was over the minute we stepped out of the courtroom."

"You mean when you ruined the company I worked for and my reputation with it?"

"You people ruined your reputations."

"I was working for the most powerful magitech corporation in America, transforming the world, spending my days briefing senators, billionaires, and celebrities. Now I'm returning to the world after thirty-five years in Trevilsom Prison. Oh, and I still have to do that community service."

"We all make our choices."

"How very true. I shall try to make better ones from now on." The elf turned to Fran and stuck out her hand. "Elethin Tannerin. So very pleased to meet you."

"I'm Fran Berryman." Fran shook the hand uncertainly. "Um, did you used to work with Gruffbar?"

"Quite the opposite. I was the head of public relations for a company he destroyed."

"For a company that the Silver Griffins took down, on account of all their dark dealings." Gruffbar scowled. "I only helped the Griffins along."

"Yes, you've always been so public-spirited," Elethin said. "Which CEO were you working for again? The one who relied on child labor in his factories or the one who was cheating on his wife?"

"We've all made mistakes. I'm trying to make up for mine."

"You're right. He was both of those, wasn't he? Although the child labor allegations only came out later. If only someone had seen the inside of that company and could've told the Griffins what they were up to."

"I didn't know," Gruffbar mumbled, looking down at his feet.

"Of course not. Or not in a legally provable way, at least." Elethin shook her head. "Whereas I knew exactly enough for a long stretch in prison. Isn't justice strange?" She smiled brightly at Fran. "A pleasure meeting you, Ms. Berryman."

The elf strode out of the shop and away.

"Poor woman," Bart said. "Sounds like she's had a very rough time. She didn't even get a coffee."

Fran looked at Gruffbar, who looked up at her from beneath a crumpled brow.

"You're not going to get me involved in child labor, are you?" she asked.

"I told you when we started this that I was looking for redemption," Gruffbar said. "For the record, I didn't know about the kids. Even then, I had my limits." He started gathering papers together. "I should get out of here."

"But the meeting…"

"I'll file these today. We can deal with other business later." He grabbed his helmet and got out of his seat. "Thanks for the coffee."

Out in the street, Gruffbar stopped by his Harley and drew deep breaths. Seeing Elethin Tannerin had shaken him, a blast from deep in his past. True, he'd been on the right side of the case that time, helping a dodgy business stand up against a truly despicable one.

Still, he could do without the reminders of who he'd been back then and without people from that past hanging around the place. Hopefully, Elethin would want to put some more distance between her and Trevilsom, and Gruffbar would never see her again.

He reached into his pocket, about to pull out a cigar and steady his nerves that way, then thought better of it. He'd said that he would file the papers, and that was what he should do. That would put Fran's business on a better footing and help to occupy him until his court appointment.

He pulled on his helmet, jumped onto the bike, and started the engine. It spluttered slightly before shifting into its familiar roar. He would deal with that later, too. Tuning the engine always improved his mood after a stressful day.

The bike wobbled as he pulled away from the curb and accelerated down the street. Gruffbar frowned. Something was shifting underneath him. He was about to hit the brakes when the whole bike jerked, twisted, and skidded down the street. His head bounced off the pavement and asphalt scraped his leathers. Traffic swerved to avoid him, and there was an enormous honk as a steam truck slammed on its brakes. Then the bike hit the curb and stopped.

Gruffbar staggered to his feet and looked down at the battered Harley. He was vaguely aware of people rushing up to him, asking if he was all right. Someone had fired up a communication spell and was calling a medical witch. He ignored them all and knelt over his beloved bike.

Something crawled out of the engine, a small, warty creature covered in oil and rust. It waved at him, then leaped down a sewer drain and disappeared before Gruffbar could get his revenge.

"Gremlins," he growled. "I hate gremlins."

Unnoticed by him, at the corner of the street, Elethin Tannerin stood watching.

"Close," she murmured. "Better luck next time."

CHAPTER TWENTY-ONE

Josie snapped her fingers, and the screen of the Manaphone lit up, unlocked. It showed the symbols for all the usual Philgard apps, a few that were new for the Manaphone Seven, and some third-party software that they'd installed for testing. Josie had been cautious about the apps she chose for that. Details of the Seven were still a big business secret, and she couldn't afford to install something that might leak data into the wider world.

While she was proud of the work she'd done setting up the test phone, she was far more proud of the change they were testing now.

"If it unlocks at a finger snap, what's to stop anyone from opening it?" Simon Green asked. He was Josie's manager, a middle-aged wizard who seemed to have few ideas of his own but who made a career out of enthusing about other people's work to senior management.

"It's magically attuned," Josie explained. "It will only respond to a snap from the owner's fingers. A slight spark of magic flies from every one, a unique energy signature that's very hard to forge. It's at least as secure as a passcode."

"Show me again."

Josie locked the screen and set the phone back down on the workbench. She'd been hoping that Green would be more impressed, but if he understood the value of what she'd achieved, he didn't show it.

The door to the test lab opened, and Julia Lacy walked in. Josie and Simon jumped to their feet a moment before Howard Phillips appeared, followed by his hulking Kilomea bodyguard.

"How's my new phone coming along?" Phillips asked.

It was the first time Josie had met the tech guru in person, but he was everything she'd expected: sharp suit, winning smile, and straight to the point. "I hear that you might have a new USP for me."

"A new..." Green's eyes darted from the phone to Josie. He still didn't get it, but he knew that they'd only added one more trick to the phone this week, and that had to be what this was about. "Of course, yes, the unlocking mechanism. Opening your phone with a distinct snap of your fingers. It's going to be very popular."

"Show me," Phillips said.

"Of course, sir." Green snapped his fingers. Nothing happened. He tried again, and still, nothing happened.

Behind Phillips' back, Julia gave Josie a sly wink, then a small nod toward the phone. Josie stood frozen for a moment. Could she do this, stealing her manager's thunder in front of Phillips? If the technology stopped working, it would be humiliating. On the other hand, if it worked, she would get the CEO's attention. She drew a deep breath and gathered her courage.

"As Simon has so ably demonstrated, not just anyone can unlock this phone," she said. Then she snapped her fingers, and the phone unlocked. "We've not only overcome the problems with the old unlocking software but added something new."

"Nice." Phillips reached for the phone.

Josie snapped her fingers again and the screen locked. She had a moment of panic, wondering if she'd gone too far locking it in the boss's hand, but Phillips smiled.

"It's perfect," he said. "Not a paradigm shift, but an attention-grabbing novelty that we can also pitch as a security upgrade. That finger snap will make for great marketing. How quickly can you run up a whole set of test models?"

Now they were in territory that Green understood and where he could take over the team's side of the conversation.

"Five weeks," he said.

"Make it three. Send me the first one you get ready." Phillips threw the phone to Josie. "Apart from this one. You can keep that..."

"Josie, sir. Josie Bullworth."

"Wait, the same tech who took out the magic transmission glitch?" Phillips turned to Julia. "Why didn't you tell me we were meeting her?"

"It was a happy coincidence," said Julia, who had told Josie to be in the lab that morning.

"It certainly is." Phillips beamed. "Josie, Simon, keep up the good work, both of you."

Then he strode out of the room, his assistant and his bodyguard with him, gone as suddenly as he'd arrived.

Josie looked nervously at Simon. Would he be mad that she got the attention?

"Good work, Josie. Perfect time for a demonstration of what we've come up with. Keep it up."

Josie stifled a laugh. "We" hadn't done anything. It was all her work, something Simon would doubtless hide when he wrote up the improvement and sent out the test models. But it didn't matter. She'd met Howard Phillips. She'd shown what she could do. She was at a great company with an excellent opportunity to prove herself. The place might have its oddities, but there was nothing worth worrying about. Her career at Philgard was off to a fantastic start.

Back in his office with Julia and Handar, Phillips sank into the seat behind his desk. He waved, and the doors slammed shut.

"All right, we've seen the trinkets and patted the heads of the minions," he said. "Now down to some real business. Have you found any sign of Kiri?"

Handar shook his head. "Little bastard's in the wind, boss. No one's seen him for weeks now. Best bet, he's taken your money and run."

Phillips slammed his fist down on the table, cracking the wood. A slender tentacle ran out beside his wrist and touched the crack, which sealed up again.

"I should've known better than to invest in that gnome.

Some people can't be trusted. I assume you've done a thorough search of his place?"

"Yes, boss. No sign of the money or of where he was going to."

"I hope you appreciate, Handar, how much this aggravates me. Kiri was supposed to be our lead, our route to a source of power that could get me into the netherworld, that could give me the resources I needed to overrun this place. Now it all comes down to hunting for this mirror."

"Maybe not, boss. We did find this."

Handar carefully drew an envelope from his pocket and laid it down on Phillips' desk. When Phillips tipped it up, an old piece of torn parchment slid out.

Phillip gazed at the parchment for a long time, then looked up at Julia and raised an eyebrow. "Is this?"

She nodded slowly, gazing at the parchment with a feverish intensity.

"The Tess prophecies," she whispered. "The parchment, the ink, the writing style, it all fits with the earliest samples." She leaned over, not touching the document but examining it with the utmost care. "This isn't a text I've seen before. It's a completely new piece, a lost part of the prophecies. This could be a real opportunity."

"And the gnome had this."

"Yup," Handar said. "Looked like it was the clue he'd been following."

"Look, here." Julia pointed at a symbol on one corner of the parchment. "The mark of the Dark Market. This has been through the Oriceran underworld, which makes sense. You could hardly sell or buy a thing like this legally without people hearing about it."

"People like whoever it was stolen off?"

"Probably." Julia nodded. "Let me have a look at the text." Still not touching the parchment, she ran her gaze down it. "It's talking about some ancient group that protects the magicals on Earth. See, here, apparently, they would watch over them for as long as the gates weren't open enough to provide them with enough magic."

"So they're redundant now?" Handar asked. "I mean, gates opening up and all, why would anyone need these losers?"

"Because they do something else too. They have a special magic, though it doesn't say what's different about it, which isn't helpful. Apparently, they use it to guard a precious store of energy, some sort of amazing power that no one else has. That could be the key you need, the way to get into the world between."

"Hm." Phillips leaned back in his chair. If this was true, what Kiri had been chasing could do more than get him his army from the netherworld. It might let him crack open the walls between worlds and unleash his nightmares at last, upon Mana Valley and Earth. It could bring his goals about far faster than expected.

He slid the parchment back into the envelope, then went to the back of the room. Tentacles emerged from his sleeve and touched specific points on the wall. The door of a safe appeared, then opened in response to his tentacle print. He placed the envelope inside, locked the safe, and waved his hand. The safe vanished into the wall again.

"You don't mention this again," Phillips said. "You understand? Not to each other, not to anyone else, not even to me unless I mention it first. Clear?"

"Yes, sir."

"Yup."

"Good." Phillips sat back down in his seat. "These guardians who protect this energy source, do they have a name?"

"Evermores," Julia said.

"Evermores." Phillips rolled the word around his mouth. "Evermores. Something else worth looking for. A clue to what I need." He drummed his fingers on the desk, lost in thought, then abruptly looked up at the other two. "We're done here. Get back to work."

They exchanged a look as they headed for the door. The boss had never seemed distracted like this before, but perhaps there had never been so much at stake.

Left alone in his office, Howard Phillips, the face that hid the Darkness Between Dreams, thought about power, and strength, and the future he would make.

"Evermores," he whispered. "I'm coming for you."

CHAPTER TWENTY-TWO

Fran sat at her desk, a tablet and drawing tool in her hand, working on designs for her containment unit. She was close to something that would work. She could feel it. She even had her experiments for proof, pieces of electronics, mechanical components, and magical parts scattered across the floor. None of them quite did what she wanted yet, but each one brought her a little bit closer.

She sat back in her chair, put the tablet down, and rubbed her eyes. It was only eleven in the morning, and she was already tired. That didn't seem fair somehow.

A Rubik's cube sat on the shelf next to her, an old puzzle of her mother's that Fran had become obsessed with as a child and eventually adopted as hers. She picked it up, twisted the worn pieces around until they were well mixed, and set to work trying to solve it. Corners clicked into place. A sense of satisfaction swept through her as colored squares matched up.

No! This wasn't what she was supposed to be doing.

She flung the cube out of reach on the bed and turned back to her tablet.

In the office, she'd been grateful for any distraction she could find to liven up her day. Now, she needed to avoid being distracted, but the habit was still there, and so were the dozens of books, gadgets, and toys that littered her room. Even when she forced herself to switch off her Internet connection for a few hours, there was always something to draw her away from her designs.

She took a firm hold on her drawing tool and started to sketch again. She could do this. Focus. Concentrate. Narrow her perspective down to that single point pressed against the screen, to this one task that needed doing, to the future of her company, to—

There was a tapping on the window. She tried to ignore it. She was supposed to be concentrating. But what if it was Smokey? She hadn't seen him in days, which wasn't like him. Maybe he was freaking out because she'd found out that he was a shifter. Maybe he'd been avoiding her, which she didn't want. Perhaps he'd come to make peace. She should take time out for that.

She set the tablet down and looked up. A crow was standing outside the window, tapping on the glass.

"You're not Smokey." Fran walked over and opened the window. The crow hopped inside. "You haven't seen him around, have you?"

The crow gave her a quizzical look.

Fran glanced from the crow to her tablet and back out of the window. Now that she'd started thinking about Smokey, she grew concerned. He really had been away for longer than usual. She should probably check on him. But how?

"You know Smokey, right?" she asked the crow. "Black and gray cat, hangs around on the fire escape."

The crow cawed. It didn't seem keen on finding Smokey, and she could hardly blame it. After all, cats could be a real menace to birds. Even if Smokey was only a menace to a plate full of chicken, it was still natural for the crow to stay away from him.

"Never mind," Fran said. "I'll go find him myself."

She pulled on her boots with the rainbow laces and the rhinestones across the toes and headed out the door.

Fran didn't know much about where Smokey went when he wasn't at her apartment. Cats normally kept to a fairly small radius, but Smokey wasn't only a cat, and she knew from the meeting he'd run that he went farther around Mana Valley. Still, local spots were the most convenient place to start and the only lead she had.

The green space next to the apartment block turned out to be a bust. There was no sign of any cats, and the presence of a group of pigeons happily pecking at the ground made her think there hadn't been any predators there for a while. Next, she tried looking around the dumpsters out back, beneath the fire escape, but all she saw was a raccoon and a trash imp fighting over the leftovers in a pizza box.

"Hi," Fran said as she walked up to the counter of the deli on the corner. "Have you seen a cat in here, gray and black, likes to be scratched between the ears?"

"Not in a while," the gnome behind the counter said, shaking her head. "He sometimes comes in at the end of the day to see if we're throwing out any meat scraps he can scavenge, but I haven't seen him in, I don't know, at least a week."

"OK, thanks. I'll look elsewhere."

"Good luck finding your cat."

"Oh, he's not my cat."

Fran walked down the street, peering under parked vehicles and up trees, wandering down alleyways while calling Smokey's name. People glanced at her as they passed, but no one said anything about her behavior. Mana Valley had that big city vibe, where oddity was expected and most definitely not commented on.

A croaking noise made Fran look up from behind a set of dumpsters. A crow was looking down at her from a window ledge. It was hard to be sure, but something about its stance made her think it was the same bird she had seen earlier.

"What are you after now?" she asked. "I don't have any food for you, and honestly, I'm a bit more concerned about the cat."

The crow cawed again, then tilted its head like it was pointing its beak at something. It fluttered down to the ground in front of Fran and pointed again.

"You want to show me something?" Fran asked.

The crow nodded, then fluttered a few steps down the alley.

"Is this about Smokey?"

The crow nodded its head.

"Okay, I'm coming."

The crow led Fran down a series of streets until they came to a park. There, it stopped beside a stand of bushes and pecked at a sandwich crust that had fallen from a nearby bin.

"You brought me all this way for that?" Fran glared at the crow. "What about Smokey?"

The crow pointed its beak at the bushes, then got back to the bread.

Fran crouched at the edge of the bushes. They were thickly grown, but if she crawled, there was a gap she could get through to the interior. She got down on her hands and knees and headed in.

Branches scraped Fran as she forced her way forward, and leaves tickled her skin, but in a minute, she emerged into a hollow space in the middle of all the foliage. Smokey lay there in his cat form, curled up around himself. He opened his eyes a crack to look at her.

"What do you want?" he muttered.

"I was worried about you."

"Don't be. I'm fine."

"But you haven't been around for days."

"I said I'm fine."

"That's cool, but you could be fine at my place too, with a nice plate of chicken."

He closed his eyes and flicked his tail dismissively.

"Come on, Smokey. It's only me."

Fran reached out to scratch the top of his head, between the ears, something that normally made him purr. Today he batted her hand away, stood, turned, and lay down again, his back to her.

"Seriously, what's the matter?" she asked.

"I don't want to talk about it." Something in his tone finally made sense to her.

"Are you embarrassed?" she asked. "Because I saw your meeting?"

"Not because of the meeting," he mumbled. "Because you give me food and shelter, like a common street cat, and now you know that I'm not one of them, so you're going to judge me like everybody else does."

"Oh, Smokey." Fran shook her head. "There's no need to be embarrassed. You're as much a cat as a dwarf, and you shouldn't feel embarrassed about being either."

"I'm a useless dwarf too. I can't find enough work to pay rent, so now I'm spending my whole time as a cat because it's easier to find shelter that way. My ancestors would be ashamed."

"You're doing your best with a tough situation. No one's going to judge you for that. No one worth talking to, anyway."

Smokey didn't respond, but his furry body relaxed a little.

"I tell you what, I'll provide you with whatever food you need, and you can come to my place for somewhere out of the weather whenever you need it. I've told you already, I'm okay with that, and no one else is going to judge you there."

"I can't go living off your handouts."

"Then let's not make it handouts. It's a loan. I'll keep you fed and warm while you need it, and you can pay me back once you've found a way to earn money."

He tipped his head back to look at her. Fran fought the urge to tickle him under the chin.

"I will pay you back," he said.

"I know. That's what I said."

"All right then." Smokey got to his feet and headed down the narrow tunnel between the branches that Fran had crawled through. The branches didn't scrape him. "I'm hungry. Is that stupid crow still hanging around out there?"

"You can't eat him!" Fran said as she scrambled after Smokey. A twig prodded her in the ear.

"I'm not going to. He's got a good eye for scraps out of bins."

"You can't eat bin food!"

"I'm a cat. That's what we do."

"Not anymore. I'm getting us some chicken on the way home and cat biscuits for you. If I have a pet cat around the apartment, I'm doing it properly, with food bowls and everything."

"I'm not a pet."

"Of course. But you will still let me pat your head, right?"

There was a moment's hesitation before he answered. "Yes, but no talking to me while you do it. I don't want this to get weird."

CHAPTER TWENTY-THREE

Having managed to distract herself once at home, Fran decided that the best way to concentrate would be to go and work elsewhere. She was at the stage in design when she needed to be working with components, not just diagrams, and she couldn't do that in a coffee shop. Once she got Smokey settled in the apartment, she headed for the maker space. The crow came with her again, fluttering overhead as she skated through the streets to the empty department store, then landed on her shoulder for the walk down into the basement.

The place was far less busy than it had been for the competition. Half a dozen creatives were occupied at workbenches or using the machines lined up around the walls. One of them was drilling holes in a plastic box, another using the large 3D printer that occupied one corner of the basement. Instead of folding tables laid out to make space for as many people as possible, there were a smaller number of sturdy benches.

Fran put her bag down on a workbench, then went to

the back wall and unfastened the padlock holding one of the many boxes in a rack there. These were the personal storage containers of individual makers, allowing them to leave half-finished projects for next time securely. In Fran's case, it was mostly full of random components she'd thought might be useful at some point and that she hoped might give her the inspiration she needed now. She took it back to her bench and tipped it out, alongside some materials she'd brought from home.

She stared at the components intently, sorted them into piles, resorted them into different piles, then took out her tablet and compared what she had with some of her design ideas. She knew that she wanted to do something with mirrors, as they were a good way to channel and store her particular magic, the type of magic that she now knew belonged to the Evermores.

What was the best way to make use of mirrors in a containment device? One big mirror to help overpower the prisoner and reflect their magic into the device? Smaller mirrors to support beams of magic around the outside, like cage bars? Maybe a mirror box to hold and amplify the power source? Her drawing tool tapped against the screen as she tried to work out what approach to take.

"Do you have to do that?" someone asked. "It's really annoying."

Fran looked up, and the crow looked up with her, its beady eyes staring accusingly. At the workbench across from them, a Willen in a flannel shirt was constructing a magical device out of old monitors and a scratched bathroom mirror.

"I know you," Fran said, setting the drawing tool down. "You were in that competition with me, right?"

"That's right." The Willen kept working. "I built something useful. You built something flashy. Surprise surprise, the pretty witch beat the rat woman." She set her screwdriver down with a distinct *thump* and picked up a soldering iron. "Imagine my shock."

Fran decided it was best not to respond to the Willen's angry tone. She couldn't undo the outcome of the contest even if she'd wanted to, and talking about it seemed sure to trigger an argument. But she did want to know more about what the Willen was doing with her mirror.

"Your name's Singar, right?"

"That's right."

"I'm Fran."

"I know."

"That looks cool. What are you making?"

Singar sighed, set her soldering iron back in its stand, and finally looked up at Fran. Her whiskers twitched irritably.

"It's an entertainment device," she said. "A 3D image projector. Something flashy."

She said the last word like it was a curse.

"I like flashy." Fran pointed at the rhinestones on her boots. "Flashy can be fun."

"Well, quite." Singar picked up her soldering iron again. "I need to get back to work."

There was a faint *hiss* and a familiar smoky smell as she started connecting electronic components. The crow hopped over to take a closer look.

Fran walked around her workbench and came to stand

close to Singar, examining what she was doing. There were crystals embedded into some of the screens and runes scratched down the sides of the mirror. Fran tried to work out what the runes would do, but she couldn't quite spot the pattern. Sometimes you had to see magic in action to understand how its parts would connect.

"What's the mirror for?" She peered more closely at it.

Singar stood stock still for a long moment, then turned to look at Fran.

"You're not going to leave me in peace, are you?"

"Do you want me to leave you in peace?"

"Obviously, yes, but that doesn't seem to be your thing, so..." Singar wiped solder from the iron and set it back in its holder, then pointed at one of the screens with its embedded crystals. "These produce the signals, but the mirror acts as an amplifier. The runes down the sides mean that magical images beamed onto it become briefly trapped, bouncing back onto themselves a few times before projecting. Understand?"

"Yes, it's like—"

"Whatever you're going to say, it's not like that. This is new." Singar thrust a plug into a socket on the workbench. "Watch."

She flipped a switch. The device hummed, and a beam of light emerged from the mirror. The crow jumped back from the light with its feathers spread wide. Above it, patterns shifted, colors and shapes moving. They formed a cartoonish picture of a Willen, slightly static-broken but clear enough to be obvious what it was.

"Oh my goodness!" Fran exclaimed. "It's even got a Willen's magical aura."

"That's the idea, yes."

The image stuttered, and the aura faded away, leaving only the visual image. Singar switched the machine off, and the other Willen vanished.

"I don't have a way to supply a steady stream of magic power into the image yet," Singar said. "The images can go far larger than this, and I can crank up the volume, but I need magic to hold it all together as well as for the auras and some of the effects. Give it a few months to work that part out, and it'll be ready to look for investors. Until then..." She shrugged. "Until then, I need to do some work."

She picked up the soldering iron and looked pointedly at Fran.

"Ooh, I have something you might like!" Fran rushed over to her workbench, grabbed her tablet, and hurried back to Singar. "I'm working on a magical power source, like a sort of battery thing. It might help with your device."

"You've got this now?" Singar peered at the screen. "It works?"

"Well, not yet, but I've started a company, and we're going to work on funding, and then—"

"So you don't have a power source. You have the idea that a power source would be useful." Singar clapped her hands very slowly. "Brilliant. Just brilliant."

Fran sagged a little in the face of the Willen's sarcasm, but she wasn't going to be deterred.

"I think we could help each other," she said. "I've seen you working here, and you're so good with hardware, far more practical than I am. Why don't you join my company? We can make your projector as one of the devices to demonstrate how the battery works, and the battery will mean that the projector does what it needs to do, and—"

"No. I work for myself. I'm not joining you for the sake of some imaginary battery that doesn't even work yet."

"But I—"

"What part of 'no' don't you understand? I don't need to join some flashy witch's amateur startup, to waste my time trying to make your dream work. I've got my own thing. Now please, for the love of all of creation, let me work in peace."

Feeling deflated, Fran slouched back to her workbench. She pushed some pieces together into a new heap and started assembling them into a reduced version of one of her concepts for the trap. She hadn't brought the broken bathroom mirror from home, so instead, she used a portable shaving mirror she'd bought from a discount store.

She glanced up again, looking across the gap at Singar's creation. The amplifying mirror and its runes were such a good idea, Fran couldn't help wondering how that would interact with her powers, the light and sound that she projected, especially the light. As Fran stared at the mirror, Singar tensed but didn't look up, instead focusing even harder on her soldering.

"Can I ask one more thing?" Fran asked quietly.

"Fine. One." Singar looked up with a scowl. "Make it quick."

"Have you considered using the mirror to amplify light as well as magic?"

Singar stared at Fran for a long moment, then looked

down at her mirror. The crow, perching on the edge of her workbench, cawed and hopped closer to her.

"No," Singar said, her tone less abrupt. "I hadn't thought about that."

"I can see how you might miss it, but the magic could contain and direct the light, so that they both get amplified, which will add to the strength and the stability of the images you're projecting, and that will—"

"Yes, I get it. I'm not an idiot." Singar looked up at Fran. "You're not as much of an idiot as you seem to be."

"Thank you." Fran beamed. "Does that mean you might come to work with me?"

"Absolutely not." Singar set her soldering iron aside and waved the crow away. "Your one question's over. Now shut up and let me work."

Smiling, Fran turned her attention back to her components. It felt good to help someone out.

The crow fluttered over and tapped its beak on the bench in front of Fran.

"I can take a hint," she said.

It was time to focus on her work.

CHAPTER TWENTY-FOUR

Cameron was behind the counter when Fran walked into the Blazing Bean. It was a quiet morning, so he had his laptop open and was typing as she approached.

"Working on that thesis?" Fran asked.

"Something like that." Cam set the computer aside. "What can I get for you this morning?"

"You don't know my regular order yet? I'm in here all the time!"

"You have a different drink every time. One day it's a chai latte. The next it's a cappuccino with extra froth, and you're the only customer we have who's ever asked for both hazelnut and vanilla syrup in the same black coffee."

"I like to experiment. There are so many exciting things in life. Don't you want to try them all?"

"There isn't enough time in life to try everything. You'll drive yourself insane."

"Who says that I haven't already?" She crossed her eyes and stuck her tongue out the corner of her mouth.

Cam laughed. "Fair point. Still, my question stands, what do you want?"

"Mocha, extra sugar, with peppermint syrup, please."

"See, who could've predicted that?"

He started making her drink.

"Can I pay for a tea and a black coffee as well?" Fran asked. "For when my colleagues arrive."

"They're already here." Cam nodded at a table near the back, where Gruffbar and Bart conversed over their drinks. "And they bought cake. Apparently, you're not allowed to pay for it three weeks in a row."

"Aw, such sweethearts." Fran paid for her drink and took the mocha Cam set down in front of her. "Time to get to work."

"Have fun at the office." Cam winked, then opened his laptop, ready to start typing again.

Fran made her way to the table where the others sat.

"Why are we back here instead of by the window?" she asked. "It's all dark and gloomy!"

"Gruffbar's feeling paranoid," Bart said.

"You're not paranoid if they're out to get you," Gruffbar said.

"Is someone out to get you?" Fran looked around in alarm, half-expecting assailants to emerge from the shadows of the coffee shop.

"Not yet, but I've been getting that tingle in my beard."

"Maybe you're jumpy because of the accident with your bike?"

He shook his head. "That was weeks ago. This is something different." He narrowed his eyes and looked all around. "I feel like someone's watching me."

"We're always being watched." Fran pointed at the security camera attached to the ceiling in the corner of the room, at Cam sitting behind the counter, at people glancing into the Blazing Bean as they walked down the street. "That's what happens when you live in a city."

"Still." Gruffbar tapped a chunky metal lighter against the tabletop. "I don't like it."

Fran took a slice of chocolate cake from the plate in the middle of the table, then took her laptop out of her bag and set it up in front of her.

"Oops," she said as she entered her password. "Sticky fingers."

Trying to wipe chocolate icing off the keys with a napkin led to the laptop thinking that she was typing and getting confused at the gibberish of it all. Fran stopped once she'd cleared the worst away. She could sort it out properly later. It wasn't like a little icing would do any harm.

"What's on the agenda today?" she asked.

"That's something you should work out before the meeting," Bart said. "Remember our talk the other day about efficient use of time?"

"Kind of." Fran shrugged sheepishly. "All that management stuff, it makes my brain start to wander. I don't take it all in the first time."

"Well, you'll have to take it in soon. You can't be a CEO without delving into the dark arts of management."

"I know. I'm sorry. I'll pay more attention next time."

"I appreciated the fact that you'll try." Bart pulled out his laptop and brought up a document. "Fortunately, I planned and wrote an agenda of my own. First up, a report from your chief legal officer."

"The accounts are set up," Gruffbar said. "Although right now, there's nothing in them..."

For the next hour, they talked about various issues relating to Mana Wave Industries, with varying degrees of excitement. Gruffbar explained where the legal process of creating the company was and some of the policies and procedures they now needed to create. Bart made Fran write those down as Gruffbar went through them so she would have to pay attention.

Then they got onto progress with the technology, and her interest level rose. She talked about the devices she'd been working on, from the batteries to a rebuilt flying carpet to a small prototype for the containment unit.

"You might need to focus on that one a bit more," Bart said. "You have a potential buyer for it."

"I do?" Fran stared at him open-mouthed. "Who? How? Why? When?"

"Perhaps one question at a time." Bart smiled proudly. "Although it is news worth getting excited about. I have some contacts in law enforcement on Earth. I've been chatting with them over the last few weeks, priming them with tidbits about you and what you're working on, then getting into the device itself. It's exactly the sort of thing they need, now they're facing more open magical challenges, and they're interested in buying."

"That's brilliant!" Fran grinned and took a celebratory gulp of her minty mocha, which had gone cold while she enthused about her ideas.

"Who exactly is they?" Gruffbar asked.

"The FBI. They've offered us a contract to provide them with a prototype, building up to a full production run if the design seems suited to their needs. There are even advance fees to help with developing the technology."

"A contract?" Gruffbar held out his hand. "Show me."

Still beaming, Bart took a sheaf of papers from his bag and handed them to Gruffbar, who quickly skimmed through them.

"They're expecting us to sign up to this?" he asked.

"Well, yes, and you'll need to act quickly: they have other people they're interested in too."

"We'll take it!" Fran grabbed a pen and the contract.

"Wait!" Gruffbar said. "Don't sign that."

"Sorry, too late." She looked at him sheepishly. "Is there a problem?"

"You just signed a contract committing us to a multi-million-dollar technology deal."

"We need to get money from somewhere."

"A multi-million-dollar technology deal to sell them a technology that doesn't even exist yet."

"Well, yes, but we're working on it, and..." Fran's voice trailed off. "Is this bad?"

Her spirits, which had risen to giddy heights at the announcement of their first customer, now plummeted. She felt like a ball of lead was weighing down her stomach. This was a huge deal.

"Can we just pretend I never signed this?" she asked. "Tell them we lost the paperwork?"

"We could." Gruffbar looked at the expressions of his colleagues and saw the whole business on the verge of collapse. They needed the money, and they needed the boost that would come with striking a deal.

There were times for brutal truths, and there were times when you had to walk more carefully, to spin a version of what was technically true, to keep people going. It seemed like this was one of those times.

He sipped his coffee and composed himself.

"This will be challenging," he said. "But we can do it." If we work insanely hard and get very lucky, he didn't add. "The money they offered for initial development will help." That last part was true. With the money, they could afford components, pay their bills, maybe even somewhere to work. "It's a big commitment, and we need to treat it very seriously, but if we do this right, it could be the making of Mana Wave Industries."

If they failed, they risked ending up in court for fraud, but he wasn't going to say that part out loud.

"So now what?" Fran asked, tense but not as terrified as she'd been a moment before.

"Now, you need to focus on this one project. No more flying carpets or smellophones or whatever other ideas you've been tinkering with. It's the containment unit all the way."

"And the power source for it," Bart added.

"And the power source," Gruffbar agreed. "That can still be the heart of our business model." He put the contract in the middle of the table and tapped one of the pages. "Now though, we have a delivery date for a containment unit, and we have to meet that deadline."

Fran stared at the date, which stared back at her accusingly.

"That's much sooner than I expected," she said. "Can't we delay it?"

"Not now that we have a contract."

"But it's only me making it, and, and, and..."

"We need more technical staff." Bart ran a hand through his cloud of white hair. "I don't suppose you've found any potential recruits?"

"I met someone who would've been great for the hardware side, but she's not interested, and I don't know anyone with the programming skills we need."

"At least we can hire people now, with the FBI money."

"Not yet," Gruffbar said. "The upfront money will need to cover components."

"Are you sure?"

Gruffbar switched to another page of the contract, with amounts and dates for payments.

"Oh." Bart frowned. "You're right. We can't afford wage commitments upfront."

"So we need to find staff," Fran said, "but we can't afford to pay them, and we needed to finish the prototype by sometime last week."

"Pretty much," Gruffbar agreed.

Fran could feel the seriousness of the situation rushing down upon her, like a great wave about to crash over a tiny boat. If she steered the boat right, maybe they could ride this out. Just like riding that wave, it was bound to be thrilling, and wasn't that what running a startup was supposed to be about?

She grinned, half-nervous, half-excited. "That's settled then. What's next on the agenda?"

CHAPTER TWENTY-FIVE

When the others had gone, Gruffbar sat alone in the Blazing Bean, staring at the contract. It wasn't the worst situation he'd ever been in or even seen a business get into. Now that his initial shock was receding, he thought it might be possible that they could get through this and come out ahead thanks to the money and prestige the contract would bring. Still, it was a big gamble, and Fran hadn't yet convinced him that she was ready to bear its weight. She was still a kid at heart, and this was a huge deal.

On the other hand, she had enthusiasm, commitment, and more than a little inspiration. He recognized something of his younger self in her. Was that why he hadn't walked away when Bart's contract left them up in the air like this? Maybe. After all, he'd had to give up his dreams of engineering. If he could help Fran achieve hers, that seemed like a hell of a way to balance his karma.

He put the contract back in his bag, then stacked up the

empty coffee cups on the cake plate and carried them to the counter.

"Thanks," Cam said. "But you don't have to do that. Clearing tables is part of my job."

"I'm trying to do good deeds, kid. Just accept it."

"Right you are." Cam took the dirty crockery. "You're a lawyer, right? Do you know anything about how people make deals with dark forces?"

"I know better than to do that sort of thing. Unless you're an idiot, you'll steer clear of it too. That's the only free legal advice I'll ever give."

Gruffbar walked out into the sunshine and went to where he'd parked his bike. He'd spent whole days repairing the Harley after the accident, straightening dented plates, filing away scrapes and scratches, replacing busted components, and giving the machine a new coat of paint. It had been satisfying work, if sad to see the bike in such a state. Still, however good the repair job was, it seldom matched the original, and he could see the accident's aftermath on the machine.

He fixed his bag in place, put on his helmet, and climbed into the saddle. He patted the poor, recovering bike.

"Let's go home."

He revved up the engine and headed out into the road, overtaking a steam wagon and a carriage pulled by giant lizards. These days, even the more traditional vehicles had modern touches influenced by Earth design, like the wing mirrors on the carriage and the fluffy dice hanging in the window of the steam wagon.

That was the good thing about Mana Valley. It was

more like Earth than almost anywhere else on Oriceran. Even the litter and the taste of diesel fumes in the air reminded him of that other world. He kind of missed it when he wasn't over there looking for work in San Francisco, but there was an opportunity here, and he wasn't going to miss out on it.

Lost in thought, he shifted into a sort of mental autopilot and almost didn't notice the sound of parting metal. However, dwarves trained their ears to alert them to the noises of a mechanical world, and especially of that world going wrong. He looked up, saw a lamppost falling toward where he was about to be, and swerved the bike aside. Horns blared as he almost ran into oncoming traffic, but he kept from colliding with anyone and stayed in his seat.

Heart racing, he pulled to the side of the road, secured his bike, and walked over to look at the fallen lamppost. Traffic had stopped on either side of it and pedestrians were walking over to look.

"Seems like the fixings holding it up came loose." A wizard pointed at the bolts that lay on either side of the lamppost's base.

"There are traces of magic on them." An elf picked up one of the loose bolts. "Do you think it was some sort of prank?"

"More likely someone tried to secure it and got the wrong spells." The wizard shook his head. "You can't get good contractors these days."

Gruffbar stared down at the lamppost. That had been alarmingly close to a second accident in the space of a month. At least he'd come out of it unhurt this time, and so had his bike.

He mounted up and headed off down the road again. With the lamppost fresh in his memory, he looked around warily as he went. When the bolt of magic flew out of an alleyway, he saw it coming. Unfortunately, it was too fast for him to avoid. The spell hit his front wheel, ice covered the tire and spread to the back, and the bike slid across the road, its wheels locked.

Gruffbar leaned into the skid, keeping upright as long as he could while the bike used up its momentum. There was only so much he could do. For the last few feet, it dragged him across the ground before bike and rider crashed into a tree.

For a long moment, he lay on the ground, dazed and bruised and trying to work out if he'd broken anything.

"Are you okay?" someone asked.

Gruffbar looked up. People were gathering around him, all of them looking concerned. Someone was lifting his bike while someone else offered him a hand, and a third person waved their hand in his face.

"How many fingers am I holding up?" they asked.

"Too damn many." Gruffbar got to his feet. His ankle hurt, but that didn't stop him from shoving through the crowd to the alarm of many concerned onlookers. He rushed back to the mouth of the alley the magic had come from.

"Who's there?" Gruffbar shouted. "Show yourself!"

A raccoon with three tails appeared from behind a dumpster, clutching a moldy chunk of bread. There was no one else.

Cursing and limping on his injured ankle, Gruffbar made his way back through the crowd and grabbed hold of his bike. The magical ice was melting, but he would need to check the machine over before he rode it anywhere again.

"Are you sure you're all right?" one of the onlookers asked. "I think you should go to the hospital."

"I think I should go home for a stiff drink. Let's see what happens there."

"I don't think I can let you leave like this."

Gruffbar rounded angrily on the witch.

"I'm a lawyer, not a cop, but I'm pretty sure you have no right to stop me," he snapped. "What do you think?"

She looked at him with wide eyes. "I'm only trying to help."

Gruffbar drew a deep breath. "Thank you, but I'm fine. And I'm going."

He walked his bike up the edge of the street, helmet hanging from the handlebars, heading for the apartment he'd found on a short-term lease. His ankle ached, the back of his hand was scraped raw, and there were bruises up his back, but it was the damage to the bike that really hurt. All those repairs he would have to do again.

Something moved in the branches of a tree by the side of the road. Gruffbar stopped. Was it a coincidence that something was happening in his path again? He didn't think so.

Bees flew down out of the tree, a large swarm angrily buzzing. People hurried away, but they needn't have worried. The bees weren't interested in anyone else. They were heading straight for Gruffbar.

He pulled on his helmet, slammed down the visor, and got the gloves on seconds before the swarm hit him.

"Try and sting me through this, you buzzing bastards," he declared, flexing the leather of his jacket.

The bees swirled around him, bouncing off his helmet and banging against his jacket as if they were determined to get through to him. He would've wondered what had gotten into them, but after the rest of his journey, he was sure that he knew. This was magic, pure and simple. Someone was out to get him.

People were gathering around, some pointing, some taking photos, some calling to Gruffbar, asking if they could help him somehow.

"Is this an art thing?" someone asked. "Like, a performance piece?"

"That's right," Gruffbar growled as a bee made it through the gap between his jacket and helmet, then stung him in the back of the neck. It hurt, but not much worse than the aches he already had. "I'm being stung by bees for your entertainment."

"It's a bit showy for my taste," said one spectator.

"And dangerous for the rest of us," said another. "I don't think that this should be encouraged."

"Look out!" A shopkeeper flung a bucket of water over Gruffbar and the bees. "Did that get rid of them?"

"No," Gruffbar growled. "Now I'm soaking wet."

"No need to get snappy. I was trying to help."

Gruffbar grabbed hold of his bike and set off down the street again. The gathered people parted in front of him, not wanting to get stung. Dripping wet and with insects buzzing around him in a slowly diminishing swarm, Gruffbar limped home, pushing his battered bike.

"I don't know who's behind this," he muttered to himself, "but I'm going to make them regret the day they ever heard of Gruffbar Steelstrike."

CHAPTER TWENTY-SIX

Fran sat at the kitchen counter, her laptop perched in front of the coffee machine, a pile of receipts and bills in front of her. She looked through the pile again, hoping that there might somehow be fewer than when she had last looked. Instead, she spotted one that she hadn't noticed before.

She pushed the papers aside and opened a spreadsheet on the laptop. On its first tab, she titled the first few columns, used headers like "earnings," "outgoings," and "date." She made those words bold, outlined the columns around them, and saved the sheet as "Accounts Year 1".

There, that was a start. Now she could get back to her prototypes, right? Except that Gruffbar had been very clear that she had to keep accounts. It was a legal obligation and one of the first things the authorities would want to see. Even their new client at the FBI had a right to some of their accounting information as part of the contract, which currently only existed in the form of crumpled receipts and unpaid debts to electronics shops.

Fran picked up the first receipt for a jar of newt's eyes

and two packs of enchanted runic chalk from a magical supply shop. That went under expenses, but what sort of expense? Which date should she give it, the one when she'd been shopping or when the money had gone from her account?

She set that receipt aside unprocessed and picked up another one. This time it was for magically coated computer cables, the reinforced kind that could carry a heavy mystical load. She hadn't used them in the project yet, so could she still put them in the expenses? If she used half, did she only put half the cost onto the spreadsheet? What about the electricity she was using while she worked? Or the electricity she was using while she thought about how much electricity she was using?

"Aah!" Fran flung the receipts in the air and threw herself to the floor in exasperation.

At that moment, the door to the apartment opened, and Josie walked in. She looked at Fran and the scraps of paper falling around her.

"What's the matter?" Josie asked.

"Nothing," Fran said without conviction.

Josie picked up and read one of the receipts.

"Can you not afford these things?" she asked. "Is it stressing you out?"

"No. I mean yes, it's stressing me out, but I can afford them. Just about. For now. The problem is the accounts." Fran pressed her head back against a cupboard door. "Accounts are haaaaard."

Josie looked at the spreadsheet and stifled a laugh.

"Don't you need to make some accounts before you know that?" she asked.

"I'm trying! Look, there's an expenses column and an earnings column, and accounting things like that. I even did headers."

"Yes, you did. Although I think you might need to add a couple of things, like what the expense is and who you paid it to. Then there's factoring in the taxes..."

Fran leaped to her feet and wrapped her arms around her roommate.

"Josie, you're my savior! You understand accounts. You can do them for me."

"No."

"But please!"

"Absolutely not. I have quite enough work of my own. The last thing I want is to spend my leisure time doing the bits you don't have enough patience for."

"You could work for me. Then you would have the time to spare."

"Three things." Josie counted off on her fingers. "First, I love my new job, and I don't want to give it up. Second, I'm a tech girl, not an accountant. Third, one of us in this apartment needs to earn a steady wage, at least until your startup gets going."

"But..."

"No buts. Either you find an accountant, or you deal with this yourself."

Fran sighed. "Fine."

She gathered the papers up off the floor and made a pile of them, even less neat than before.

Taking pity on her roommate, Josie wrapped an arm around Fran's shoulders. "Tell you what, why don't you take a break? Knowing you, you've been staring at this for hours, failing to get the boring thing done. At least you've got your spreadsheet now, which will make it easier to get started when you come back from skating."

"Skating?"

"Yes, skating." Josie picked up Fran's skates and shoved them into her hands. "Go get some fresh air and exercise. No more than an hour, then you're back here to fix this."

"You sound like my mom telling me to do homework."

"I'm sure you listened to her even worse than you do with me. Now go, skate, clear your head."

Fran wasn't going to say "no" to orders like that. She walked down to the street, put on her skates, and headed for the skate park with a crow fluttering along beside her.

"I don't suppose you like doing accounts?" she asked the crow. Its only response was a croaking sound.

The skate park was busy, with a roller derby team practicing on one half of the track and a bunch of skateboarders using the pipes. Bart was rolling back and forth on the empty half of the track, dressed in his usual layers of padding and protection. He waved hello as she skated over.

"Great to see you practicing again," Fran said. "You're here almost as much as I am."

"Got to keep myself entertained," Bart said. "I started a watercolor class too, but that's only one evening each week." He wiggled his fingers. "I've been learning some new things, though. Watch."

Magic shone from his hand, and he started to speed up, accelerating away from her. He hunched over, keeping himself stable, and held his other hand out in front of him.

"One hand to go faster," he called back. "The other one to stop me."

He waved the hand in front of him, and there was another flash of magic. Instead of stopping, Bart somersaulted over that hand. He flipped twice through the air and landed on his back with a *thud*.

"Are you okay?" Fran skated over and knelt beside him. "Don't move. I'm going to check you for broken bones first."

"That looked so much easier on the Internet." Bart groaned. "What did I do wrong?"

"Basic physics." Fran prodded his arms and legs. "The people you saw in videos will have put the brake on higher, lowered their center of gravity, or slowed down first. If you don't do that, your momentum carries you over the casting point. This is why you should work on your basic skating first and throw the magic in later."

"Good to know." He pushed himself up on his elbows. "Will I live?"

"You'll be fine. Nothing broken but your dignity."

"I'm too old to care about that."

Fran stood and offered him her hand. Once they were back on their feet, they started slowly skating back and forth, Fran giving Bart someone he could grab hold of until he'd found his confidence again.

"I've been meaning to apologize," he said after a while. "That whole business with the FBI contract, I shouldn't have arranged it without you. I'm not even really part of your company, only an old man keeping himself busy by meddling in your life, and thanks to me you're stuck with this big commitment."

"Are you kidding? I could never have gotten us a contract like that myself. It's an amazing opportunity, and it'll keep me focused on the work." She looked around guiltily. "OK, so it'll mostly keep me focused. Just not today. Today I needed, like, a break from the paperwork of it all."

Bart chuckled. "We really are different people. I love a good bit of paperwork."

A couple of crows landed on Fran's shoulders and started cawing in her ears. She glanced at her watch. It had been nearly an hour since she left the apartment.

"Did Josie send you?" she asked the crows. "Or are you just manifesting my guilty conscience?"

The crows cawed again, then took off into the air.

"Sorry," she said to Bart. "I've got to go now. The accounts aren't doing themselves."

"Ah, accounts. The joy of numbers, making the money dance." Bart waved his hand like he was conducting an imaginary orchestra. "The symphony of the spreadsheets. I miss it."

Fran stopped where she was.

"Wait, you used to be an accountant, didn't you?" she asked.

"Oh, yes. Until I got too senior and ended up running a finance department instead. I should have stayed more junior. The figures were where my real passion lay."

"Would you like to be an accountant again?"

"You know that I'm retired, don't you?"

"I know that you're bored, and being in a startup is, like, the total opposite of boredom."

He laughed. "I suppose I'm practically part of the company already. Why not make it official?"

Fran's heart sank.

"I've just remembered why not. I can't afford to pay you."

"Then why don't I take the same deal as Gruffbar? A seat on the board and a promise of future fortune, assuming that we succeed. It'll give me a good motive to help you save money."

"You could be my chief financial officer."

"Why not? But once you're big enough to hire more accountants, I want to be demoted straight away. No more running departments for me. It's spreadsheets or nothing."

"You're on." Fran held out her hand, and they shook on it. "Would you like to come and start on those accounts now?"

"Why not?" Bart rubbed his bruised back. "I think I've skated quite enough for one day."

CHAPTER TWENTY-SEVEN

Singar sat on a high stool by a workbench in the maker space, hunched over the latest iteration of her magical image projector. That annoying Fran girl had been right. It was possible to use the mirror to amplify light as well as magic, and the result was a big improvement in the power of the projector. Sin hadn't had a chance to test it in a large, open space yet, where she could see the power and range of the projections, but interference was down, clarity of images was up, and the whole thing was running better.

She flipped a switch, and the projector stirred into life. An image of a Willen sprang into the air, twice life-size. The illusory Willen wore a suit with a gold chain hanging from her pocket and held the keys of a sports car in her hand.

"One day," Sin whispered.

She held up a sensor to take some readings of the magic radiating from the illusion. It seemed to be steady and projecting the sort of field she'd been after, but the details still weren't quite right, and this thing needed to be perfect.

How else was she going to convince a company to take her on? If they saw shoddy Willen craft, they would see another shoddy Willen too, and she would never get past the prejudices that had stopped her from finding work at the Mana Valley companies she'd applied to before. Skills weren't everything, as people from her neighborhood knew all too well.

A flip of the switch killed the image again. Sin unplugged the machine and started dismantling the outer case so she could reach the components inside.

A chill ran down her spine as if a sudden draft had swept across the room. She looked around, but the door wasn't open, and no one else was around who might have opened it. She had the place to herself. No wonder she was getting so much done.

She slid the two halves of the device apart and slid the mirror out from between them. The runes along its edges still looked good, but she took the time to examine them in detail. The devil was in the details where magic was concerned, and a slight tweak to the lines of those runes might make all the difference.

Frost appeared in the middle of the workbench and spread out toward its edges.

"What the..." Sin stared at the surface of the bench, then at her machine. This couldn't be a side-effect of her work, could it? There was no frost on the other benches, and though correlation didn't necessarily imply causality, she'd been using magic. Weird things could happen when you did that.

A ghostly hand appeared through the frost and grabbed for the mirror.

"Hey!" Sin grabbed the mirror and leaped down off her stool. She peered suspiciously at the solid side of the workbench. "Get away from my tech!"

A figure crawled out of the side of the bench. It was ghostly pale, draped in ragged gray robes that looked as insubstantial as its body. A featureless face stared at Sin.

"Give it to me," the spirit hissed, reaching for the mirror.

"No way." Sin gripped the mirror tighter. "This is mine."

"Feeble creature, give it to me."

The spirit grabbed the mirror, its hand becoming substantial as it took hold. It was stronger than Sin expected. It pulled on the mirror, almost dragging it from her hands.

Sin was tough, but she couldn't win this as a tug of war. Gambling on the fact that she could hang on briefly with one hand, she let go with the other and reached into the pocket of her flannel shirt. She pulled out a screwdriver and slammed its point into the spirit's hand. The creature howled and let go of the mirror so suddenly that Sin staggered back, banging into the next workbench over.

"Liked that, did you?" she said, waving the screwdriver at the spirit. "There's plenty more where that came from."

Sin had grown up in a rough neighborhood, and she was well-practiced at using whatever came to hand to defend herself. She slashed the air with the screwdriver, its point looking as dangerous as any knife.

"Give it," the spirit hissed, "or I will suck the warmth from you and leave you a cold, dead thing."

"Like hells am I giving this to you." Sin stayed defiant,

even though her breath froze as it left her body and the growing chill made her shiver. "You want it, come get it."

She backed away, screwdriver held out but was brought up short by a tugging on the corner of the mirror. Looking down, she realized that it was firmly attached to the power cable that she used for the projection device, which in turn plugged into a socket on the edge of the workbench. She tugged on the cord, but the angle was wrong to get it free.

The spirit lunged at her. Unable to go back, Sin went forward, rolling under the spirit's arms, her body curled around the mirror. She came to her feet on the far side of the spirit and jumped up, first onto her stool, then onto the top of the workbench.

"Help!" she shouted. "Someone get the Griffins. Something's attacking me!"

"No one to help you." The spirit drifted back toward her. "No one else to hear. Me. You. Mirror. Give."

Sin kicked the stool over. It fell into the spirit's path, but the spirit went through it. Any time it wasn't touching the mirror, it was too insubstantial for her to hurt.

Sin wished that she knew more magic. That might have been able to touch a creature like this. All she had was her claws and teeth and the tools lying around her. She flung a soldering iron at the creature, just in case, but it sailed through the ghostly body.

"Foolish creature." The spirit extended a hand, but this time it didn't try to grab the mirror. Instead, a stream of Arctic cold reached for Sin, like a frozen hand closing around her throat. She gasped, barely able to breathe. It felt as though ice was forming in her very veins.

She looked down at the mirror. Her mirror. She

wouldn't let anybody take the things that she'd made, the things that were going to drag her out of the slums. She'd sweated and bled and gone hungry to get this thing made.

No ghost was going to steal it from her. Except the cold was spreading, and now her mind was starting to feel numb as a terrible ache took hold of her lungs. Her vision grew blurry as she stared at the runes around the mirror's edge.

The runes. Those held magic. Maybe she could use that. But how?

She pulled a piece of circuity off the back of the mirror and used it to scratch a new line over one of the runes, breaking its shape. She was running out of breath and sank to her knees on the workbench, surrounded by the pieces of her device, but she wasn't giving up. The circuit's edge rasped across the mirror one last time. Then she flung the circuit at the spirit.

"Foolish. Weak. Dying." The spirit's words were a hiss. "You cannot resist."

Sin jabbed the power switch next to the mirror's plug with her toe. Electricity ran down the cable, triggering the mirror's mechanisms, powering up its magic. The mirror, detached from the rest of the machine, trembled in her hands.

She really, really hoped this worked.

"Mine." The spirit, sensing that something was amiss, grabbed the mirror. The runes along the edges lit up. The mirror had encountered magic that was different from and far more powerful than what it had dealt with before. However, she'd made it to work with magic, and it dealt with it in only one way: trap it long enough to amplify it.

The mirror's magic grabbed hold of the spirit and sucked it in. Within the thin layer of enchantment across the mirror's surface, the spirit cried out in frustration.

"Release me!" it screeched. "Release me, or I will destroy you!"

The mirror had turned icy cold, but the freezing grip on Sin's throat was gone. She laid the mirror down on the workbench and stared at it. The runes were active, doing their work of trapping and amplifying the magic that was the spirit.

Normally, they would've released that power after a few moments so it would come out stronger and form a projection. The rune she'd scratched over was the one that would release the power. Without it, the mirror would hold onto the spirit as long as its magical technology was powered up.

Sin hurried across the room to where the collective behind the maker space kept components. She grabbed a couple of battery packs from a box and hurried back to the workbench. It wouldn't take much to give the mirror a portable power source. Then…

Honestly, she didn't know what came then. Was she going to keep this spirit trapped forever, find a way to dispose of it, or hand it over to the Silver Griffins? That was a decision for future Sin. What mattered now was that it mustn't get out.

Nobody messed with a Willen from the wrong side of the tracks, not even creeping cold ghosts. She might need a different mirror to finish making her projector now.

CHAPTER TWENTY-EIGHT

Fran set the prototype down on her bed. It was a foot across, a framework of metal rods with a mirror in the bottom, crystals, and tiny electrical fittings decorating the corners where pieces joined. She'd painted the rods black, and their lines were stark against her rainbow-colored sheets.

Wires trailed from the device down the bed and across the floor. One went to a power socket and another to the computer on her desk, the one with all the extra processing power to run software her laptop couldn't handle. Eventually, the device would need a processor, but that was a lot of design work and many test iterations away. For now, what she needed was a way to connect it to the draft control software, to test whether it even worked in principle.

Tapping on the window made Fran look up. A crow was there, peering in at her. She opened the window, and it fluttered in to perch on top of the prototype.

"I don't think you should do that," Fran said. "Not unless you want to be my first test subject."

The crow cawed and lifted its wings in something like a shrug, then hopped down into the body of the device, like an animal stepping into a cage.

"All right," Fran said. "I suppose I might as well make use of you."

She switched on the device, which started to hum gently. A trail of smoke drifted from one corner, and for a moment she wondered if she should switch it off in case she set her bed on fire. The smoke didn't last, so it was probably all fine. Besides, she needed somewhere to test this, and home was where all her tools were.

With a key tap, she triggered the software that controlled the device. Theoretically, it should use the sensors on the corners to evaluate the magical and biological strength of the device's occupant, as well as their biological needs, then use that information to set up a containment field of appropriate power. Feeding off the occupant's energy and catering to their needs would come later, once she'd perfected this part of the device.

Lines of magical light shone from the crystals on the corners of the frame. Some of them shone on the crow, which looked down in curiosity at the bright points against its feathers. Those were the sensor beams. The rest ran between the rods of the frame, like shining bars for an illuminated cage.

"It's working," Fran exclaimed and clapped. "It's really working!"

"What is it?" a familiar voice asked from the window.

Fran looked around to see Smokey standing there, paws on the windowsill, peering in at the device.

"It's a containment unit," she said. "For holding magicals."

"You're running a prison business?" He swished his tail from side to side. "From here?"

"A magitech business. Yes, from here, at least until I can afford an office."

Smokey jumped in, prowled across the room, and jumped up onto the bed. The crow, alarmed at the grinning cat only a few feet away, spread its wings and flew. There was a brief crackle as it hit the magical bars, then it was through them and out.

"Oh." Fran looked in disappointment at the cage and then at the bird sitting on top of her wardrobe. "That was supposed to hold you in."

"This?" Smokey waved a paw through the magical bars, which crackled and sparked but did nothing to stop him. "Doesn't seem very strong."

"It's supposed to respond to the power of the creature it's containing, using the sensors and the control software."

"Well, I'm feeling particularly powerful today, and this isn't responding to me." Smokey turned and tried waving his tail through the bars, which still didn't grow in strength. "Looks like it needs work."

Fran sighed and switched off the prototype. The magic faded, leaving only the rods with their crystals and sensors.

"I need a snack," she said. "You want anything?"

"I wouldn't say no to some cat biscuits."

"Really? Don't you want something more…"

"More like a magical should eat? Not really. When I'm

like this, I have a cat's senses and a cat's needs, which gives me a cat's tastes. I'd rather have good cat food in this shape than almost anything I could eat as a dwarf."

It made sense, but not in a way Fran had expected. She liked surprises like that and pondered what it meant as she went into the kitchen to fetch a cupcake and a bowl of biscuits. It would've been a fine line of thought to follow if she wasn't supposed to be thinking about the device and how to make it work. By the time she came back into the bedroom, she was no closer to an answer than she'd been before.

She put the bowl down on the floor and sat in front of her computer.

"Try it again," Smokey said as he sniffed at the biscuits.

"I know it doesn't work."

"Just try it."

"All right." Fran looked at the crow. "Would you mind?"

The crow looked at Smokey warily, but he seemed occupied eating, so it flew down and took its place in the device, claws resting on the mirrored base. Fran flipped a switch, hit the "Enter" key on her keyboard, and the beams of magical light reappeared.

"Wave your wing through them so I can see what happens."

The crow pressed its wing against the bars, but this time it didn't pass through. Thwarted this time, the bird spread its wings and tried to fly, only to be held back by the magic. It flopped down on the mirror and cawed angrily.

"It's working." Fran grinned. "How is it working?"

"Feedback loops," Smokey said.

"Huh?"

"You were missing a couple of feedback loops in the software."

She turned to the screen and scrolled through her code. Sure enough, a few lines hadn't been there before, which let the program assess and reassess the information it was receiving until it got the balance right on the power it was putting out.

"You did this?" she asked.

"Uh-huh." Smokey nodded and kept crunching through his biscuits.

"You did this in the few minutes while I was in the kitchen?"

"Uh-huh."

"That's… Wow, you're really good at this."

"Uh-huh. But can I get a job? No, because no one wants a cat at the keyboard."

Fran thought back to her previous coding problems and some solutions she didn't remember finding.

"Have you done this before, changing things in my programs?"

If Smokey had been in dwarf form, he would've blushed. Instead, he hid his face in the big pile of biscuits.

"A few times," he admitted. "If I see a problem in the code, I want to fix it. Perfectionist. That might be why I have trouble keeping jobs. Most people are looking for good enough, and I refuse to stop until I've done the absolute best."

Fran switched off the machine. The crow leaped out and flew back up onto the top of the wardrobe, where it perched, glaring down at them.

"Don't you go sulking," Fran said. "You didn't have to be in there." The crow cawed. "Yes, of course, I'm grateful. Thank you very much."

Now she knew that the containment could work in practice, but could it adjust as she wanted it to? She needed another test subject to see how the software and the magic responded. Her gaze fell on the cat.

"Smokey, you've been a huge help already, but I was wondering..."

Smokey looked from her to the cage. "Do I have to?"

"If it helps, you could think of it as working off your debt."

"I suppose." He brushed a few crumbs off his whiskers, then jumped up onto the bed and from there into the containment unit. He curled up on the mirror and looked out at her. "All right, let's do this."

Fran flipped the switch and set the software running. Magical lights danced across Smokey's fur and glowing beams appeared between the rods.

"Go on, try to get out." Fran leaned forward eagerly, watching to see what happened.

Smokey batted at one of the bars with his paw. It held steady. He hit it harder and got the same result. Then he stood, tensed his legs, and tried to leap. The bars bent like rubber bands, then flung him back down into the cage.

"Yep," he groaned. "That's working."

"Brilliant!" Fran looked again at the code he had written. "This is so clever, the way it deals with the information from the sensors. It's simple but effective, far easier to deal with than any of the solutions I'd come up with."

"Told you I was good at this."

Fran thought about the challenges she was facing. She enjoyed coding, just like she enjoyed building things, but she knew that she needed other people to help if she was going to make this business work. If those people could take her ideas and quickly and elegantly fix their problems, all the better.

"Would you like a job with my startup?" she asked. "There's no pay yet, but you'll get a place on the board and a profit share once our big contract pays out, and I can keep you in cat food while you're working."

"A job? A real job?"

"Depends on how you define 'real.' Like I said, no wages yet. But the company's real, we've got a big government contract, and I could really use your skills. What do you say?"

"Sounds good. I've only got one other condition."

"What's that?"

Magic crackled as Smokey ran his paw across the bars. "Let me out of this cage."

CHAPTER TWENTY-NINE

A couple of hours later, Fran sat cross-legged on the bed, pieces of her device scattered around her. She adjusted a line of crystals along the side of the mirror panel, trying to make them more like the ones on her portal mirror, which was lying on a pillow next to her.

At the desk, Smokey was typing away on the keyboard, coding incredibly fast for someone using a cat's paws instead of fingers. It had been a little difficult to make a setup where he could work, but by pushing the monitor back and raising the height of her swivel chair, Fran had made space for a cushion he could sit on while operating the keyboard.

"All set." Smokey stepped back from the computer. "You ready?"

"Almost." Fran fixed one last crystal in place, then set the mirror down on the bed. "Okay, let's do this."

Smokey hit a key and the crystals lit up around the sides of the mirror. Without the framework of rods and components around it, the magic glowed in a soft cloud over the mirror, a swirling and shapeless mass. Fran picked up a sensor from the pillow and stuck it into the cloud.

"Three-point-two," she said, reading the sensor. "Three-point-five. Three-six. Back down to three-two." She scratched her head. "That's enough to hold you in cat form, but not a full-size magical."

"So, like, a gnome or a Willen?"

"Not even that. We're not getting the power levels I hoped for."

Fran set the sensor down, and Smokey switched off the power.

"This is bad," Fran said. "We promised the FBI a containment unit for large magicals, and right now we have a cat trap."

From its place on top of the wardrobe, the crow cawed.

"Yes, or a bird trap."

The crow cawed again and pointed its beak at the bedroom door.

"What's up?" Fran asked.

The crow cawed again. It almost looked like the bird was rolling its eyes. Then the buzzer by the apartment door sounded, and the crow pointed again.

"Oh, you were trying to tell me that someone was coming!" Fran leaped up from the bed. "Sorry, I think I need some lessons in bird talk."

She rushed into the living room and pressed the intercom button.

"Is that the delivery guy?" she asked. "I could really use those circuit boards right now. Or the wires. Or even those fancy new crystals. Really, whichever delivery guy you are, this is perfect timing."

"Do I sound like a damn delivery guy?" a female voice replied.

"No, the delivery guy is always polite. You do sound familiar, though. Who is this?"

"Singar."

"Wait, Singar with the magic projector?"

"No, one of the dozens of other Singars you're always meeting around town."

"I don't think I have—"

"Yes, of course, it's that Singar. Now let me in. I have something I need to show you."

Fran pressed the button to unlock the building's front door.

"Come on up. We're on the third floor."

"I know. I'm fluent in apartment numbers."

Fran opened the door and peered out into the hallway. She liked to take the stairs when she could, for the extra exercise and the fun of trying to jump across the last three in a single bound. Singar wasn't as much of a stairs fan. The elevator *pinged* open a moment later, and she stepped out, carrying a large, flat object wrapped in trash bags and duct tape.

"Hi there." Fran smiled warmly. "It's great to see you. How did you find me here?"

"Got your address from the maker space people." Singar waddled past her into the apartment. "Where can we make a mess?"

"Through here." Fran showed her into the bedroom. "Singar, this is Smokey, definitely just an ordinary cat, and, um, crow the crow."

"Crow the crow?" Singar shook her head. "Real imaginative." She stared at Smokey. "There's nothing suspicious about pointing out that someone's an ordinary cat. What are you, a familiar, some sort of changeling?"

"Shifter," Smokey said grumpily. "But don't ask me to show you."

"Wasn't going to. Don't really care."

Singar pushed the pieces of Fran's prototype aside and set her package down on the bed. Frost was forming across the surface of its wrapping. She pulled a switchblade from her pocket and sliced through the duct tape, then tore the trash bags open, revealing a mirror with runes etched along its edges, electronics fixed underneath, and a hefty battery pack strapped to one side. A thin layer of ice covered the surface.

"Isn't this part of your projector?" Fran reached out to touch the ice.

"Don't." Singar slapped Fran's hand away. "I don't want to risk letting it out."

"It?"

Singar explained the attack by the icy spirit and how she'd trapped it in the mirror.

"So now I've got dung knows what trapped in the central component of my prototype, and I don't know how long this will hold. It's burning through batteries like nobody's business. I remembered that you were good with mirror magic and that you were working on some power source, so I figured you might have an idea."

"I've got an idea," Smokey said. "Take it to the Silver Griffins."

"Are you kidding?" Singar snorted. "I've accidentally found a way to trap a ghost in a mirror. That's new technology and new means money in the tech sector. Do you think the Griffins are going to care about protecting my ideas more than warning everybody about what I've caught?"

"I'm sure the Griffins would understand if you ask nicely," Fran said. "They're here to help, right?"

"Were you born in a bubble, or did someone replace all your common sense with cotton wool?"

"She means well." Smokey had dragged a cable over to the mirror with his teeth and plugged it into the electronics at the side. "She doesn't have a lot of street smarts."

"I am here, you know." Fran picked up her magical sensor off the pillow. "Let's see what's going on." She set the sensor against the mirror and stared in amazement at the reading. "Wow! Three hundred and nine! How is your magic holding this?"

"Amplification, remember?" Singar pointed at a layer of fuzzy air above the mirror's surface. "Magic and light rebounding multiple times, cranking up the power level. There's enough energy in that inch of air to contain an enchanted rhinoceros."

"Or an elephant?" Fran asked as casually as she could, despite the grin spreading on her face.

"Yeah, sure, an elephant."

"Or a really powerful wizard?"

"Yes, yes, a wizard. Right now I have an angry spirit that's threatening to escape and choke me to death with its icy grip, so maybe we could focus on that?"

"I've got some good news." Smokey looked around from the computer screen. "We can adapt the software we're using for our unit to manage your mirror. That'll let us run it more efficiently, which will save on battery life and means I can set up an alarm in case your spirit tries to escape."

"Great." Singar peered past Smokey at the computer screen. "Wait, why do you have software for this?"

"You know that company I asked you to join?" Fran asked. "We're trying to make a magical containment unit using mirrors and light. Smokey's writing the software and I'm working on the hardware."

"You?" Singar snorted. "So that's what this is for?" She peered at the mirror from Fran's containment unit, then tapped one of the runes with the tip of her knife. "You know there's a better rune for this part, right?"

"Really?" Fran grabbed a book of runes off the shelf. "Which one?"

Singar ignored her and flipped the mirror over.

"You call this mystic circuitry?" She tugged out the ends of half the wires, cut some of them off, and reconnected them in a different order, running some through a dial that she pulled from between the folds of her skin. Then she set the mirror back the right way up. "Try that."

Smokey switched on the control software, and the mirror flickered into life. Fran pressed her sensor against its magical glow.

"Ten-point-two," she read. "Eleven. Twelve-point-three. Hey, this is far better! Although it's nothing compared with what your mirror's doing."

"Problem with my mirror is that the magic's only an inch thick." Singar tapped the ice-cold glass. "Works for spirits and other insubstantial bodies, but nothing with a physical form. Maybe if we combined what we're working on…" She pressed a hand against her eyes and groaned. "I'm going to have to join your stupid company, aren't I?"

"Really?" Fran smiled. "That would be brilliant."

"What's the pay like?"

"There isn't any."

"Medical plan?"

"Not yet."

"Workspace?"

"This room."

"How are the finances?"

"Our one contract is covering basic expenses, like components. Everything else will come out of my savings for now."

"You have savings?"

Fran grimaced. "Not for much longer."

"Wriggling dung, this might be the worst job I've ever considered. Is there anything good about it at all?"

"A seat on the board and a profit share on our big contract with the FBI."

"You have a big contract with the FBI?" Singar stared at Fran, incredulous. "You?"

"I have to be honest up front. We're struggling with that contract. If we fail, we'll be in a lot of trouble."

"That might be the worst pitch I've ever heard." Singar shook her head and looked at Smokey. "Please tell me this idiot's not responsible for recruitment."

"Without my software, you can't contain your ghost," Smokey said. "Without that, you can't monetize your accidental invention."

"At last, someone with brains." Singar turned to Fran and held out her hand. "All right, I'm in."

CHAPTER THIRTY

Half a dozen Evermores crept through the woods outside Seattle, with Winslow leading the way. Dressed in jeans and sweaters, carrying nothing more deadly looking than a walking stick, the Evermores could've passed for ordinary hikers. Still, a walking stick could be a powerful weapon in the right hands.

"Are you sure this is the right place?" Enfield asked. "It seems a bit exposed."

The younger Evermore looked around with a mixture of curiosity and incredulity. He hadn't been out into the world much, and he didn't like what he saw. The trees here were smaller and weaker than he'd expected, the air didn't taste right, and occasional litter made for ugly points amid the woodland beauty.

"I haven't been sure of anything in twenty-six thousand years," Winslow replied. "That's how I avoid making foolish assumptions."

"Almost all our previous reports have said that the Source was moving through underground spaces."

"It was, and that's why it will end up here."

Winslow gestured at the other Evermores, who spread out through the surrounding trees. Night was falling, and as their movements slowed, they became almost invisible amid the gloom, more gray shapes in a world of tangled shadows. The Evermores understood light, and they understood how to avoid it, a necessity for staying secret through the centuries.

"This isn't the classroom," Enfield said. "Cryptic phrases aren't going to help me learn. They're just going to leave me confused and unable to fulfill my duty."

"You're right." Winslow gave a small nod. "Force of habit." He pointed through the trees to a clearing. "There is a kemana under there. It's one of the closest points between an underground kemana and a woodland in the whole of North America.

"From below, you can see the roots reaching down through the ground. The Source is used to being around trees. While they can be useful in binding it, they're also something familiar, potentially comforting. When it reaches that kemana, it will want to follow the trees, and so..."

"It comes up here, where we use the trees to bind it."

"Exactly."

The Evermores took their places around the outside of the clearing. A few minutes later, the ground beneath their feet started to shake.

Winslow looked at his watch. "A little early, but I would be surprised if that isn't our prey."

Fallen leaves bounced across the shaking ground in the center of the clearing, then flew aside as the ground burst open. Light shone from the hole, flickering and shifting, changing color and brightness. Discordant noises followed it.

The Source reached out with an arm that became a tentacle, then the grabber of a crane. It pulled itself out of the hole, its shape constantly shifting. One moment it was a bear-like monster, the next a gleaming chrome machine, then an abstract pattern of dots and swirls. Throughout it all, two things remained constant: the glow radiating from it and the strange, unsettling noises.

Winslow stepped into the clearing, one hand outstretched, the other wielding his walking stick like a sword. The other Evermores followed his lead, stepping out to surround the Source.

"Come back with us," Winslow said. "Back to the trees. Back to the roots."

"Back?" The word emerged from the cacophony around the creature. "Roots. Caged. Trapped."

"Safe, secure, cared for."

"Imprisoned." The Source became a cloud of faces, all baring their teeth. "No!"

It raised a hand and shot a stream of magical light straight at Winslow. He deflected the magic with his walking stick and sent it toward Enfield, who bounced it on to the next Evermore, who sent it to the next, and the next, the magical light running from stick to stick until it formed a blazing ring around the Source.

The Source stopped the flow of magic, but the circle of power around it remained.

"We didn't want to do this," Winslow said sadly. "Remember that."

The Evermores raised their hands. The circle of light rushed in, tightening around the source. It formed arms to fend off the attack, but the magic drew them in, pinning them to its sides. The Source howled in frustration.

"I am sorry." Winslow stepped closer and raised another hand. The sounds from the Source grew quieter as Winslow absorbed the noise, draining it away before it could draw attention. "This is necessary. The kemanas must be empowered, and that means we need you."

The Source's agonized howl emerged as little more than a whimper. Seeing it weakened like this, Winslow came even closer, ready to set the seal on the spell.

Even after twenty-six thousand years, he could still make mistakes.

The Source shrank, then suddenly expanded. The magical light binding it shattered. A strand of power whipped out and hurled Winslow from his feet. As he landed in the dirt and half-rotted leaves, he looked up to see a monster towering over him, a glowing beast with four arms and two heads.

The other Evermores charged. They flung blasts of light ahead of them, hoping to blind the Source, but it absorbed the power and spat it back out at them. One of the Evermores sank screaming to her knees, clutching her blinded eyes.

The Source opened one of its mouths, and a shrill, piercing noise emerged. The Evermores clapped their hands to their ears as the noise sent daggers of pain into their heads.

While they stood clutching their heads, the Source charged. It slammed into one of the Evermores, flinging him back against a tree. Another one charged the Source from behind, a walking stick raised and blazing with light. The Source turned its second head to see the attack. It caught the walking stick with a clawed hand, wrenched it from the Evermore's hand, and hit him in the chest. He fell, groaning.

Enfield advanced, hands raised. As the Source flung noise and light at him, he caught it between his hands, a growing ball of energy that shone and howled but stayed in his grasp. The ball grew as the Source flung more power at him: a blast of blinding light, a screech that could've pierced his eardrums, a low, throbbing wave of sound designed to throw the Evermore from his feet. Enfield caught it all in that single ball of energy.

"Let it go," Winslow shouted, struggling to make himself heard above the noise of the Source and its magic.

"I've got it," Enfield replied.

"Let it go before it becomes too much."

"I said I've got it!"

The Source advanced on Enfield, still howling and blazing with light, flinging everything it could at him. Another Evermore charged at it from the side, hoping to catch the creature while it was distracted, but the Source batted her away with a hand like the front of a snowplow.

"I've got it," Enfield said between gritted teeth.

The power between his hands throbbed and rippled. He pressed against it, knowing that if he could pull this off, if he could trap the Source's power and turn it against the creature, they could win. It was what the Evermores did.

It was too much. With a crash like thunder and a blast of light that seared the leaves from nearby trees, the power exploded from Enfield's grasp. It hurled him to the ground, hands burned and face stinging, as the world around him shook.

When he opened his eyes, the Source was standing over him.

"Crush you now," it said, raising a fist that became a tentacle, a boulder, an anvil ready to pulp him.

A high, clear note sounded through the clearing. The Source's body rippled, and it seemed to shrink a little. It lowered that anvil fist and turned to the source of the sound.

Winslow stood with his mouth wide and his hands raised in front of his face, fingers curled to shape the magic of his voice, turning it into something more than singing, into a weapon against another being powered by light and sound.

For a moment, the Source seemed shaken, stopped in its tracks by the power of the sound. Then a tentacle of light whipped out and struck Winslow in the throat. His singing turned into a gasping croak, and he clutched his bruised neck.

Enfield forced himself to his feet. Everything ached, but he had a duty: to the Evermores, to himself, to the whole world. With no one else left standing, he had to make his power count. He raised his hands and channeled light.

The Source turned to look at him. It had eight heads now, and it shook all of them. As Enfield formed his spell, it jumped back into the hole it had emerged from and disappeared into the ground.

Enfield let the magic go and staggered over to Winslow.

The older Evermore was on his knees, his breath a rasping wheeze.

"Here." Enfield took a potion from his pocket, pulled out the stopper, and handed it to Winslow, who gratefully gulped it down. The bruises around his neck started to fade.

"Thank you," he whispered.

"What now?" Enfield asked.

Around the clearing, other Evermores staggered to their feet. Everyone seemed to be alive, which was something, but it wasn't much of a victory.

"Now we continue," Winslow said. "We track its movements, predict where else it might appear, and get ourselves ready to tackle it again."

"That's it? More of the same, when it didn't work this time?"

"When you get to be as old as I am, you come to understand the value of persistence."

"What if that doesn't work? I don't want to spend my whole time being beaten on by that thing. Isn't there anything different we can do?"

"Perhaps, if all else fails, but we can't do it alone. For now, we persist. It is the Evermore way."

CHAPTER THIRTY-ONE

Gruffbar pulled up in front of Fran's apartment block and maneuvered his Harley into a gap between a steam car and a delivery van. It was perfect. Enough space for him to park and with enough other vehicles around it to give any potential saboteur cover as they approached. An opportunity for whoever was out to get him to give in to temptation and to fall into Gruffbar's trap.

He climbed down carefully, unstrapped his briefcase from the back of the bike, and checked the extra compartment he'd installed behind the seat. He didn't like to use magical augmentations on his bike since they felt like a violation of its pristine mechanical beauty, but setting a physical trap was fine. It was practically traditional for a dwarf vehicle.

Fran buzzed him into the building, and he hurried up the stairs to her apartment. Singar was already there, constructing an extendable metal frame on the coffee table while Bart did accounts and sent emails to potential investors from the kitchen counter. Frantic tapping sounds emerged from Fran's bedroom as Smokey worked on new code.

Fran herself sat on the bed, sketching outlines for different versions of the containment unit, though as he walked through, Gruffbar noticed that some other sketches were lying close to hand. However hard she tried, Fran couldn't concentrate on one thing the whole time.

"This leads down to that bit of garden, right?" Gruffbar pointed out the bedroom window at the fire escape.

"That's right," Fran said. "Do we need to have some sort of fire escape plan too, now that there are five of us? That wasn't on the list of documents you gave me."

"This isn't a company thing. I just need to get outside."

Gruffbar put his briefcase down and climbed out the window. His heavy boots *clanged* against the fire escape.

"You know we have a door, right?" Fran said. "If you're going to smoke, can you please close the window? I don't want that smell in here."

"Back soon."

"But you only just got here!"

Gruffbar hurried down the fire escape. The sounds of the city would be enough to cover the noise of his descent, and he didn't want to be only halfway down when the saboteur struck.

If the saboteur struck.

A crow glided past him and croaked as it went. Gruffbar ignored it. Those birds always seemed to be hanging around Fran, but he had no interest in them. Too much like nature. A magpie he might've gotten along with, given their taste for shiny objects such as mechanical components, but the crows were someone else's business.

The stairs ended with a ladder down to the green space next to the apartment block. Gruffbar jumped down the last few steps and hurried over to the corner of the building. He peered around. From here, he couldn't quite see the Harley, but he could see either end of the car in front and the van behind it. If anyone approached, he would see them.

He settled down behind a bush, peering through its tightly packed leaves at the parked vehicles, scrutinizing everyone who went past. He was looking for anything like a familiar face: a past client he'd failed, someone he'd beaten in court, a criminal who'd competed for the same work as him. In a long and inglorious career representing the disgusting and the disreputable, he'd crossed a lot of people. The question was, which one of them cared enough to hunt him down, and were they right to be mad at him?

All sorts of people went past. Humans, elves, dwarves, gnomes, Willens, people of all shapes and sizes, genders and ethnicities, wearing a wide variety of fashions. Some looked like he might've met them before, but were they people he knew or the sorts of faces that looked instantly familiar?

The crow fluttered down onto Gruffbar's shoulder.

"Shoo!" He waved it away. It fluttered down onto the pavement and stood glaring up at him. "I said go. You'll give me away."

Someone else drew his attention away from the crow. A tall, slender woman had stopped by the parked vehicles. She wore brand-name sneakers and fitted jeans, but a baggy hoodie hung off her figure and covered her face. She carried a weighty backpack. She glanced around, but all

Gruffbar saw inside the hood was a brief glimpse of aviator shades. Then she stepped into the gap between the car and the van, right where he'd parked his bike.

"Got you," he hissed.

Gruffbar stepped out from behind the bush. There was no need to creep. Plenty of other people were noisily walking up and down the street. Still, he approached the parked vehicles with caution.

There was a *crack* like a gunshot, a yelp, and a cloud of blue powder burst out around the bike. Gruffbar darted around the car.

The woman in the hoodie stood over his beautiful Harley with a saw in her hand. The package he'd set behind the seat had burst open, spraying her with blue powder designed to stain would-be thieves. A metal trap had sprung out with the powder and pinned its jaws around her arm, which she was trying to wrench free.

"Got you!"

Gruffbar grabbed the edge of her hoodie and tugged. The hood fell back, revealing the long blond hair and pointed elf ears of Elethin Tannerin.

"You!" Gruffbar growled. "Get the hell away from my bike."

"You!" Elethin snarled and wrenched her arm out of the trap. She flung the saw at him, and he ducked. It *clanged* against the door of the car behind.

Elethin launched herself at Gruffbar with her teeth bared and hands out like claws. She slammed into him, and the two of them tumbled across the sidewalk. People looked at them in confusion, then stepped around them, not sure what to make of the dwarf and the blue-painted elf rolling on the ground.

Elethin tried to pin Gruffbar to the sidewalk, using her height to give her an advantage. He was stronger and easily broke free of her hold. He pressed his feet against her midriff and rolled back, flipping her over him. She landed on the grass beside the apartment building.

Before she could catch her breath, Gruffbar strode over. He pulled his foot back to kick her in the ribs, but she grabbed his other foot and pulled it out from under him. The two of them rolled again, kicking, punching, and gouging, doing everything they could to hurt each other as they rolled into the bushes.

"You ruined me!" Elethin screeched as she scratched his cheek.

"You ruined yourself."

"Hypocrite."

"Criminal."

"Lawyer."

She pulled a shock baton from the pocket of her hoodie and jammed it into his side. An electric jolt ran through him, throwing him off her. Elethin got to her knees and looked down at him, grinning maliciously.

"Got you now, you little prick."

However, a stun baton calibrated for elves and humans didn't have the punch to take out a dwarf for long. As she brought it around for another hit, Gruffbar grabbed her arm, twisted, and pulled her face down onto his fist. The baton fell from her hand, and she slumped to the ground, groaning.

"I hate you," she whimpered. "I freaking hate you."

"I don't like you much right now either." Gruffbar got to his feet and finally got a good kick in, curling her up around her stomach. "You started this."

"You started this when you—"

"Oh, quit your whining! We were criminals. Paying the price if we got caught was one of the risks. You're not exempt from that because your crimes were big corporate ones."

"It wasn't supposed to go like that. We were going to be masters of the world, me and Finn and, and, and…"

She started sobbing, the sounds of a broken, wretched woman, so sad and pitiful that Gruffbar almost bent over to pat her on the shoulder. Then he remembered who he was dealing with.

"You can cut that crap out too," he said. "I'm not falling for the lies of a PR master."

The sobs continued a moment longer, then abruptly stopped. Elethin peeked out from between her fingers, evaluating him, trying to work out if her bluff really and truly had been called. She sighed and sat up, grim-faced but not crying.

"Fine," she said. "You win. Happy now?"

"Do I look happy?" Gruffbar brushed stray twigs out of his beard and gingerly touched a bruise on his hip. "I've almost been killed a dozen times in the past month. My bike's a mess again. I'm out here wasting time with you when I have work to do."

"My heart bleeds for you. I can't imagine what wasted time feels like. I mean, apart from my thirty-five freaking years in Trevilsom."

"You'll get over it. But if you take a shot at me again,

you won't get the chance. I might have reformed, but I still know how to wield a shotgun, how to get into an apartment unseen, and how to hide a body. If I ever see you again, it's going to end very badly for you. Understand?"

Elethin glared at him, and for a moment he thought she might be dumb enough to give it another go. Instead, she sagged, arms hanging by her sides.

"Fine," she said. "We're done."

"Glad to hear it, but I don't trust you for a minute, so you'd better believe that I'll be ready if you come at me again."

He strode out of the bushes, grabbed the bottom of the fire escape, and started climbing up the metal steps. Halfway to Fran's apartment, he remembered her rule against smoking, so he stopped on the second floor and lit up a celebratory cigar. Leaning against the metal rail, he watched Elethin limp away, her face blue and her bottom lip swollen. Gruffbar smiled. That had felt far more satisfying than it should. He almost missed the old days.

A crow landed on the railing next to him.

"Fine," Gruffbar said. "This time you can stick around. Seems like you're a lucky omen."

CHAPTER THIRTY-TWO

With his cigar finished, Gruffbar brushed off the remaining sticks and leaves from his tumble in the bushes, then climbed back in through the apartment window.

"All done," he said. "Where can I work?"

"Why do you have blue in your beard?" Fran asked.

Gruffbar brushed his fingers through his beard. "Gone yet?"

"No."

"Then I'll live with it." He looked around. There wasn't space in the bedroom. "I'll find somewhere to work through there."

He picked up his briefcase and headed into the living room. With the kitchen counter full of Bart's papers and the coffee table covered in Singar's construction work, there wasn't a spare surface for him, so he sat on the sofa, put his feet up, and opened his laptop on his knees.

"How are the finances looking?" he asked Bart while he waited for the computer to power up.

"We don't have any money," Bart said, "but we have

almost everything we need for the sample containment unit, so that's progress."

"This is how startups are supposed to be, right? No money for bills, big red marks against our accounts, just hoping we can pay for a sandwich sometime next year."

"Until we get some investors, yes."

"How's that going?"

"I'm working on it."

Gruffbar turned his attention to the coffee table. The new containment unit used extending poles so it could grow and shrink. It looked impressive, all the more so thanks to the control unit that Singar was fixing onto the side.

"How's the prototype?" Gruffbar asked.

"It would be going a lot better if I could get some quiet time to concentrate," Singar said. "But someone keeps making calls."

"I can't help it," Bart said. "Persuading people to give us money needs a personal touch."

"I get it. I get it. Still..." Singar waved. "This is not a great space to work in."

The apartment door opened, and Josie walked in. She stopped and looked around.

"Have you got your boots on my sofa?" she asked.

"Sorry." Gruffbar hastily swung his legs around.

"Are those soldering marks on the coffee table?"

Singar picked up the device and looked at the tabletop. "Ah, yeah, sorry about that. I'll put a protective mat down next time."

Josie walked stiffly through the apartment to the kitchen. Along the way, her foot got tangled in a heap of cables, and she had to shake it free. She reached for the coffee pot, but when she picked it up, a pile of papers slid from in front of it, falling across her feet. She put the coffee pot down.

"Fran," she called as she strode across the room. "Apartment meeting on the fire escape."

Fran looked up from the designs she was working on. Josie was usually fairly relaxed, but now she sounded super tense. Had she had a bad day at work? Climbing over a pile of components, Fran clambered out onto the fire escape and shut the window behind her.

Josie was already out there, arms folded.

"Are you all right?" Fran asked. "Tough day at the office?"

"This is not about my work," Josie said. "It's about yours."

"Mine?"

"Yes." Josie pointed through the window. "That. Our apartment is a dump. There's nowhere to sit. Stacks of paperwork are blocking the way to the coffee. I can't even cross the room without tripping over pieces of your devices."

"I guess we could tidy up a bit…"

"Tidy up a bit? There are five of you working here, in an apartment that's barely big enough for the two of us to watch TV."

"I'm sorry. It's only temporary until we can afford somewhere proper to work."

"No, I'm sorry, this has to stop. You're my friend, Fran, and I love you dearly, but I need to be able to relax in my own home."

"You said we could work here."

"Yes, when it was you and a house cat, with a quiet little gnome popping 'round one morning a week. What you've got now is a whole other level."

"Oh. I'm sorry." Fran stared at her shoes, crestfallen. She hadn't realized that she was upsetting Josie, and now the thought was upsetting her.

"Don't get me wrong." Josie laid a hand on her friend's shoulder. "I'm immensely proud of you and everything you're doing. I just need you to do it somewhere else."

Fran sighed. "I guess."

"Could you maybe try working in the maker space?"

"It's shut for refurbishments."

"Oh." Josie bit her lip. "How long for?"

"At least a month."

"Sorry, sweetie, but I can't put up with another month of this."

"That's okay. We'll work something out." A thought made Fran's expression suddenly brighten. "Maybe we could work at the Blazing Bean."

"Maybe." Josie looked dubious. "But there's a big difference between doing some coding or having a meeting there and taking all this stuff you guys are doing now."

"Cam will help us if he can." Fran hugged Josie. "Thanks for your help. And thanks for letting us get started here. We'll get out of your way now."

She opened the window and climbed back into the apartment, bracing herself to tell the others the bad news. To her surprise, they were already packing up, Bart cramming papers into his briefcase while Singar carefully put each of her tools into its place in her toolbox.

"We have to..." Fran began.

"We guessed," Gruffbar said.

"And we understand," Bart added. "So what's the plan now?"

"We'll try the coffee shop."

"Seriously?" Singar asked, looking pointedly at the device she had been assembling.

"I've seen skateboarders changing their wheels in there. Are we that different?"

"Yes, but let's give it a go." Singar pointed to the mirror she'd trapped the spirit in, and which leaned against the wall, still covered in ice, its magitech components plugged into the mains. "What about that?"

"Better leave it here for now. Hopefully, we'll have a workspace before we have to do anything with it."

Working in the coffee shop was one thing, unleashing a dark spirit there quite another. Fran knew she didn't have other people's limits, but she had to draw a line somewhere.

With all their equipment gathered, they headed down the street, Fran and Singar leading the way. As they walked, a crow circled overhead as if keeping watch over them.

"You know, it's a funny thing," Fran said. "I got attacked by a weird spirit thing too, in my bathroom."

"Huh." Singar stroked her whiskers thoughtfully. "Maybe he was coming to get his friend out?"

"Oh no, this was before he attacked you. He came through the bathroom mirror."

"There was another spirit attack."

"Yes."

"Involving a mirror."

"Yes."

"And you didn't think it was worth mentioning?"

Fran shrugged. "I didn't think about it."

"Even though they're clearly related."

"They are?"

"Yes. Obviously. Two spirit attacks, close together in place and time, both involving mirrors. That's not random chance."

"Oh." Fran thought about it for a moment. "I suppose you could be right."

Singar groaned. "For someone so smart in many ways, you're incredibly dumb in others."

Fran thought about the mess they'd made in the apartment.

"I think you might be right. Can you tell me when I'm being dumb, so I can fix it?"

"It'll be my pleasure."

"What do we do about these spirits?"

Singar shrugged. "Catch them if they turn up again, I guess. Not really our problem though, are they?"

The staff of Mana Wave Industries reached the Blazing Bean and trooped inside, leaving the crow to search for scraps in a nearby bin. Cam smiled at Fran as she approached the counter.

"Hi there," he said. "Looks like you brought your whole crew today."

"Um, yeah, about that…" Fran looked around. The place was pretty busy, but they could probably find a couple of tables somewhere. "We were wondering if we could maybe work here for a bit? We'll be super quiet, and we'll buy plenty of coffee and cake of course, but we don't really have anywhere else to go, and, um..."

She looked at Cam uncertainly. Now that she was here, with bags full of laptops, paperwork, and components, as well as everyone working for her company, it seemed like a pretty big ask.

"No problem." Cam smiled and looked around. "Wait here a second. I'll push some tables together out of the way near the back of the room so the other customers won't disturb you. Maybe you can all decide on what you want to order while I do that?"

"Brilliant! Thank you." Fran gave the rest of the team a big thumbs-up. "Cam's finding us a place to work. Does this mean that we can put coffee and cake on our expenses?"

"The coffee, maybe," Bart said. "Though it doesn't really matter until we've got some money to pay expenses with."

Smokey, still in cat form, jumped up onto the counter and peered at the cakes.

"Didn't you want to come here as a dwarf?" Fran asked. "Then you could have coffee and cake and maybe help carry our stuff."

"Are you trying to force me to conform to your rigid bipedal norms?" Smokey asked sharply.

"No, no, no! I thought that you know..."

"I thought being a cat sounded like an excuse to avoid work," Singar said. "So the rest of us can do the heavy lifting."

"It is not an excuse," Smokey said. "If I could've carried things, I would've, as long as I don't have to join you in the biped realm to do it."

"Duly noted."

Something in Singar's voice made Fran think this conversation wasn't over, but for now, the Willen turned her attention to the drinks menu.

"I'll have a black coffee," she said. "And one of those oat cookies."

"Table's ready," Cam said, reappearing behind the till. "It's not much, but it's better than making you work out in the street." He leaned across the counter and scratched Smokey between the ears. "What a cute kitty. Do you think he'd like a saucer of lactose-free milk?"

Smokey meowed.

"I think that's a yes," Fran said. "Thanks, Cam. Come on, gang, let's make ourselves at home."

CHAPTER THIRTY-THREE

The coffee cups were piling up at one end of the table, a precarious tower of white crockery and brown dregs, accompanied by a pile of plates covered in cake crumbs and flakes of pastry. Occasionally, one of the Mana Wave Industries team would shake the table, either hammering the keys of their computer too hard or while slamming together pieces of hardware, and the cups would wobble precariously, porcelain skyscrapers threatening to crash down onto the floor. No one on the team thought of clearing them away. They were too preoccupied with their work.

"Maybe I should take some of these," Cam said, approaching the table with a large tray. "Then I'll have some cups to spare for the other customers."

"Huh?" Fran looked up from the tablet on which she had been sketching designs for a battery compartment. "Oh, hi Cam! Do you need us to get out?"

Cam laughed. "Not at all. You keep ordering coffees, and you're all good. But I need some of these back."

Fran scrambled out of her chair and helped him pile the cups on the tray. She didn't want to annoy the person providing them with workspace, and it was nice to spend a few minutes with Cam, maybe even better than spending time working on her invention.

"What's all this for, anyway?" He nodded at the heap of pieces on the table. "Trying to find out who's the fairest of them all? Or technology for beauticians, maybe?"

"Why beauticians?"

"All the mirrors."

Several reflective surfaces were on the table, including the one from Fran's experimental device, her portal mirror, and a couple of cheap hand mirrors that Singar was using to test connections.

"Oh, so, like, for people to check their makeup?"

"It's my best guess so far, and I've been guessing for hours." He smiled. "So go on, spill the beans. What are you all making?"

Fran glanced at Gruffbar, who shook his head.

"Sorry," she said, "but I can't tell you. There's a confidentiality clause in our contract with the feds." Her eyes went wide. "Wait, I probably shouldn't have said who the contract's with. That's totally not confidential of me!"

"Don't worry." Cam patted her on the shoulder. "Your secret's safe with me, at least the little part of it that I know. I probably don't want to know about mirrors at the moment anyway. They seem to have become dangerous."

"Really?" Fran raised an eyebrow. "Why's that?"

"Haven't you heard? There have been all sorts of weird things happening around mirrors in Mana Valley. Thefts, assaults, attacks by magical creatures. A lot of them seem to be targeting unusual, expensive, or enchanted mirrors, but there have been other ones too. Bathroom mirrors going missing, mirror shops getting trashed, that sort of thing."

He shook his head. "This town, it never stops surprising me."

"Does everyone know about this?" Fran realized to her shame that she hadn't checked the news in weeks, too busy with her business to care about the rest of the world.

"No, but more people are starting to talk about it. I pay attention to weird events, so I spotted the pattern sooner than most, but you can bet the Silver Griffins are on it by now. Although whether they can catch the culprits…" He shrugged. "Well, if we run out of mirrors first, it's going to make shaving difficult."

He picked up the tray full of crockery and headed back to the counter.

"Hey Sin!" Fran slid back into her seat and leaned conspiratorially across the table. "Did you hear that?"

Singar didn't respond.

"Sin!" Fran tapped the Willen on the paw.

Sin looked up with a frown, then took a tiny pair of headphones out of her ears. "What?"

"It's not only you and me. Lots of people have had problems with mirrors. Thefts and supernatural attacks."

"Huh." Singar leaned back in her seat, toying with one of her whiskers. "Maybe we can do something with this."

"Like what?"

"I don't know…"

"Turn it into a trap," Gruffbar said from down the table.

The others looked up from their work, curious about what was going on.

"How does that help?" Fran asked.

"If magicals are going after mirrors, and we can lure them in, that gives us test subjects," Gruffbar said. "It can help prove to our clients that the technology works."

"Sounds risky," Bart said. "Inviting something to attack us and our project."

"We're working with mirrors. Apparently, that's already inviting trouble, so why not lean into it? I'm a lawyer, not a general, but isn't it better to lay an ambush than to be on the receiving end of one?"

"We'll need something to bait the trap," Smokey said. "Like the cheese that catches mice."

"A special mirror then. Anyone know where we can get one of those?"

"Ooh ooh ooh!" Fran bounced in her seat with excitement. "I do." She looked at Bart with her most winning smile. "Do you think your friends Raulo and Gail might help us?"

"Are you sure this is all right?" Bart asked as he, Fran, and Singar followed Gail down the steps to the basement below the Worn Threads carpet shop.

"Of course it's all right." Gail pushed her long blue hair back behind her ears. "We're always happy to help."

"It might bring some danger..."

"We run a carpet shop. We could do with a little more excitement in our lives."

The basement was every bit as vast and dusty as Fran remembered, with cobwebs obscuring the corners of the ceiling and ancient, chunky machinery piled up against the back wall. The machinery wasn't what interested her today.

"Here." She pulled the dust sheet off the vast mirror along one wall. "That's pretty special, right?"

Singar rubbed her hands together. "Oh, yes."

The Willen set her toolkit down on the floor, opened the lid, and started carefully selecting her measuring instruments.

"That mirror's older than I am," Gail said. "I've always loved having it here, but it's not really doing anything, so it'll be nice to have someone make it useful. What are you going to do with it?"

Fran hesitated, partly because of the confidentiality clause in the contract, but mostly because she wasn't sure yet. They might use the mirror to build another prototype for their device, though that would be tricky. The size would mean hugely scaling up their hardware and potentially rewriting the control software, and they couldn't exactly take this mirror to show the FBI. What they gained in power might not make up for all the disadvantages.

On the other hand, they could simply use this mirror as bait, with their mirror trap set up nearby. A lot depended on what Singar made of the mirror.

"I can't really talk about what we're making." Fran smiled at Gail. "But I promise, once I can, you'll be one of the first people I tell." She went to stand next to Singar, who'd pressed a device against the mirror and was reading its display with a thoughtful expression.

"What do you think?" Fran asked.

"It's in remarkably good condition for its age," Singar said. "Magical conductivity per square inch is good, though obviously, the size is going to cause us some issues."

"Obviously." Fran blushed, realizing how many of these technical considerations she wouldn't have thought about. It was great to have a team who understood parts of the business better than she did. "Can we turn it into a you-know-what?"

Singar took out a tape measure and handed one end to Fran. "Go down the end. I need to get some measurements."

"But can we?"

"Maybe." Singar walked the length of the mirror, spooling out the tape measure as she went. "I want to run some tests, try attaching bits of what we've built. It's the perfect bait for our trap, but it might not be the right component to make the containment unit work. We're probably better off setting up the prototype down here and waiting to see what happens."

"So the prototype's ready for testing?" Fran clapped. "That's so cool!"

Gail clapped too. "Yay for whatever it is!"

Singar rolled her eyes. "Don't get overexcited yet. It's still a prototype, and we're still a long way from ready to show it to our clients."

"But the FBI are waiting. We've only got—"

"Fran," Bart said, "remember about the confidentiality?"

Fran clapped a hand over her mouth.

"Oh my goodness!" she mumbled through her fingers. "I am just, like, the worst at this."

"Then we won't put you in charge of data security." Bart looked at Gail. "Could you perhaps pretend you didn't hear that?"

Gail ran a finger across her mouth as if closing an imaginary zipper. "Don't worry. My lips are sealed. If you want to set something up down here, that's fine. I can give Bart a spare key."

Singar rolled the measuring tape back up and returned her instruments to their places in her toolkit. The lid snapped shut.

"That's everything I need for now," she said. "Next step is to assemble the parts of the prototype down here and check that it'll run around another mirror. There's a slim chance of magical interference." She frowned and brushed the dust from her shirt. "I'll get as much prepped in advance as I can. The less time I spend in this dirt pit, the better." She glanced at Gail. "No offense."

"None taken." Gail smiled. "This place does need cleaning. Now come on upstairs, and I'll make us all a coffee before you go."

CHAPTER THIRTY-FOUR

"How's it going?" Cam asked as he walked past the Mana Wave Industries table. "Cracked your super-secret project yet?"

"If you mean the project of tasting every muffin you serve, we're almost there." Fran wiped the last few crumbs from her plate. "If you mean the tech thing, we're still working on it."

"Good for you. Chase that Mana Valley dream."

Cam took the empty plate and headed back to the counter.

Distracted from her work, Fran peered over Smokey's shoulder to see how he was doing. The shifter was still in cat form but not typing as rapidly as before. Instead, he seemed to be scrolling through a message thread. At the top was an advert for his activist group.

"Hey, your ad's getting some attention this time," Fran said. "Well done."

Smokey swiftly switched tabs, a stream of code hiding

what he'd been looking at. "Don't know what you're talking about."

"It's okay. We don't have office hours. You can advertise your activist group too."

"I said I don't know what you're talking about." Smokey flicked his eyes toward the rest of the team, then back to Fran.

"Oh!" She lowered her voice. "You don't want me to talk about…"

"Exactly." He looked at the time, then closed the laptop he'd been working on. "I should get going. I've got a thing."

"And by a thing you mean…"

"Yes." He jumped down off his chair and headed for the door.

"Will you be back today?"

"Maybe. Or maybe I'll be too busy changing the world."

He prowled out of the door and away, one more cat roaming the city streets.

"What was that about?" Bart looked up from his emails.

"Who cares?" Singar said. "And whose turn is it to get the coffees?"

Smokey walked into the lobby of the burrow building where he ran his meetings. The place wasn't ideal since the low ceilings might put off some larger magicals. Still, the owners committed to giving some of their space to community causes, which meant he could have the room for free, and that was the most important consideration when he was funding the whole thing alone.

To his surprise, there were people in the room already when he arrived. It was the first time that had happened, and for the first second, he instinctively assumed that they were in the wrong place or that the owners had double-booked the room. Then he remembered the responses to his online advert. At last, he'd gotten through to people who cared, people who would be as passionate about a world biased toward bipeds as he was.

He smiled and strolled to the front of the room, his tail swishing from side to side. This was going to be a great day.

Apart from him, there were three people in the room. One was a large winged lizard that sprawled across three chairs, its tail curled in underneath. It sat in splendid isolation, apparently indifferent to the world around it. The other two sat together, talking to each other in whispers.

One of them was a human-looking guy in his late teens, wearing an anime t-shirt and a pair of baggy jeans. The other was a troll with bright blue hair, currently at his default small size. Smokey wasn't sure why the troll was at a non-biped support group, but he assumed the teenager was a shifter.

Smokey jumped up onto a stool, giving himself as much height as possible to address the rest of the room. "Good evening. Welcome to Paws and Claws. It's great to see so many of you here today."

"It's great to be here." The teenager grinned. "Sooooo many people. We're so psyched up for this cause. Right, Tabber?"

The troll made a bunch of noises that Smokey couldn't understand but that sounded enthusiastic.

"That's good to hear," Smokey said. "Because I know how hard it can be to deal with this world alone, but together, we can be much stronger."

"Totally." The teenager grinned. The noises from the troll next to him almost sounded like laughter, but Smokey assumed that only showed his ignorance of trolls.

"My name's Smokey, and I founded this group. I'm sick of living in a world where people design everything for those with two legs and two arms, and they ask us to adjust to that instead of the world adjusting for us. Being bipedal isn't a default. Magicals are far more varied than that, and people shouldn't get away with disadvantaging us by acting like we don't exist.

"The moment that made me aware of this was trying to get into a building where I worked. The door was supposed to be motion sensitive, but it only responded to people standing tall on two legs. I was stuck outside my office because the people who made that thing had assumed we were all one shape.

"Now, why don't we go around the room? You can tell me your names and what made you aware that the world was biased against you?"

He turned to look at the lizard.

"My name is Vaudrek," it said in a voice that was probably feminine. "I saw your advert and was curious. I am not convinced that the world is against us, but I am prepared to learn."

"An open mind is a good start," Smokey said. "How about you guys?"

The troll made a bunch of noises, some of which sounded like farting.

"This is Tabber." The teenager struggled not to giggle. "He's, uh, he's here to support me."

"It sounded like he said more than that," Smokey said.

"Oh, yeah, sure, but that's trolls for you. I'm, um, Timmy Thomson, and I, um, I turn into a rhinoceros."

"A rhino shifter? That's unusual."

"Oh yeah. Real rare. There's hardly any of us around, which is why you might not have heard of it. And it's really hard to find seats made for you or to get through doorways."

"I hear you, comrade." Smokey raised a paw in salute. "Society is biased against us, and we have to change that."

"Oh yeah. Like, when I put my head down and charge at things, people get real mad, but a rhino's got to rhino, right?"

"I guess..." Suspicion was starting to creep through Smokey.

"And there's never any..." Timmy struggled to get the words out past his laughter. "...never any rhino food in the school canteen, and... and... and..."

"You're not really a shifter, are you?" Smokey glared at the teenager and the troll, who were high-fiving each other as they laughed. "You're here to make a joke out of this group."

"We don't need to make a joke out of it. It already is one." Timmy stood, and the troll jumped onto his shoulder. "Thanks for the laughs, buddy."

He walked out of the room, still laughing.

"You weren't even funny!" Smokey shouted after them.

He sank into his seat and drew his tail in, curling up around himself. He had felt so optimistic, coming in to see real people at his meeting, but it had all been a lie. Apparently, he was a joke, and so was everything he stood for.

"What do we discuss next?" Vaudrek's scales shifted as she raised an eyebrow.

"Nothing!" Smokey snapped. "We don't discuss anything because this meeting is over."

"A shame." Vaudrek stretched her wings. "That idiot child has demonstrated to me that you might be right."

She got up onto all fours and walked out, leaving Smokey alone with his disappointment.

"Half an hour until closing," Cam said as he walked past the table where the Mana Wave team was working.

Fran looked up in surprise. Sure enough, it was dark outside the coffee shop, and most of the other customers had left. Aside from her company, there was only a group of skaters sitting at window seats and a tired-looking wizard trying to cast enchantments on his coffee. A Silver Griffin walked in, one of Cam's colleagues handed her a takeout order, and she was gone again.

"I guess we should pack up." Fran yawned. Now that she thought about it, she was pretty tired. The amount of coffee she'd been drinking should've countered that. Instead, she'd reached the point where her legs kept jiggling, but her thoughts had slowed to a slug's pace—tired and wired, the worst possible combination for either work or a good night's sleep.

Never mind. The team had done an excellent day's

work. They'd developed a new plan for testing their prototype. Everything was finally coming together.

A small, dark shape stalked into the coffee shop and over to the table. Smokey jumped up onto his seat and turned his laptop back on.

"Just in time," Fran said. "You can help us pack up."

"Hmph." Smokey snorted and glared at his screen, on which his advert and the responses were showing again.

"How did it go?" Fran leaned in close to whisper to him. At least, she thought she was whispering. It was a little hard to tell at this level of caffeine.

"Not talking about it," Smokey said.

"Oh, sure, sorry, of course, secrets." She pressed a finger to her lips.

"No, I don't want to talk about it because it was a disaster, and now I'm a laughingstock. All this..." He waved a paw at the messages on the screen while his voice rose in volume. "Lies. Jokes. People trolling, and I didn't even realize."

He slammed the laptop shut and sat scowling at it.

Down the table, the rest of Mana Wave Industries carefully didn't look at the furious cat.

Fran wasn't great at comforting people at the best of times. She was doubly lost dealing with the strange issues of the shifter cat.

"Um, there, there." She patted him uncertainly on the head. "Better luck next time, maybe?"

Smokey only snorted.

CHAPTER THIRTY-FIVE

By the time the early rush finished at the Blazing Bean the next morning, the staff members of Mana Wave Industries were already well installed at the same tables they'd occupied the previous day. At one, Bart and Gruffbar talked about the business plan and called potential investors. At another, Singar and Smokey faced each other across a pile of components, testing parts for the prototype. At the last table, Fran sat with her head resting on her arms, fast asleep.

"She was awake until at least four in the morning," Singar said. "She sent me a message then about the shape of the device. It barely used whole words."

"You think we should order decaf for her in the future?" Cam extracted an empty cup from between Fran's limp fingers.

"Maybe after midday. She's going to need some caffeine once she's finished her nap."

"I'll keep an eye out and bring her something interesting once there are signs of life."

Cam headed back to the counter, leaving the team to their work.

Singar clipped a board dotted with microchips and magical crystals onto the side of a mirror. These temporary fixings weren't an ideal way to build a device, but they were proving useful now when things were constantly changing as they refined designs and ironed out problems. A properly constructed, permanent fixture could come later.

"How's the code looking?" she asked.

"Ugly." Smokey glared at his screen. "Good enough for testing, but this is going to need work before it goes into the wild."

"Sounds like every part of this project."

With the tip of his paw, Smokey pushed a lead into a jack on his laptop, then flicked the other end across the table. Singar plugged it into a socket on the board, then clipped the whole thing onto the framework that filled the table between them. It was a cube a foot across, made of extendable poles they could expand once they got into the basement at Worn Threads. In the bottom sat a mirror, with runes etched along its edges and a glow of magic around the rim.

"Time for the moment of truth." Singar looked around. "Where's one of those pesky crows when you need them?"

A dark shape croaked at her from the back of a nearby chair.

"Make yourself useful," Singar said. "Hop in here." The crow shook its head. "Not even for her?"

Singar pointed at Fran, but the crow just fluttered its wings and clung tight to the chair.

"All right then, one choice left." Singar reached over, took the hand of the sleeping Fran, and laid it on the mirror. "Fire it up."

"Is that a good idea?" Smokey asked.

"'Course it is. Let's do this."

Smokey tapped a key and the device hummed into life. There was a brief crackling noise, and Fran's palm pressed flatter against the mirror.

"Wuzzat?" Fran mumbled, rubbing her eye with her free hand. Blinking, she looked over at the device. "What's happening?"

"Just a test," Singar said. "You can go back to sleep."

"My hand feels like it's stuck in treacle. Oh, hey!" Fran smiled. "It's working."

She stood and, one hand still stuck in the trap, stepped around the table to come closer to it. As she approached, the magic tugged at her arm, pulling her in up to the elbow.

"Now it's my whole arm," she said. "All tingly and syrupy. That's good, right?"

"It sure is." Singar looked more closely at the runes on the mirror. "Just be careful. We don't want to—"

"It's got my other hand now." Fran had placed her free hand against the device as she examined it, but now it was sucked inside, both hands pressed against the mirror. "Should it be doing this?"

"In principle, yes, but I hadn't meant to test it this far yet. Stand still, and everything will be fine."

Points of magic sparkled across Fran's hands.

"Oh, look!" She leaned closer for a better look. There was a snapping sound as the device extended itself, frame expanding to enclose Fran's head and shoulders. "Um, guys..."

With a sound like the sucking of a gigantic drain, the magic hauled Fran inside the frame, on top of the coffee shop table. The frame expanded easily to contain her, but the table couldn't handle this treatment. It toppled over, and the trapped Fran crashed to the floor with Smokey's laptop and a scattering of loose components around her.

The coffee shop's occupants all looked around.

"Nothing to worry about," Gruffbar said as he and Bart rushed to block the view. "She just tripped over."

"Guys, I'm trapped," Fran whimpered. "I can't move my arms and legs, and it's really tight in here. I think it's getting smaller. Ow ow ow!"

"Better switch it off." Singar crouched beside Fran.

"Screen's broken." Smokey looked at the laptop that controlled the trap. "The code's on our cloud, though. Someone pass me another device."

"Seriously, this is not nice," Fran said. "Does our contract say it has to be nice?"

"Definitely not." Singar slid a tablet to Smokey. "It's for imprisoning bad magicals, remember? We're not in the business of making criminals comfortable."

"Oh yeah! Then great work, team, we've done it! Now can someone get me out?"

"Working on it." Smokey tugged the cables out of the laptop with his teeth and plugged them into the tablet. There was a frantic tapping of paws against the screen, a flicker of magic, and Fran flopped out of the containment unit.

"That was intense." She shook her head. "I think I need a coffee to recover."

"Here." Cam appeared at her shoulder, holding a cappuccino flavored with nut and cinnamon syrups and three sugars. "That should liven you up."

"You're a star. You know that?"

"Does this mean it works?" Cam peered at the deactivated device.

"Sort of." Singar was already starting to dismantle the prototype so she could make improvements. "It's not operating in a layer an inch deep anymore, but we need to get better control over it."

"Better stop talking there," Gruffbar said as he set the table upright. "Don't want to give away anything we shouldn't. I think it's time for another round of coffees while we contemplate our next steps..."

While Cam went to fetch their order, the team huddled around one of the tables.

"That is it, right?" Fran said. "We've got something we can show to the feds."

"Give us a couple more days on the controls," Singar said. "For now, it's good enough to try laying a trap in your friends' weird basement. Or it will be once I've straightened the control boards."

"You guys are the best." Fran hugged Singar, who stiffened at the gesture, and patted Smokey on the head. "Bart, you give Gail a call. I'll ask Cam if we can have takeout. Gruffbar, please pick up the pieces we dropped. I don't want to leave a vital component behind."

Left alone, Smokey and Singar leaned across the table

toward each other. Smokey held out a paw, and Singar gave him a high-five.

"We did it," Smokey said.

"We did. That's not the only thing I've been working on." Singar took a bag from under her seat and slid it over to the cat. "For you."

Smokey opened the bag. Inside was something made out of straps and pouches, with plastic buckles holding it together.

"It's a harness," Singar said. "You should be able to get in and out of it whenever you want and to fasten it with your paws. You can use it to carry things around when you're in cat form."

"That's..." Smokey looked at it uncertainly.

"You've said it yourself. This world's design is for a certain sort of person. This will help you to do what you want in their world. Pick up your shopping. Take your phone with you when you go hunting mice. Even help us carry our kit from Fran's place to here to wherever else we work."

"This is to make me carry my weight?"

"This world hasn't been kind to me either, or to a lot of people like me. We all need a hand sometimes. Don't be a dick about it."

"Sorry."

Smokey wriggled into the harness and clipped it shut. It fit snugly against his sides, with an assortment of pouches that he could carry tools in.

"There's a trailer that hooks on the back," Singar said. "For carrying bulky materials and shopping."

"Thanks. This is great. I mean, it doesn't address any of

the underlying systemic problems facing those of us who aren't bipeds, but it will at least help me live my life."

"You're not the biggest idiot around here. I figured you deserve it. Besides, I wanted a change from messing with mirrors."

Fran returned, carrying two cardboard holders full of coffee cups and muffins.

"I've got supplies," she said. "Now we need to… Ooh, neat! Now you can carry some parts, Smokey."

"See? I'm still a servant of the man."

But Smokey didn't take off the harness, and his tail happily swished from side to side.

The cat picked up tools and slid them into his pouches while the rest of the team bagged their components, paperwork, laptops, and everything else they needed to take with them.

"Are you deserting us?" Cam asked as they headed for the door.

"For a few hours," Fran said. "We need to do a thing I can't tell you about in a place we can't reveal."

"Intriguing." He handed her a napkin. "Here, that's my number. Text me when you're nearly ready to come back. I'll clear a group of tables for you again."

"Thanks, Cam. You're the best."

With a big grin on her face and her team following her, Fran headed off to set up her test run.

CHAPTER THIRTY-SIX

Josie sat at her desk, a sandwich in one hand and her e-reader in the other. Dostoevsky wasn't exactly light lunchtime reading, but *Crime and Punishment* made a change of mental gears from working on technology. She was happy to lose herself in nineteenth-century Russia for half an hour, even if that was a pretty bleak place.

"Bullworth," Simon Green called as he walked down the office, carrying a large cardboard box. "We have a new device to test."

Josie put the e-reader down and hastily gobbled up the last of her sandwich. Ten minutes wasn't much of a lunch break, but like the other tech places she'd worked at, Philgard wasn't the sort of company where people respected the value of time off. If she wanted to create a good impression, she had to be ready to work at the drop of a hat and willing to put in extra hours whether they were asked for or not.

She followed Simon into the test lab, where he put the box down on a workbench and opened the lid. Inside, amid a large mass of loose packing chips, was a much smaller item. It was roughly the shape and size of a grapefruit, but black rather than yellow, and with markings around its diameter.

"Get the test artifacts out of the cupboard," he said.

Josie did as instructed, retrieving a dozen assorted magical items from a cupboard at the back of the room. They were an eclectic mix, from a broken wand to a bucket that generated water to an old ceremonial dagger. Most of them were relatively low power, and none of them were hugely valuable. No two had the same or even similar powers. The one thing uniting them was that they were enchanted.

"So what is it?" Josie spread the items around the table. Their whole purpose in the lab was to test other products close to them, check for magical interference, unexpected interactions, or other side effects that didn't show up when they operated a device in the isolation of the production lab.

Simon wasn't putting the new product down next to one of the test artifacts. Instead, he set it down in the middle of the table and pulled up a document on his phone, consulting what looked like a set of instructions.

"It's for detecting magical items," he said.

"In Mana Valley? That sounds like looking for a needle in a needle factory."

"Specific magical items. Or at least specific types of items. We're supposed to test it on…" He scanned down through his instructions. "Artifacts that summon or act like portals."

"Really?" Josie didn't try to hide her surprise. Though

magicals often used portals to pass between Mana Valley and Silicon Valley, they cast them using spells, not items. The only artifact she knew about that acted like a portal was Fran's mirror, a custom device that her roommate had made for herself. There wasn't a lot of call for such items, so no one made them.

"I don't write the specs. I just test against them." Simon put his phone away. "Do we have anything even close to that specification?"

Josie considered the available items.

"The spell cloning bracelet," she said. "It imitates something you cast near it and can keep the spell going for half an hour at a time. Cast a portal through that, and you'll have a temporary portal device."

"Good enough." Simon picked up the bracelet and cast a small portal near it. Another one appeared above the bracelet. When he dispelled his portal, the duplicate remained. "Put that down at the end of the room."

Josie took the bracelet and hung it over the handle of a cupboard door. The small portal hung next to the cheap silver-colored jewelry, providing a view through the gap between worlds. It showed her a sunny day in Silicon Valley, with cars rolling back and forth as people headed for work in all sorts of strange buildings.

She wondered what it was like to work on that side of the divide, where most technologies didn't have a hint of magic, but the tech itself was often more advanced. Exciting, probably. Challenging, not being able to fall back on magic to fix the bugs.

"According to the instructions, this thing should glow green on the sides closest to the powers it's looking for, and red on sides that are their opposite." Simon looked at Josie. "Is there an opposite to a portal spell?"

"I don't think so."

"Then we shouldn't see any red."

"You know those color choices are a design flaw, right?"

He hesitated. He didn't know that, but he didn't want to admit it. His determination to look good at all times was starting to get on her nerves. How could you test technology if you weren't willing to admit to flaws and mistakes? Their work was all about acknowledging limitations.

"Well spotted," he said. "Now show me you can explain the flaw properly."

It wasn't the most subtle bluff, but it wasn't Josie's job to call him on it. She just wanted to get on with her work.

"Color blindness," she said. "A user with red-green color blindness won't be able to tell the difference between results for what they want and ones warning them away from its opposite."

"Quite right. Now start up a test record and make a note of what we've found."

There was a row of tablets at the side of the room, all of them connected to a test results database, with sensors covering everything from ultraviolet light to infrasonic sounds to esoteric magic. Josie logged into one of them, took a photo of the device they were testing, and started a record for it.

"I'm switching it on now." Simon tapped the top of the orb. Its black surface swirled in a variety of colors before settling into white. "Nothing. What a start."

"Try turning up the sensitivity."

He pulled out his wand and used it to tweak the enchantments on the device. A point of green slowly emerged on one side.

"That's more like it." Carrying the device in front of him. Simon walked slowly down the room. A green spot emerged as he walked, but instead of pointing at the bracelet, it seemed to be pointing at one of the artifacts on the table: a sacrificial knife. "What's that about?"

He put the orb down on the table and Josie came to stand beside him. He drew the enchantments out of the artifact again, and they stood examining them.

"You don't think I broke it when I turned up the sensitivity?" he asked nervously.

"I doubt it. That's a quantitative change. It shouldn't affect the direction." Josie took out her wand and used it to pull out several strands of magic, examining what they did. "I don't understand all of this, but it looks coherent. Is it set to detect the wrong thing?"

She loved this sort of work. Not only spells as practical tools but getting into the guts of them and tweaking apart the fine filaments of magic that together made something much bigger, seeing how they interacted. So few people understood spell theory, never mind magical engineering, and they were all missing out on one of the true wonders of the world. She wondered if this was how physicists felt when they saw a new particle revealed.

Simon unfolded part of the spell. Inside it was an unmistakable trace of portal magic.

"According to the instruction manual, that part's supposed to define what it's looking for," he said. "So unless it's somehow using another source instead, this isn't the problem."

They carefully folded the magic back together and returned it to the orb. The green dot was still pointing in the wrong direction. Simon tried switching the device off and on again just in case.

"Still the wrong way." He scowled.

"Maybe it's about this." Josie picked up the knife and examined it, looking for any sign that there was more to its magic than they had thought. That was the problem with running tests on cheap, discarded artifacts. Sometimes they weren't quite what they seemed. The previous week, they'd tried to switch on a protective charm and instead summoned a luminous yellow elephant.

If there was anything odd about the knife, she couldn't find it. She was about to set it down on the workbench when she noticed something else. The green dot hadn't moved to keep pointing at the knife. It still pointed at the spot on the workbench where the knife had been.

She put the knife down and tried moving some of the other items. The green dot never moved. Finally, she picked up the bracelet. The dot moved but kept pointing in the wrong direction, ninety degrees away from her.

Josie laughed, hung up the bracelet again, and picked up a screwdriver.

"What?" Simon demanded.

"We were so focused on the magic that we forgot this is magitech." Josie opened a panel on the orb. She started shifting things around. "The spell is working fine, and so are the sensors. There's also a projector putting the results on the surface, and that..." She pulled out a component, turned it, and put it back. "…is ninety degrees out of sync. Or was."

She closed up the device and switched it back on. The green dot pointed straight at the bracelet and its miniature portal.

The dot shifted across the surface as Simon waved the device back and forth.

"Good work," he said. "Write up the results and send them to me for approval."

By approval, he meant putting his name on her work before it went to the managers. It annoyed Josie, but not enough to protest. She would be glad to be done with this one anyway and to get back to the Manaphone. Why would anyone want to detect portal devices?

CHAPTER THIRTY-SEVEN

The trailer that Singar had made rolled along behind Smokey as he made his way down the street toward the corner store. He had to admit that this thing was pretty sweet. He'd been able to cart parts back and forth while setting up the prototype earlier instead of carrying a few cables in his mouth.

The pouches on the harness let him keep his phone, keys, and some cash close to hand instead of having to stash them in a secret spot when he left the house in cat form. Sure, he looked a little odd, a cat wrapped in something almost like clothes, but he also looked like he was wearing military webbing, which made him feel ninety percent more like a badass.

Oh yes, he could get used to this.

He stopped at the bottom of the steps leading up to the convenience store. There were only two steps, but still, that was two more than the trolley could simply roll up. This was going to take an extra effort.

Smokey climbed the steps, hauling the trolley up

behind him. When he got to the top, the trolley seemed stuck, the wheels hanging down between the first and second steps because of its low clearance.

"Next time, I'm going to the supermarket," he grumbled as he twisted to shift the trolley's weight and hauled it up into the shop. At least this would be easier going down on the way out.

Inside the shop, he headed for the aisle with the cat food. As convenience stores went, this one was relatively large, with half a dozen aisles holding different products. The pet food was near the back, of course, adding to the awkwardness of his journey as he maneuvered the trolley around display stands and the feet of other customers.

"Excuse me," he said as he approached a man standing directly in his way. The man didn't move. "Hey, asshole, shift!"

The man looked around, then finally down, and scowled at him. "No need to be rude."

"No need to take up the whole aisle. Now move."

The man snorted but got out of the way.

At last, Smokey was at the back of the store, next to the pet food. This was it, a great moment in the history of four-legged magicals. For the first time, he would not only eat his pet food in cat form, but he would also buy it that way.

Except that the cat food was two shelves up, out of reach. Smokey sat glaring at it.

"Hey, little fellow." A gnome leaned down and patted the cat on the head. "Are you hoping someone will feed you if you sit there long enough?"

She chuckled at her joke while Smokey glared at her.

This was supposed to be his great moment of emancipation, not another chance for his fellow magicals to patronize him.

"Look, he's got a little cart," an elf said. "Did your master send you to fetch the shopping? You must be the cleverest little kitty! Oh, but it's out of reach. You want me to fetch something down for you?"

He reached for a packet of cat food.

"No, I do not," Smokey snarled. "I can do this for myself."

"Oh, you talk. Okay." The elf backed off from Smokey's glare.

Left alone in the aisle, Smokey looked up at the cat food again. He could do this. He'd got to plenty of high places before.

He tried to jump up onto the shelf, remembering the trailer only when its weight stopped his jump and slapped him back into the floor. Cursing and hissing, he unhitched himself. This time he was able to get up onto the shelf and wriggle in behind a bag of cat biscuits. With a strain of feline muscles, he pushed it off the shelf. It landed with a thud in the trailer. Success. He followed that with a box of wet food and a packet of treats—after this, he'd earned them. Then he hopped back down and hooked himself to the trailer again.

That seemed like enough shopping for a trial run. Besides, the trailer was pretty heavy now. Smokey hauled it down the aisle and joined the queue of people waiting to pay for their purchases. A minute later, a dwarf wandered up with a pack of beer and tried to step into the space occupied by Smokey. Smokey meowed loudly, and the dwarf looked down.

"Are you in the queue?" The dwarf looked confused. "But you're a cat."

Smokey hissed at him. Sometimes looking threatening was the only way to deal with people.

"Okay, okay!" The dwarf stepped into line behind Smokey. "Not going to mess with you."

"Aw, what an adorable kitty," said a passing witch. She stopped and leaned over to stroke Smokey's head. He almost purred, then remembered that he was strong and independent, no human's pet, so he shook her off instead. "Is he yours?" she asked the dwarf.

"I am no one's," Smokey declared. "I am an independent animal, and you bipeds had better remember it."

The witch laughed nervously and returned to her shopping.

At last, Smokey reached the front of the queue. When the dwarf didn't step up to the counter, the clerk behind the till looked around in confusion.

"Down there," the dwarf said quietly, pointing with his beer.

"Yes, down here," Smokey said, trying his best to sound intimidating and not like a plaintive, meowing cat. It was hard not to let those animal instincts take over when life was this frustrating. "Not all of your customers are human height, you know."

"Sure, cool, whatever," the clerk said. He appeared to be a young wizard, spotty-faced and nervous looking. "Just put your purchases on the counter."

"How am I supposed to do that?"

"How do you normally do it?"

"I don't. I only just got this trailer."

"Then can't you, I don't know, grow bigger or something?"

"I'm a cat buying cat food. That shouldn't be too difficult for you to work with. Come around and take the products."

"I can't do that. Store policy. You have to put the items on the counter."

"Why?"

"Because it's policy."

"Why is it policy?"

"I dunno."

"Then why follow it?"

"Because it's policy."

"That is a stupid answer."

"No need to be rude."

"Why don't I help?" the dwarf behind Smokey said. "I'll put them on the counter."

He reached for the bag of biscuits. Smokey spun, hissing, and batted his hand away.

"You will not! I'm a customer, and it is this store's job to sell me my groceries. That makes it their job to sort this out."

"But I want to buy my beer, and you're holding the rest of us up."

In the queue behind him, other customers made frustrated noises.

"I'm not holding you up. This guy is." Smokey glared at the store clerk. "Now, how are you going to fix this?"

"I don't know. Ask my manager."

"Where is your manager?"

"I don't know. It's his day off."

"Then how can I ask him, you dolt?"

"For crying out loud." The dwarf picked up the bag of cat food. "Let's get this over with."

"Don't you dare!"

Smokey leaped at the dwarf's arm. The trailer dragged him back, but he managed to latch on, wrapping his paws around the arm.

"Ow!" the dwarf exclaimed as Smokey's claws dug into his skin. He lifted his arm, dragging Smokey and the trailer up. "Ow, shit, get this crazy cat off of me."

The clerk grabbed hold of Smokey, trying to drag him off the dwarf's arm. Smokey's shifter instincts kicked in now that he faced two far larger opponents. He needed to be bigger and more menacing. Without meaning to, he started to change. The harness popped open and fell off. The trailer *clanged* onto the floor. Smokey twisted around, fist raised. The clerk, now holding up a naked, hairy dwarf instead of an ordinary house cat, staggered and collapsed beneath the weight. The two of them fell behind the counter in a tangle of limbs, both flailing with feet and fists.

"Help!" someone shouted. "Help! It's a mad shifter attack!"

The store door burst open, and a pair of witches raced in, amulets around their necks and wands in their hands.

"Silver Griffins," one of them announced. "What's going on here?"

The whole shop full of customers pointed behind the counter, where the clerk was trying to fend off a furious

Smokey, naked and bearded and at the end of his patience.

"How dare you touch me?" the dwarf shifter shouted in outrage. "How dare you?"

"You're under arrest," one of the Griffins said.

"This is Oriceran. You have no authority here."

"We have in Mana Valley. Special license. Now put your hands up."

It was all so unfair. They shouldn't be able to touch him. This place wasn't supposed to be run by witches and wizards. Hell, why should he let them get away with it?

"Yargh!" He ran straight at the Griffins.

"Refrigero!" one of the Griffins shouted. A bolt of icy magic shot from her wand and struck Smokey, freezing him in place.

"Don't worry, son," the other Griffin said as she pulled the frozen shifter off the bewildered clerk. "We've got him."

Coated in ice and frozen in place, Smokey was suddenly very aware of just how naked he was. His beard, which went down past his waist, went a little way toward protecting his dignity, but he was most definitely showing his ass to the world. He was naked, cold but unable to shiver, and he couldn't even explain himself.

"We'll take him down to the station," the Griffin holding him said. "We can come back for your statements in a moment. Nobody leave."

The shoppers groaned.

"You should take that, too." The dwarf with the beer pointed at the harness and trailer. "It belongs to him." He looked at Smokey with some sympathy. "I don't think he was trying to be a jerk, just having a bad day."

Smokey wanted to scream at them all about how bad a day could be, how difficult it was to do simple things in the form that made him comfortable, how stupid it was to have a world full of magical creatures but build it like everyone was a human or a dwarf. But he couldn't say any of that: his mouth was frozen shut. Instead, he stood in silence as the Silver Griffins summoned a portal.

He tensed his fist as his anger and frustration at the injustices of the world flowed through him. The ice started to crack.

CHAPTER THIRTY-EIGHT

"Hey, Fran," Cam called across the coffee shop. "Your company's in the news."

"It is?" Fran's head shot up like a meerkat emerging from its hole. Had word gotten around about their innovative ideas? Were they the shiny new example of Mana Valley innovation already? She'd known that she would get there one day, but she'd thought that she'd have to achieve more first. Maybe they'd got the right idea at the right time. Perhaps the media was looking for a bright new thing to focus on and had picked their ragtag crew of technologists. This was fantastic.

"Yeah, but not in a good way..." Cam winced as he watched something on the screen of his laptop, which he'd propped up behind the register. "I'll send you the link."

A notification *pinged* on Fran's screen, and she clicked on it. As she did so, Singar, Bart, and Gruffbar gathered around to see what was going on.

A video appeared, a new upload from a local news channel. In the paused image, a reporter stood in the street outside a convenience store down the street from Fran's apartment. The text in the lower third read,

Mana Wave Executive Goes On Rampage.

"That's weird," Fran said. "None of us is on a rampage. Do you think someone else has the same name?"

"Smokey's not here," Gruffbar said. "What's he been up to?"

"Smokey wouldn't go on a rampage." Fran thought about the look on his face after his meeting went wrong. "I mean, probably not..."

She hit "Play," and the news reporter started talking.

"I'm coming to you live from the scene where an executive at a tech startup has gone on a wild rampage, shocking residents and customers in this convenience store. The magical, a dwarf shifter named Smolden Haggerhold, known to acquaintances as Smokey, allegedly started a fight in the store after staff refused to serve him in his animal form."

Another dwarf appeared on the screen, a half-drunk tin of beer in his hand.

"It was wild," the dwarf said. "He just went for me. Look at these scars!"

He held up his arm for the camera to see, then belched.

"Those aren't scars," Singar said dismissively. "They're barely scratches."

Back on the screen, a teenage convenience store clerk had appeared.

"I was just following the rules," he said, his voice wavering. "But that guy went totally nuts."

The video cut to shaky footage of Smokey in his dwarf form. He was naked, covered in chunks of ice, and running down the street, pursued by Silver Griffins.

"See the oppression!" Smokey screamed. He was wide-eyed, his beard flapping down his front, chunks of icy hair bouncing off his skin. "I'm a tech executive, and they won't even let me buy my biscuits! They won't even let me—"

One of the Griffins waved a wand and chains shot out, wrapping themselves around Smokey. He fell to the ground and half a dozen witches and wizards leaped on him. The video cut back to the news reporter.

"Haggerhold, who according to public records is director of software at magitech company Mana Wave Industries, is now being held by the Silver Griffins. Many in the local community are asking why a company would employ someone so unhinged in such a senior role."

The video ended.

"This is bad, right?" Fran whispered. "The first time we're mentioned in the news, and it's for this."

Her phone buzzed with a call from an unknown number. There were also several messages she hadn't noticed, all claiming to be from news agencies looking for a quote.

"Don't answer any of those," Gruffbar said. "Until I say otherwise, you don't answer any message or call that isn't from me. Understand?"

"But what if—"

"Whatever it is, don't answer. I'm your lawyer. This is a situation with legal implications. Everything goes through me. In fact, you head over to Worn Threads and take all our work with you. Get out of sight and stay out of sight. I'll find you once I've cleared up this mess."

"You're going to the Silver Griffins?"

Gruffbar shook his head.

"I'm a lawyer, not an influencer, but the reputational damage is our priority here. Before I even think about getting Smokey out of jail, I need to get us a PR professional."

"We can't afford those sorts of fees."

"Then how would you feel about adding one more person to the team? I know just the magical. She's great at her job, ruthless in pursuing her objectives, and very motivated to prove her worth. She'd be an asset to the company far beyond dealing with Smokey's frozen junk."

"Sounds like your friend is the perfect person for us. Go ahead and offer her a position, same terms as everyone else. A seat on the board and a profit share."

"Oh, she's no friend of mine, but she's exactly what this company needs."

Gruffbar grabbed his briefcase and headed out the door. Behind him, Singar pressed play on the video.

"Just one more time before we go," she said. "I want to watch the bit where the ice bounces off his—"

"How did you find me?"

Elethin stood in the doorway of her tiny room, glaring down at Gruffbar. Instead of her professional skirt and blouse, she wore yoga pants and a sleeveless t-shirt. Her hair was greasy and tied loosely back so that her elf ears poked out between the strands. Behind her, a battered secondhand laptop and a bowl of ramen noodles sat on an unmade bed. The curtains were closed.

"It wasn't hard," Gruffbar said. "I've worked with the city's halfway houses before. Didn't think you'd have got yourself back into private accommodation yet, so I made a few calls, and here you are."

"It's hard to rent an apartment when you've got a criminal record and no job. One more reason why I should turn your guts into molten lava."

She raised her hand and magic flowed between her fingers.

"Two things," Gruffbar said. "Number one, you don't know that spell. If you did, you'd have used it on me weeks ago. Number two, I'm here to offer you a way out of this."

A cockroach scuttled across the floor between them, then disappeared into a gap in the wall. One of its legs knocked the peeling paintwork as it went, and a strip of paint fell away to join the rest of the detritus on the floor.

"Maybe I like it here," Elethin said.

"Really? You like sitting in a room the size of a prison cell watching daytime TV?" Gruffbar peered past at the screen. "Seriously, you're watching soap operas? I expected better of you."

"Screw you, Gruffbar. You got me locked away. I changed, became the person I needed to be to survive. I don't need your judgment, and I really don't need your charity."

She slammed the door in his face.

Gruffbar sighed and turned away. Maybe it was for the best. Working with her, he would have spent the whole time watching for poison in his coffee and thumbtacks in his sandwiches. But where was he going to get hold of a PR person now?

The door creaked open behind him. He stopped but didn't turn to look at her.

"How were you going to get me out?" Elethin asked, her voice tight as a guitar string.

"A job. It's exactly your sort of thing, PR for a magitech startup."

"I don't like startups. Too many greasy young geeks."

"You'll like this one. The kid behind it, she's got passion, drive, and a head full of fantastic ideas. She's built a decent technical team, not your usual tech bros, but a mix of talented magicals. Now she needs someone who can do PR, sell the company to the media and the big-league investors. No one on Earth or Oriceran has better skills than you when it comes to magitech PR."

"I am brilliant."

"So come and use those skills again."

"What does it pay?"

"Nothing yet, but you get a profit share, a seat on the board, and you can call yourself director of public relations. We've got a big contract we're working on, so soon we'll be able to—"

"Don't bullshit a bullshitter." Elethin snorted. "Come back to me when you've got something that pays."

"This will pay in time, but we need someone to do PR right now, this news cycle. So either you're in now, or you're out forever."

He turned to look at her. Elethin's face was pinched, one hand clutching the door frame.

"I do like the job title," she said. "And the board position. But I need to get out of this dump, and that means I need something that pays."

Gruffbar hesitated. Nothing he could do would give Mana Wave Industries the money to pay Elethin's wages, but they need her right now, her or someone like her.

"I can't believe I'm about to do this," he said. "A few days ago, you were trying to kill me. But if you take the job, I'll lend you the money for rent."

"Glad to see that one of us has done well out of life," she said with a sardonic curl of the lip.

"I'm not doing well, but I'll manage. I believe in this kid. I believe in this company. I might not believe in you, but she needs you, so I'm making it happen. It's decision time. You in?"

"I'm in."

"Good. Get cleaned up and meet me at the local Silver Griffins station. I need you to come up with excuses for a naked dwarf popsicle."

"You need me to what?"

"I'll explain later. One thing you can be sure of with this job, it's not going to be dull."

CHAPTER THIRTY-NINE

Fran, Singar, and Bart stood around the counter of the Worn Threads carpet store, drinking coffee with Gail and Raulo, while a crow watched them from on top of the register. The coffee wasn't as good as the coffee in the Blazing Bean, and Fran missed the pastries almost as much as she missed Cam's coffee-making skills, but it was touching how the couple had taken the Mana Wave team in during their time of need.

"Are you all set down there?" Gail nodded toward the cellar door.

"Pretty much," Fran said. "It's a great space to work in. Thank you so much."

"It's a filthy space to work in," Singar said. "And we need to wire some of the power outlets back in. But it is appreciated."

"Most use anyone's gotten out of that space in years," Gail said. "Maybe it'll motivate us to clean it out."

"Let's not get carried away." Raulo chuckled. "Cleaning

it out would mean doing something with all those old machines, and I have no idea what that would be."

"What are you doing down there anyway?" Gail asked. "Or is that all secret?"

"Interference tests." Singar set her cup down on the counter, a foot away from Gail's, and wobbled it until ripples formed in the top of the coffee. "Some magical devices use related frequencies, which is fine most of the time. They go along, doing their thing, completely separate from each other."

She pushed her cup down the counter until it touched Gail's. Her wobbling made the two cups rattle against each other, setting up ripples in Gail's cup too. "But if devices with similar magical frequencies operate close together, their magic can interfere with one another."

"So put a wand and a Manaphone together, and the wand starts taking calls?"

"Maybe. Or maybe they turn into a frog. Magical interactions don't always work out in an obvious way." Singar pulled her cup away and took a gulp. "Our device uses a mirror. That's no corporate secret. So I've run an enchantment through your giant mirror, then set up our device and Fran's magical mirror next to it, with a load of sensors to see what happens."

"Any frogs yet?" Raulo asked with a grin.

"Not yet, but we can hope."

The shop door opened, ringing the bell above it, and a gnome walked in. She held a device the size of a grapefruit in a hand that was missing two fingers.

"I'm looking for a new carpet," the gnome said.

"Then you're in the right place," Gail said. "Let me show

you around." She emerged from behind the counter. "Say, what's that thing you've got there?"

"This? Oh, it's a new sort of personal organizer I'm testing out for a friend." The gnome shook her head and laughed. "Mana Valley, it's always throwing you something weird, right?"

"Oh yes!" Gail laughed and led the customer out of sight, between the rows of carpets.

"Do you think Smokey's going to be OK?" Bart asked. "He looked very agitated."

"He'll be worse than agitated after all those Griffins piled in on him," Singar said, scowling into her coffee. "You can bet they put the boot in on the way to the cells to make sure he doesn't cross them again."

"Gruffbar got me out of jail," Fran said. "I'm sure he can do it for Smokey too."

"You got arrested?" Singar laughed. "I don't believe it."

"Really, I did..."

Fran started telling the story about the flying carpet and the San Francisco Silver Griffins. Gail returned partway through and laughed along with the rest as they heard about Fran's misadventures.

"...which is how I ended up with Gruffbar on my team," Fran finished. "Funny how life works out, isn't it?" She glanced down the store. The door to the basement stood ajar. "Gail, did you go downstairs while you were away?"

"No, dear. Why do you ask?"

Fran set her coffee aside and headed down the store, accelerating from a walk into a run as she went. That customer with the missing fingers, she hadn't left the store, had she? And she had been carrying that weird device, a sort of orb with a green dot on one side. Something about it all seemed off.

Fran flung the door open and dashed down the stairs, the crow fluttering after her.

In the basement, the gnome was standing with the orb in her hand in the middle of their testing area, right between the prototype, the giant wall mirror, and Fran's pocket-sized portal mirror. The underside of the orb was a swirling mass of green patterns.

"Damn stupid device," the gnome muttered, thumping the top of the orb. "Which one is it?"

She looked up as Fran came dashing down the stairs.

"What are you doing here?" Fran asked.

"Got lost." The gnome held up the orb. "This new assistant device, it's terrible at navigating."

"That's the most terrible excuse I've ever heard."

"Had to give it a try."

The gnome raised her empty hand and cast a spell.

Suddenly everything seemed fine to Fran. Of course, the gnome was supposed to be here, and Fran was supposed to help her. Why wouldn't she?

"Which one of these makes portals?" the gnome said.

"The little one," Fran replied. "I made it myself. Super cute, right?"

"Sure, whatever."

There was a sharp pain in Fran's shoulder. The crow was pecking her, hard. She yelped in pain and knocked the crow away, but that pecking had done its job. Clarity returned, the gnome's spell broken.

"Hey, you're not my friend!" Fran shouted.

The gnome was reaching for the hand mirror. Fran

summoned her Evermore magic and launched a narrow beam of sound. It shook the mirror and sent it bouncing away across the floor, underneath one of the machines.

"Oh no, you don't." The gnome cast another spell, an icy blast this time. Fran dove onto the heap of abandoned carpet samples, and the spell hit the wall behind her. Dust billowed from the carpets, a cloud of it that made her cough and close her eyes.

There were more footsteps on the stairs, the rest of the gang coming down behind Fran. When she opened her watering eyes, Bart, Singar, and Gail all stood facing the gnome, who had one hand under the machines, stretching to reach the mirror.

"No one messes with my friends and me." Singar pulled out a switchblade. Gail drew her wand, and magic sparkled around the tips of Bart's fingers.

"Oh for..." The gnome intruder stood and pulled a short-barreled revolver from inside her jacket. "Put your hands up, all of you."

A beam of light shot from Fran's hand and struck the gnome in the face.

"Argh!" Temporarily blinded, the gnome clutched her agonized eyes.

Singar ran across the room and slammed into the gnome, knocking her to the floor. The gun fell from her hand and slid under the machines. The gnome and the Willen rolled across the floor, kicking and punching while dust rose into the air around them.

The rest of the gang charged over to help. Before they could get hold of the gnome, she shoved Singar off and got to her feet. With her back against the wall and her hand raised, magic swirling around her fingers, the gnome stared at them with watering eyes.

"Just give me the damn mirror," she said. "You'll only regret it later if you don't."

"It's my mirror," Fran said. "I spent years getting it right. You can't take it like that."

"If I don't, someone else will, and believe me, they'll make you regret this."

"I don't give in to bullies."

The gnome laughed. "Bullies? Oh, this is so much bigger than you think, little girl. Powers are coming that would crush you without even seeing you were there."

"Big talk," Singar snarled. "But right now you're outnumbered and surrounded. Bart, I will almost never say this, but call the Griffins."

The gnome pulled a piece of wood the size of a domino from her pocket. A painted rune showed on one side. "Domum." She snapped the piece of wood in half. There was a flash of light, and she disappeared.

"The mirror." Fran ran over to the machines and peered into the shadows underneath. Was it still there or had the gnome magicked it away with her when she went?

A glint of silver shone in the darkness. With a big sigh of relief, Fran drew the mirror out. It was dusty and a little scratched but otherwise intact.

Singar also reached under the machines. She pulled out the gnome's pistol, dusted it off, and carried it to her toolkit.

"I'll keep this." She opened the box. "In case of any other trouble."

"Do you really need something like that?" Bart looked at her with concern.

"I've needed this enough times." Singer waved her knife. "So yeah, I reckon I can find uses for a gun."

Clutching her mirror tight, Fran walked over to Gail.

"I'm sorry about that," she said. "I know I warned you that there might be trouble, but I'll understand if you don't want us here anymore."

"Are you kidding?" Gail grinned. "That's the most thrilling thing I've seen in months. Wait until I tell the rest of my crochet club about it."

"And Raulo?"

"Oh, he'll be fine. Probably more bothered that I left him minding the shop while we did this. Now, shall I make more coffee and get us some cookies?"

"Yes, please, but we'd better have ours down here." Fran looked at the prototype containment unit. "The sooner we finish our tests, the sooner we can get out of your way."

CHAPTER FORTY

Smokey sat in the Silver Griffins' interrogation room, his hands cuffed to the table. The Griffins wouldn't let him shift back into cat form and had used a spell to make sure he stayed dwarf for a while, but at least they'd given him a t-shirt and some jogging pants, as well as a cup of coffee to warm him up after the freeze spell wore off. They'd asked a lot of questions, but they hadn't listened. No one ever did. That was why things didn't get better for non-bipedal magicals.

He wasn't only angry at the world. He was angry at himself too. Losing his temper like that hadn't helped anyone or done the cause any favors.

Sure, the convenience store kid should've been more helpful, but if the owner had set up the place properly, he wouldn't have needed to be. That was the company's fault. Smokey would be writing them a very strongly worded email from the official Paws and Claws account as soon as he got out of here. If he got out of here and wasn't flung into Trevilsom forever by the man.

The door opened, and Gruffbar walked in, accompanied by a Silver Griffin. The Griffin unlocked Smokey's handcuffs and stepped back but kept her wand in her hand, pointedly watching him.

"What's happening?" Smokey asked.

"You're being released." Gruffbar handed him a pair of sneakers. "Here, these should be your size."

"Released? But how?"

"I talked with the watch commander about your arrest and what might be considered a disproportionate force in the pursuit of magical policing. There's an argument to be made that freezing a naked magical isn't the best way to deal with a disturbance, especially when you haven't even tried talking him down."

"So I'm free to go?"

"There's a small fine for disturbing the peace, and you won't be allowed in that shop for the next month, but other than that, you're free."

"I can't afford..."

"Bart paid your fine. Apparently, being friends with a public troublemaker makes him feel young. From the glint in his eyes, I'm worried that he's going to go shoplifting now, just to feel like he's fifty again."

"I... Thank you."

"Thank Bart. I'm doing my job, looking after the company's legal interests. Which reminds me, there's an elf in the lobby and some people from the press. Nod and smile and agree with everything the elf says."

"If I'm going to be in front of the cameras, can I get something to cover these bruises?" Smokey pointed at the blue marks left on his skin by the Griffins' magical chains.

"Definitely not. Nothing makes you sympathetic like pain. In fact, try to look tired and miserable as they lead you out. It'll help Elethin." Gruffbar flashed a smile at the Griffin guard, who was watching him with narrowed eyes. "What can I say? We have better PR than you."

Smokey, still in his dwarf form, followed Gruffbar through a portal and out onto a street in Silicon Valley. The air there tasted different than in Mana Valley. It didn't have the breeze off the mountains or the tang of spent magic. For all the problems with Mana Valley, there was nothing like leaving it to make him realize how much he loved the place.

"What are we doing here?" he asked as the portal shut behind them.

"Going for a drink."

"Shouldn't we get back to Fran and the rest? There's still space for improvement in the control software, and I don't want us showing something inferior to the client."

"The client's not coming around any time soon. Besides, you just got out of jail. Having a drink is traditional."

"There are traditions for getting out of jail?"

"Oh yes." Gruffbar grinned. "If you move in the right circles."

They walked into a bar decorated with images from old video games. On one wall, a giant yellow ball was chasing what looked like a mustachioed gnome in plumber's overalls, while opposite it, a strange-looking elf was waving a magical sword in the air.

"Forty years ago, we'd have had to pass for humans to come into a place like this," Gruffbar said. "Hell, they would've assumed we were humans. But the world keeps changing..."

There was a step in front of the bar. He climbed up onto it, ordered a pitcher of beer and two glasses, and carried them to a table in the corner of the room. Before sitting, he fed change into a vintage jukebox, then flicked through the selection until he found what he was after. The first bars of a classic rock anthem belted through the bar as Gruffbar took a seat opposite Smokey and poured them both a beer.

"Here's to your first run-in with the law," he said. "Congratulations. You made it out."

"Thanks." They *clinked* glasses. Smokey took a long drink, then made a face. "This is what they call beer?"

"You know humans. A few of them have worked out how to brew properly, but they don't have the lifespans to really master the craft. We put up with what we can get over here."

"Still..."

"When you're the one picking up the tab, you can moan about the booze some more. Until then, drink up."

If there was one thing that dwarves were good at, it was quaffing beer. They were halfway through their second pitcher before the conversation got started again.

"I thought you said it was okay for us to be here," Smokey said.

"It is. In this economy, they'll be glad of any business."

"Then how come people keep looking at us funny?"

"Because, in their heads, we don't belong here. A generation ago, most of them would've had no idea that magicals even existed. Can you imagine that? Being so ignorant that half the sentient beings in existence weren't part of your worldview?

"Anyway, they haven't properly adjusted yet. To a lot of humans, we're still a novelty, for good or for bad. They don't understand us, they're not used to us being here, and our existence is a constant reminder that their world is going through a radical change."

"So they don't want us here?"

"Some of them. Some want more of us, want to spend their whole time around magicals, to experience the hot new thing. Then there are the ones in the middle who are curious and uncertain, trying to cope with it all."

"I don't like it." Smokey glared at a woman who'd looked at them for too long. She hastily looked away.

"You shouldn't." Gruffbar refilled their glasses. "But you see why this is better than some of the stupidity back on Oriceran, right?"

Smokey turned his glass in his hand while he contemplated the question, trying to get to the bottom of what Gruffbar meant. Eventually, he shook his head.

"I give up. Explain it to me."

"This lot doesn't know any better." Gruffbar gestured over his shoulder at the room full of humans. "They're not used to us. For centuries their society was built only for them, at least as far as they knew.

"When they treat us like novelties or they don't think to build a society that fits us, even when their adjustments are something pathetic like putting a single step in front of the bar, that's understandable. They don't know any better.

"In Oriceran, there are no excuses. We've always been there. Some businesses, some governments, some people, they've adjusted what they do to prepare for shorter people like gnomes, dwarves, and Willens. That's fine. The ones that haven't? That's insulting because it's not treating us as equals, not treating us as people like them, after all this time.

"So here, I'll accept the ignorance and the lack of adjustments. I'll swallow my pride with my beer because they don't know better. But I can't accept that back home."

Smokey nodded thoughtfully. "I think I get it. You're saying that, for non-bipedal magicals in Oriceran, it's the same situation as for dwarves here. People don't know enough, but they'll get there with time."

"Don't be stupid." Gruffbar poured the last of the beer into their glasses and waved his pitcher at the barman. "There have been four-legged magicals in Oriceran as long as there have been two-legged ones. It's people being idiots again.

"My point is, remember that they're idiots. Here or there, you're better than them, and it's not worth letting them get to you. If you do, you'll end up in the crazy wing at Trevilsom."

"Ha, you're right!" Smokey looked up a little fuzzily as the barman set down a fresh pitcher of beer. "Hey, I'm better than you!"

"Buddy, as long as your tips are good, you can think whatever you like," the barman said. "But there's nothing better about an asshole who pukes all over the bathroom, so don't keep drinking if you can't take it."

Smokey rested his chin on the edge of his glass and watched the barman depart.

"I need to cool it, don't I? To stop hammering everyone about being better, about bipeds and all that."

"To the depths with that," Gruffbar said. "You keep up the fight. Just maybe remember, not everyone's smart enough to understand what you've got to say. Shift your message to fit the idiots." He held up his glass. "Here's to being better than the rest of them."

"To being better!" Smokey *clinked* glasses with Gruffbar, and they got back to the serious business of quaffing.

CHAPTER FORTY-ONE

Gruffbar and Smokey walked into the Blazing Bean, both wearing sunglasses. The Silver Griffins' magic had worn off, and Smokey was back in his feline form, but he had found a tiny pair of shades from somewhere, shaped to suit a cat. The two of them walked slowly and stiffly as if they were afraid to make any sudden moves.

"What can I get you?" Cam asked loudly, smiling over the counter at them. "Something with extra sugar and caffeine? And maybe a painkiller on the side?"

"Coffee," Gruffbar muttered. "Black. Many sugars. And the most solid, stomach-settling muffin you have."

"Of course. And how about you?"

Smokey, who had hopped up onto the counter, peered over his sunglasses with bloodshot eyes. "Saucer of oat milk, and try to be quiet about it."

Fran looked up at them brightly as they approached the tables at the back of the shop. Her expression turned to concern as she took in their pasty skin and pained expressions.

"Are you two all right?" she asked. "Did the Silver Griffins do something terrible to you?"

"I think they did this to themselves," Bart said.

"Huh?"

Bart mimed drinking.

"Oh, you're hungover?" Fran asked. "Why didn't you just say?"

"Ssh." Smokey pressed a paw to his mouth. "Quiet now. We work."

He took a compact laptop out of his harness and started typing, moving slowly and carefully to avoid the sharp keyboard sounds.

It was Saturday morning, and the coffee shop was bustling. Teenagers played videos for each other and snippets of music from their phones. Small children screamed for cake. Parents tried, at increasingly loud volume, to cheerfully persuade said children that they didn't want cake.

Gruffbar winced at every last sound. Through it all, the only empty area in the room was around the table where Singar was fitting components to the sides of a mirror. The smells of solder and solvents were enough to drive the other customers away.

"Shouldn't someone be at Worn Threads?" Bart asked. "In case that gnome comes back for the mirrors?"

"I set an alarm." Singar pointed at a small box on the table before her, with a green light flashing on the top. "Plus I've increased the sensitivity on the containment unit. If anybody tries any funny business down there, we'll have solid proof that our invention works."

"What if they get to the mirror first?"

"I have the one they were after." Fran showed him her portal mirror. "Although I still have no idea why they wanted it or how they even knew about it."

Elethin strode over to join them, carrying an espresso. Her stiletto heels *clacked* against the floor.

"Good morning, Gruffbar," she said.

"Is it?" Gruffbar peeled his head up off the table. "Everyone, this is Elethin, our new head of public relations. Elethin, this is everyone."

"Your manners remain as strong as ever." Elethin extended a hand. "You must be Fran. It's lovely to meet you properly."

"And you." Fran shook the hand. "You've met Smokey, right?"

"In a very different form."

"Oh yeah, I keep forgetting the dwarf thing, which is kind of surprising after seeing you all—"

"No need to talk about that," Smokey said.

"Really? But it's the most exciting part of the week."

"Really."

"I think so. Anyway, this is Bart, our director of finance."

"Charmed." Elethin reached across the table to shake Bart's hand.

"And this is Singar, director of hardware. Though we're all one-person departments right now, so 'director' sounds a little too grand."

"Grand is good. It can make you sound like professionals and imply a far larger operation." Elethin extended a hand to Singar. "Delighted to meet you, Singar."

"Sure." Singar nodded and continued with her soldering. "Could someone fetch me a coffee without paint chips in it? This stuff gets everywhere."

"Do we really not have anywhere better to work?" Elethin looked around. "Working in coffee shops is very of the moment, and we can spin it as showing a flexible, no-frills operation, but there are times when you want to be able to show your grown-up side."

"Once we've got some money, we can get an office," Bart said.

"And a workshop," Singar added. "Plus storage, a manufacturing floor, hazardous waste disposal…"

"An office," Gruffbar said. "A nice, quiet office. That's what I need right now."

"Um, guys?" Cam had appeared at the end of the table, holding a tray and a collection of cardboard cups. "I'm really sorry about this, but I'm going to have to ask you to leave. The manager says that your devices are taking up too much space at a busy time and that you're putting other customers off."

He looked at the empty tables around Singar, then at how crowded the rest of the coffee shop was. "I don't like to do this, but he's not completely wrong, so could you pack up and take this elsewhere? I brought takeaways for your drinks."

He put the cardboard cups down on the table and started collecting their cups and plates.

"Should I go and talk to this manager?" Elethin asked. "I'm sure that I can persuade him to let us stay."

"No, that's okay." Fran packed up her laptop and notebooks. "Cam's been so helpful. I don't want to do anything that might make more hassle or lose these guys business."

"You can come back when things are quieter," Cam said. "You know that I'm always happy to have you working here."

"Thanks," Fran said. "That's, like, really sweet of you."

"It's not much use to us, though, is it?" Singar asked. "We need somewhere we can work in working hours, not only in the evenings."

She meticulously fixed her tools into their spaces in her toolkit, then started packing components into a bag.

"Where do we go now?" Smokey asked. "Back to Fran's apartment?"

"I don't think we can do that," Fran said. "Josie was settling in for a morning of coffee and cartoons. She won't appreciate us bringing all our noise and mess again."

"Anyone else got an apartment we can use?"

Despite the noise around them, the lack of response among the Mana Wave board somehow became a special sort of silence. They had seen the chaos they created together, and even those with enough space to work in didn't want to see their homes overrun.

"You could take the day off," Cam suggested. "It is the weekend."

"We could…" Fran hesitated. That sounded like a good idea in theory. She could watch cartoons with Josie, go skating, maybe play some video games. But it was hard to imagine a day right now where she wasn't working on Mana Wave Industries and its future.

"Maybe you losers want to slack off," Singar said, "but I'm not. We've still got a deadline to hit."

"That's right." Smokey found some energy for the first

time that morning. "We've got to get this finished for the client."

"I'm still sorting out the paperwork for the business," Gruffbar said. "Hungover is the best time to face the really dull bits. They'll numb the pain."

"I am not going back to my room," Elethin said sharply. "The cockroaches are noisy today."

"I could make some calls to my old contacts," Bart said. "See if anyone can lend us some office space for the afternoon."

"Or a workshop," Singar said as the whole group headed out the door. "Then I can make all the mess I need to…"

With the Mana Wave team gone, Cam wiped down the tables and set the space around them in order. Soon that part of the shop was bustling, as more Saturday shoppers came in searching for somewhere to relax.

"I'm going for my break," Cam said to his colleagues as he grabbed his laptop from under the counter. "Back in twenty."

Taking a coffee he'd made for himself and one of the previous day's slightly stale croissants, he went to sit in the last remaining seat by the window. He opened a document containing his dissertation, always a useful cover for anything else he was doing. Then he opened the file he really cared about.

It was a big document, full of research. There were pages from history books, snippets of local gossip, reports from Mana Valley news outlets, both recently and in previous centuries. He'd sorted some of it by themes, events, or even people. Some was just a jumble, things that had caught his attention but he was sure would form part of the puzzle he was trying to complete.

He scrolled to the most recent section of the document. Under the heading of Mana Wave Industries were a series of subheadings: Members, Objectives, Methods, Esoteric Connections, Timeline, Possible Links to D. Under members, he added a new section.

Elethin Tannerin, head of PR. Former criminal. Probationary. Elf. Worked for Nuada. Agent of D?

In the timeline, he added the date of Elethin's arrival with the company, as well as the fact that they still didn't have a permanent base. That had been a feature of his records on Mana Wave since the start. Their homelessness had been useful, keeping them in the coffee shop, where he could keep an eye on them. What would happen when they got an office of their own? How would he watch what they were doing then?

That was a problem for another day. For now, he scrolled up to the section on Fran and read a note he'd made weeks before.

Innocent? Villain? Hero? Does she understand what she's opening the way for?

He shook his head. One day, he would work out the answer. He hoped that day wouldn't come too late.

He turned to another page of the document, where he kept a photo of a piece of parchment, an ancient page with the symbol of the Dark Market stamped on one corner. A page of the Tess prophecies. He'd been lucky even to see it, never mind take a copy like this. He hoped that his contact hadn't got in trouble for allowing that before they sold the sheet on to someone far wealthier than him.

"Evermores," he muttered to himself, reading the page of prophecy again. "What does it even mean? How do I find out more?"

CHAPTER FORTY-TWO

Winslow and his team of Evermores sat around a restaurant table, bathed in the glow coming through the window from the kemana's central crystal. Willens were cleaning the area around the crystal, clearing away gifts left by superstitious locals in the crystal's shadow. *It was funny,* Winslow thought, *how these traditions grew up, how what was normal in one place could seem bizarre or extraordinary elsewhere, a truth that held both here on Earth and across the gap in Oriceran. Perhaps even more so when you looked at the two together.*

An elf waitress setting a selection of plates on the table drew him out of his reverie.

"Stuffed undervine leaves," she said. "Steamed dumplings. There's our selection of dips and sauces. And of course, plenty of flavored flatbreads to tear and share." She smiled at them. "Enjoy."

The Evermores didn't wait for the waitress to leave before they dove into their meal. Their journey across America had been a long one, with as much walking and climbing as using magic or finding their way onto vehicles. They couldn't always take the quickest or most restful route while looking for clues along the way or while trying to lay traps for the Source.

"Four times now." Enfield dipped a dumpling into dwarf-style barbecue sauce. "Four times we've found it, and four times it's got away. We need to get more help."

"Patience," Winslow said. "How many times must I say it to you?"

"Too many." Enfield stabbed another dumpling into the saucepot so hard that he tipped it over. He grabbed a fistful of napkins and started wiping up the mess, never meeting the older Evermore's eyes.

"Will it be different this time?" one of the others asked.

Winslow smiled. They were all so young, the ones who'd volunteered to come with him, none more than a few centuries old. So fresh-faced. So naïve about the world.

"Perhaps," he said. "Perhaps not. But we will persist. We will stick to the path laid before us. We will do what we need to do to protect the magic in the world and the kemanas that sustain it."

The other Evermores nodded, apparently happy with this view. Enfield still scowled as he set the sauce-stained napkins aside and reached for a piece of spiced bread.

"Here." Winslow pushed the food to the edges of the table and spread out the map they'd been navigating by, a map of North America marked with colored symbols to show where they'd been and what they'd learned. "The Source is on a looping path that will carry it to California.

This kemana is our next chance to catch it, but if that fails, we have another here and another here before…"

"Before what?" Enfield snapped. "What aren't you telling us?"

"The Source," one of the other Evermores said. "It's nearly here."

"He told us that already."

"No, I mean, it's really nearly here." The Evermore pointed out the window at the kemana crystal. Its magic was flickering to the alarm of the Willens working around it.

Winslow popped a stuffed vine leaf into his mouth.

"It's time," he said, through a mouthful of spiced rice and mince. "Time to get ready."

He dropped payment for the half-eaten meal on the table, stuffed the map away in his pocket, and led the rest of his Evermores out into the kemana.

The flickering of the crystal grew more intense as the Evermores spread out around it. It was like being in a strobe-lit nightclub, something Winslow had never experienced before their recent trip into the world and which hadn't been to his tastes. He went where he needed to for his contacts, but he was several millennia too old to become a dance music fan.

"Brace yourselves," he called to the other Evermores. "Prepare the net."

Around them, other magicals watched the crystal with doubt, uncertainty, or excitement, not knowing what the flickering meant. Winslow knew all too well, but he wasn't there to soothe their fears. Instead, he and his team started singing, casting their magic out as they did so. The magical sound waves bound themselves around the song, turned it, formed it into something almost solid, translucent strands hanging above the crystal. A nearly invisible net made from thick strands of air and light, supple yet strong as steel.

The ground burst open, and the Source flew out. Its form was becoming more settled. Now there was always something animal about it, with wings, arms, and claws, vast muscular shoulders, and legs underneath it all. Although how many legs changed as often as the wing color or the shape of the arms, or the features of that looming face.

The Source was starting to understand what the world expected from a monster.

The Evermores stood their ground and kept singing as the other magicals fled screaming past them. A pair of Silver Griffins, wands in hands, rushed up to face the Source. One of them flung a magical chain at it, but the Source tossed it back with a flick of its power, slamming the Griffin against the wall. The other one tried a freeze spell, but the ice evaporated against the Source's incredible energy. A swing of its tail knocked the Griffin out.

Winslow kept singing, but his note changed, sending a vibration through the net, a signal to the others that it was time.

The whole song shifted. Rolling, repeating choruses turned into a staccato verse. The net dropped, and its edges swept in, engulfing the Source.

Quickly, the Evermores grabbed the ends of the net. Sonic magic flowed from their hands, drawing out strands of thickened air that they flung to each other and pulled tight, drawing the net in under the Source. It howled and struggled, strained its arms and wings, but remained caught.

Winslow nodded at Enfield, who gathered the loose ends of the net and pulled them together into a knot.

"We did it!" Enfield laughed in delight. "We actually did it!"

The Source slumped, leaning against the kemana crystal. Its roars gave way to a low rumble, then to a deep, humming note that shook the world around them.

"What is it doing?" Enfield asked.

"It's copying our song." Winslow frowned. He'd never seen anything like this. As far as he knew, no one had. That didn't have to mean it was bad. Millennia of witnessing the new had taught him not to make that knee-jerk assumption. Still, as the sound throbbed through him, he felt an inescapable dread.

"Enfield, check the bindings." He raised his voice over the Source's song. "The rest of you, keep up the song, keep up the spell."

"The bindings are tight," Enfield said. "But the strands, the way they're throbbing, I'm not sure that—"

The net tore open, its strings of air and sonic energy ripping apart. A cacophony filled the kemana, a storm of noise that shattered windows, turned water to vapor, and made stalactites fall like stone javelins from the roof.

Winslow leaped aside as one hit the ground near him and exploded into stone shrapnel. He clutched his ears, trying to keep out the terrible noise, but it was a sound filled with magical power, a sound that the Evermores themselves had created with their magic, and it was impossible for him to keep it out.

The Source stepped out of the ruined strands of magic. It wasn't howling anymore, wasn't humming or singing. It stalked over to the kemana crystal while the sound of the broken magic echoed through the cavern around it.

The Source placed a paw on the crystal. That paw became a hoof became a talon became an eight-fingered hand. Those fingers splayed across the smooth surface of the crystal. The magical light glowing from it started to fade.

"Stop it!" Winslow flung a sonic blast at the Source, but the noise still echoing around the cave disrupted his magic, and it faded to nothing before it hit the beast. Enfield threw a blast of light, but the Source flung up a wing, sheltering itself from the blast. The wing charred and blackened as the light turned to heat, but the creature didn't flinch.

The crystal cracked, a sound so ominous it cut through the noise ringing in Winslow's ears.

"We have to stop it." He ran toward the Source, jumped, and hurtled toward it with a flying kick. The Source caught him with its tail and slammed him to the ground.

The crystal cracked again, a line running up one side as the Source drew more power out of it. The creature grew in strength as the power flowed.

Enfield had rallied the other Evermores. They started chanting, and a rope of light flowed between them, ran around the Source, surrounded it. They tightened the strand of light, drawing it in.

The Source saw the light closing on it. For a moment, it

seemed as though it was about to charge at Enfield. Instead, it turned its face, a snarling mass of fur and teeth, and roared. The ground shook until a tunnel opened beneath it, and the creature disappeared into the darkness.

The Evermores let go of their spell. The magic dissipated and the kemana fell silent, except for the tinkling of broken glass falling from shop windows. Winslow pushed himself to his feet. He was aching all over and trying not to feel ashamed of his defeat.

"Very well," he said. "Enough patience. It's time for us to seek some help."

CHAPTER FORTY-THREE

Fran sat nervously in the green room of the TV studio, with Gruffbar on one side of her and Elethin on the other. The elf seemed perfectly at ease, exchanging small talk with anyone who passed, casually flicking through the messages on her phone while she waited for the producer to call them in. Fran, on the other hand, was a bundle of raw nerves. She'd never been interviewed for a news site before. She wasn't sure she was ready for it. No, scratch that. She was certain that she wasn't ready for it.

"I'm going to go." Fran reached for her skates. "You're the head of PR. You can impress people on your own."

"I'm sorry, Fran, but that's not how it works." Elethin laid a hand on Fran's arm, softly but firmly, stopping her from getting away. "You're the chief executive officer of this company. If you want us to create a good impression, you have to do your bit with the media."

"But they're... It's... I'm not..."

"You'll be fine. Just look at you, the perfect young CEO."

Fran looked down at herself. She wore plain black

slacks and a white blouse. Both of them fit tighter than she usually liked. The only concession to color was her sequined boots, which Elethin had declared to be "a delightful quirk" and "just the little touch of personality that Mana Valley craves." Fran wanted to be back in her jeans and t-shirt, but she had to get through this first.

"It's time," said a man with a clipboard.

"Good luck," Gruffbar said.

"Aren't you coming with us?" Fran looked at him in alarm. Elethin was on her side in theory, but Gruffbar was someone she knew. She needed him there.

"I'll be right back here cheering you on."

The man with the clipboard led Fran and Elethin into the studio and to their seats in front of the camera. The interviewer was a wizard in a pinstripe suit and a red tie. He was having his makeup fixed as they sat and ignored them until someone started counting down. Then the makeup lady dashed away, a light flashed above a camera, the countdown went silent, and the presenter put on a big smile.

"Welcome back." He beamed into the camera. "I'm Don Karelsky, and this is the MVTV3 Morning Program. I'm joined today by the CEO of a new startup whose name made the headlines last week but whose work remains something of a mystery to the Valley. Francesca Berryman of Mana Wave Industries, thanks for joining me today."

Fran stared at the camera like a rabbit trapped in the headlights. She'd always wanted to be one of those executives she saw on TV, but now she was terrified of saying the wrong thing. Her clothes were uncomfortable, the lights were too hot, and she couldn't remember what she was supposed to be doing.

Elethin tapped her foot with one toe, enough to remind her to open her mouth.

"Um, hi," Fran managed.

"With Ms. Berryman is an industry veteran, although one who's been out of the limelight since her days at the infamous Nuada Industries, Mana Wave's director of public relations, Elethin Tannerin."

"It's a pleasure to be here, Don," Elethin said with a warm smile. "Thank you so much for having us on your show."

"The pleasure's all mine," Don said. "Now, Francesca, could you tell our audience a little about Mana Wave Industries? What's your mission? What makes you stand out from the herd of magitech startups?"

"Um, yes, um, you can call me Fran." Fran twisted her fingers together and tried her hardest to look at Don, as Elethin had told her to, instead of straight at the unblinking eyes of the cameras.

"OK, Fran." Don smiled some more. "Should I be shortening Mana Wave Industries too?"

"Only if you want to."

"Only if I want to." Don chuckled. "That's not what I hear from most companies."

"Mana Wave isn't most companies," Elethin said brightly. "I know we fit a lot of the clichés, the plucky young startup with fresh faces and big dreams looking for investors, but we're so much more than that. What Fran has built in the space of only a month is a remarkable business full of the sort of outsider talent that the Valley habitually scorns.

"We have Willens working their way up from the tunnels. Non-bipedal magicals who have to work twice as hard to use the tools you and I take for granted. Veterans with decades of experience, forced into retirement. And of course, as you hinted at earlier—" She touched a hand to the center of her chest. "—ex-cons."

"Since you brought that up..." Don leaned forward, and it seemed to Fran that he was almost hypnotized by Elethin's beauty, shifting in his seat to be a fraction closer to her. "Given your involvement in the Nuada affair, why should any investor trust their money to a company with you on the board?"

"I could give you all sorts of answers." Elethin laughed lightly. "Because I've served my time. Because everyone deserves a chance for redemption. Because we all know how much scrutiny will be on me. Ultimately, answers about me aren't what you need to hear because this story isn't about me. It's about Fran."

Elethin laid a hand on Fran's shoulder. "It's about her ideas, her vision, and her incredible gift for combining magic and technology. Isn't that right, Fran?"

Fran smiled. Perhaps Elethin had her hypnotized as well, or perhaps it was the power of hearing someone say such nice things about her, but suddenly she believed in herself, believed that she should be there, believed that this was her moment to shine.

"I wouldn't say that it's about me," she said. "It's about the whole team and about what we're creating."

"What is it that you're creating?" Don asked.

"It's a new magitech power source, and all the devices we'll make along the way to prove its value. A flying carpet. A 3D film projector with magic as well as pictures and sounds. Our take on magical phones, sending smells as well as spells."

Elethin gave Fran's shoulder the tiniest squeeze, and she paused for a moment, giving Don and his crew time to laugh. Hopefully, the viewers at home would do the same.

"I'm not saying that everything we make will be a winner. We have a lot of ideas, and some of them are pretty out there. Sometimes it takes unexpected ideas to transform people's lives.

"When I met our director of hardware, she was creating a machine to teach people sign language. Sure, that's not useful for everyone, but it could hugely improve the lives of deaf people and those working with them. Our director of software has a relentless focus on assisting under-represented magical groups.

"We're going to come up with devices that make the world better. Of course, we're going to come up with some fun ones too. We're going to be a fountain of new ideas. Ultimately, our devices are going to be grounded in one core, solid product: the battery that will power them all, and that can power the rest of Mana Valley."

"Some big ideas there." Don winked at the camera. "We've heard big ideas before. You first came to attention when one of your board members was arrested buck naked in the street. Is that the impression you want to present to the world?"

Fran could see Elethin preparing to answer, but this

was her moment, and if someone was going to fight for her company, it was going to be her.

"I skate around the house," she said. "Our main programmer types with his paws. We're currently running our top tests in the basement of a carpet shop. Yes, one of our staff got naked and arrested by the Silver Griffins, who released him when they realized their mistake.

"You want conventional? Invest in Philgard. They're doing solid work. If you want to invest in people who might surprise you, then come invest in Mana Wave."

"There you go, ladies and gentlemen." Don turned to the camera. "A bold mission, a quirky chief, and a staff born outside the box. Do you think Mana Wave is a company with a future? Our lines are open now, and we'll be taking your calls right after this break."

The lights above the cameras went out, and Don snapped his fingers at the makeup woman. Elethin stood and gestured for Fran to do the same.

"Shouldn't we be here for the questions?" Fran asked.

"Never answer questions you haven't prepared for," Elethin said. "Especially when they'll taint the memory of such a fine performance."

She led Fran away, back toward the green room.

"So I did well?" Fran asked.

"For your first time? Fantastic. We need to work on your presentation, but I couldn't ask for better material to work with. Next time let's have you wear the skates. I think that quirk is going to become our brand."

Gruffbar was waiting for them in the green room, a half-drunk cup of coffee in his hand.

"That was great," he said. "Just what we needed. Well done, Fran."

"Just Fran?" Elethin arched an eyebrow.

"When you've gone a full month without trying to kill me, you can have some praise."

"I promise, my homicidal days are behind me. Cross my heart."

Elethin waved in front of her chest, but Fran noticed that the other one was twitching behind her back, sparks of magic flashing as she cast a spell.

Without taking his eyes off her, Gruffbar took a sip from his cup. He grimaced. Something green was clinging to his lip.

"How did this turn into runny mold?" He peered into the cup. Then he looked at Elethin with a flash of anger. "This was you, wasn't it?"

"We're colleagues now," she said with a vicious smile. "I'm not going to try to kill you. That doesn't mean we're even yet."

CHAPTER FORTY-FOUR

Smokey paced restlessly around the meeting room, straightening seats and fluffing cushions with his paws. He'd made sure to arrive good and early this time, just in case. After all, he'd been on the news, shouting about the cause. Sure, he'd done it in dwarf form, naked and screaming and covered in ice, while being arrested by the Silver Griffins, but it had to count for something, right? Any publicity was good publicity.

Except that last time, his publicity had brought jokers and the bad kind of trolls, one of whom had been an actual troll. Was he going to get his heart broken again?

He jumped up onto the refreshment table and checked the biscuits for the third time. Maybe he could have a small saucer of milk to calm his nerves. Except that all the milk they had here was dairy, which would play havoc with a grown cat's bowels, and that was no way to start a meeting. He should write an angry email to the people who ran the burrow, point out to them that their catering was biased against all sorts of people, from vegans to kitten shifters.

Or maybe he should ask nicely. Sometimes all people needed was a little explanation.

He took his seat on a stool at the front of the room and waited. The clock ticked around, its hands counting off the minutes to meeting time and past it. So much for publicity, good or bad. Smokey sank despondently into his cushion. The meeting was going to be a bust again.

Footsteps sounded in the lobby, probably one of the people who lived upstairs returning to their apartment. Except that the footsteps were heading straight toward Smokey's meeting room. He raised his head, not quite allowing himself to believe.

Fran poked her head around the door and peered in, then waved at him. "It is the right place? Hi, Smokey!"

She walked in, carrying her roller skates and her backpack, glittery boots shining in the glow of the room's neon light. Singar came behind her, looking around curiously, then Bart, who smiled and waved. Elethin stooped slightly to get through the doorway, disdain creeping out around the edges of her forced smile. Gruffbar brought up the rear, like a teacher on a school trip, following his students to ensure no one wandered off and got lost. He gave Smokey the smallest of nods before taking a seat with the rest.

"Sorry we're late," Fran said. "The traffic was, like, totally snarled up around the TV studio, something to do with an overturned troll cart. Then we had to pick these guys up from Worn Threads, and there were roadworks in the student district, and… Well, we're here now!"

She smiled brightly and gave a big thumbs-up.

Smokey looked at them with narrowed eyes. He'd had

quite enough of being taunted recently. He wasn't up for being mocked by his colleagues too. Or worse yet, subjected to their curiosity, tourists come to watch how the other half lived.

"You know that this is a meeting for non-bipeds, right?" he said sharply. "You lot all have two legs full-time."

"We know," Fran said. "You've shown us that there are things we didn't know, things about how we automatically set up stuff in the world, the way we don't build for people who have lots of legs or are bigger, or smaller, or, like, have tentacles or something. I don't know. I'm new to this."

"That is very clear."

"Right, so, we want to learn. Just because we didn't know about these things doesn't mean they didn't matter. Now that we do know, we have no excuses, so they matter to us. We want to help, and that starts with learning about how much we don't know." She glanced at Bart. "That's it, right?"

Elethin sighed and shook her head. "The woman was so clear and coherent on television. I feared it wouldn't last."

Gruffbar kicked the elf in the foot, and she glared at him.

"Do you know how much these shoes cost, beard stain?"

"Fran's right," Bart said a little too loudly. "We want to learn more and to make the world better. I've never been an activist before, but I rather like the idea. I've seen young people marching and making protest art and doing civil disobedience, and I could still get arrested for a good cause."

Smokey pressed a paw against his eyes.

"So you're here because, what, you want to feel young again? Or it's easier than reading a book?" He sighed. "I'm trying to do something serious here."

"We're trying to support you," Singar said. "So stop being a jerk, accept that good things happen, and get this meeting started."

Smokey stood glaring at her, his back arched and tail on end. Still, she was right. This wasn't the time to get hissy. He had people in his meeting for once, and even if they weren't the people he'd hoped to reach, it was a start. His colleagues had turned up for him.

No, not only his colleagues. His friends.

"All right. If you're here to learn, we should start with the basics. A lot of the time, people talk about non-bipeds' problems as if they're our fault, or because of something wrong with us, as if the solution is for everyone to become human-shaped.

"But if society can't accommodate all the people living in it, the problem is with society. It's about structural change, from architecture to education to encouraging simple consideration. Let's start with…"

His words trailed off as more footsteps approached the room, heavier this time. There was a *hiss* of scales scraping across the floor, and a large winged lizard lumbered into the room.

"I'm late, aren't I?" she asked as she climbed up onto a row of chairs and flopped down on her belly. "Sorry, the skies are heaving this evening, and some idiots started buzzing me with camera drones. Like I don't have anything better to do than feature in an art school documentary about the wonders of the skies."

With a claw like a knife blade, she picked a piece of plastic rotor from between her teeth and flicked it across the room. It landed perfectly in the bin. "They won't be doing that anymore."

"You are so cool," Fran whispered, wide-eyed. "Is it all right for me to say that?"

"Of course." The lizard flexed her wings. "I am awesome."

"It's Vaudrek, right?" Smokey asked. The lizard nodded. "After last time, I didn't think you'd come back."

Vaudrek shrugged. The movement made her wings sway, and the scales ripple along her back.

"I'm curious. You weren't the stupidest person in that meeting."

"That wasn't a high bar to cross."

"No. Let's see how you do tonight." She winked lazily at the others, then waved a talon at Smokey. "Tell me how society oppresses me and what we're going to do about it. I want to see if you still make sense."

Smokey cleared his throat and sat up straight, forepaws planted in front of him, looking out across the room. His friends were smiling at him, and his recruit was watching him with curiosity. He finally had the group he'd dreamed of, even if it wasn't quite how he'd pictured it. Sure, they weren't doing anything yet, but they would get there. First came education, then came action.

"You won't be surprised to hear that I've been thinking about shops," he said, and for the first time let himself smile about his misadventure with the Griffins. "About how and why they fail on accessibility when in theory it should be in their financial interests to improve everyone's ability to buy things.

"Some of the answers are obvious, but they point at deeper issues, so it's worth talking about them and about the barriers we face to instigating change. That starts with —" A *beeping* interrupted him. "For crying out loud, are they testing the fire alarm again? No one warned me."

He looked around, but the lights that usually accompanied the alarm weren't going off, and now that he thought about it, the sound wasn't the same as usual. In fact, it didn't seem to be coming from the ceiling but his audience.

Singar pulled a small box from her pocket. The sound became clearer. A red light was flashing on the top of the box.

"Shit," she said.

"So that's how seriously you're treating this?" Smokey snapped. "Come along to support me, but only until something more interesting comes up?"

"It's the alarm I set at Worn Threads." Singar tapped the box. "Someone's messing with our prototype."

"Oh!" Smokey leaped down off his seat. "In that case, meeting adjourned. Sorry about this, Vaudrek, but it's an emergency. I have to help my friends."

"Not a problem," Vaudrek said. "It means more post-meeting biscuits for me."

She slid off her seats and across the floor to the refreshment table while the board of Mana Wave Industries rushed out the door.

"Smokey?" Vaudrek called after them.

The shifter turned and looked back. "Yes?"

"Same time next week?"

CHAPTER FORTY-FIVE

Gail always enjoyed cashing out at the end of the day. It didn't matter that Worn Threads very seldom made sales in cash anymore or that some days they didn't make any sales at all. It was the ritual of it that soothed her—emptying the register, downloading the digital transaction roll, checking sets of numbers to make sure they matched up. It was like a sort of spell that transformed the working day into the evening.

Raulo emerged between the heaped rolls of carpet, a notebook in his hand, whistling as he strolled down the shop.

"I think we should get more of that luxury deep pile carpet with the dirt-repelling enchantment," he said. "Some people like not having to clean."

"Everyone likes not having to clean," Gail said. "That's why our basement's such a mess."

"And our living room, our kitchen, and pretty much every part of our lives that isn't for customers."

"Good point. I wonder if we can get our apartment enchanted to tidy itself?"

A bell *tinkled* as the door to the shop was pushed open.

"Sorry, we're closed for the day," Gail called. "Come back tomorrow, and we'll cater to all your carpeting needs."

"We're not here for the carpet," said the gnome who stood in the doorway, holding the door open with a hand that was missing two fingers.

A witch and a wizard walked in past her, silver-haired and with remarkably similar faces, dressed in loose black clothes. An elf with a scar on his cheek followed them. A spirit emerged from the shadows, its face pale and its body swathed in gray rags that faded into the air around it. An icy chill swept through the store.

"I recognize you." Gail drew her wand. "You're the gnome who tried to steal that mirror."

"You can see what's in front of your face," the gnome replied. "You really should pay attention to what's behind you."

"I'm not falling for that." Gail raised her wand.

"Suit yourself."

Ghostly hands gripped Gail's shoulders. She tried to turn her head, but icy magic had hold of her, freezing her in place. One of the hands knocked the wand from between her fingers, and it rolled away between the carpet stacks.

"Get away from her!" Raulo shouted, pulling out his wand and aiming it at the spirit standing behind his wife.

"Really?" The gnome's fingers sparkled as she cast a spell at Raulo. "Is that what you want?"

For a moment, Raulo's eyes went blank, then he smiled.

"Of course not," he said. "We're always happy to see you and happy to help. What can I do for you today? New carpets, perhaps? A cup of coffee? Or would you like the money from the register? There isn't much, we mostly take electronic payments now, but I could arrange a bank transfer."

"Tempting, but we're more interested in the contents of your basement."

"The machines?" Raulo asked. "You should've said so. We don't want those, so it's no sacrifice. Although it might be a little difficult to get them out. I think the original factory owner bricked the access up after installing them. Perhaps I could hire a digger to break the wall open and some trucks to carry them away?"

"That won't be necessary. We're here for the mirror."

"Well, we'll still need to make a hole. That thing is nearly the size of the wall. It'll never fit up the stairs. Unless you're happy to take it in pieces, in which case I'll go grab a sledgehammer."

"Not that mirror. The little one."

"Little one?"

"The one that witch had down here." The gnome frowned at Raulo. "Don't you pay any attention to what's happening in your building?"

"Not really. Gail's the organized one. I just like to say yes, don't I, honey?"

He smiled at Gail, who stayed rigidly still, frozen in place and desperately wishing that her husband would find the wits to fight back against the intruders.

"Locked." The elf rattled the door at the back of the room.

"Oh, yes, that nice Willen installed some new locks for us," Raulo said.

"Should I break it down?" The elf flexed his muscles.

"No need." Raulo ducked under the counter. "The keys are around here somewhere, I'm sure. Let me see, keys, keys, keys, where do we keep keys…"

The pale-haired witch leaned across the counter to whisper to Gail.

"Seriously, this is the best you could find? I'm sure there are better options out there. We can get rid of him for you if you want. Very reasonable fees, no body to be found."

Inside her head, Gail was screaming, but there was nothing she could do. A single tear seeped from the corner of her eye and froze as it touched the frost on her cheek.

"Here!" Raulo emerged with a bundle of keys and bustled down the shop. "It'll be one of these." He pushed past the elf and started trying keys in the lock. "At least, I think it will. Though now I look at them, these might be the old keys. Is that a problem?"

"Enough!" The elf kicked the door with all his strength. There was a splintering of wood, and the door *banged* back against the wall, shaking loose a shower of dust and several spiderwebs.

Unnoticed by the intruders, a sensor on the wall blinked. Across town, in the activist meeting, Singar's alarm sounded.

The magicals strode down the stairs into the basement. In front of the wall-mounted mirror, a device with a mirror at its base sat on the floor. Crystals, runes, and pieces of circuitry dotted its edges. A framework of slender metal rods rose from it.

Next to that, another mirror lay on the floor with a battery pack attached to its side. An inch-thick magical haze hung above it. The air around that mirror looked like breath emerging on a winter's day, a swirling, frozen cloud.

The spirits raced across the room and peered into the frozen mirror. They pawed at its surface, trying to release their companion trapped inside.

"Where is it?" the gnome asked. "The other mirror?"

"You mean that one?" Raulo pointed at the frozen mirror. "Or the one in the cage?"

"The other one."

Raulo laughed. "It's on the wall, silly. Can't you see it?"

"The other one!" The gnome grabbed Raulo and, with surprising strength, flung him against the wall. His head hit the brickwork, and he fell unconscious to the floor.

The elf, witch, and wizard gathered around the mirrors.

"This must be it." The elf peered at the prototype's frame. "You could summon a portal inside that framework."

"No, that's not it," the gnome snapped.

"I think you're only saying that." The elf looked at the gnome. "You brought us here in case there was trouble, but now you want to take it to Handar by yourself, so you won't have to share the pay or the kudos."

"Don't be an idiot. We had a deal."

"I'm not being an idiot. I can see the portal machine when it's right in front of my eyes, and now I'm going to take it to him myself."

The elf grabbed hold of the framework. As he did so,

his fingers passed through the gap between some of the rods. A sound like someone slurping a milkshake through a straw and a blast of wind raced through the room. With a flash of magic, the containment unit sucked him inside the expanding frame.

"What the…" The elf tried to push his way out, but he couldn't move his arms or his legs. "I'm trapped. Get me out of this thing."

"Interesting." The gnome stepped around the prototype, carefully not touching it. She looked from it to the other mirror and the spirits pawing at its frosted surface. "Two traps. There must be something of value down here."

"Yes, me, now let me out!"

"Shut up, you idiot." The gnome pulled out the detection device that Handar had given to her. There were faint signs of green on one side of its pale surface but nothing substantial. "Interference. Something's stopping me from finding the mirror, but it must be around here somewhere."

"A detection ritual," the silver-haired witch said. "That will cut through the fog and find it, especially if we use your device in the ritual."

"I like rituals," her twin said with a sinister smile.

"All right," the gnome said. "Come on, you two."

The spirits glared at him.

"Not until our sibling is released," one of them hissed.

"This first. If we succeed, you can ask our employers to break your sibling out as a reward."

"Very well. But do not think that we will obey you in future just because we have cooperated now."

The spirits and the gnome stood in a triangle while the

witch drew chalk runes on the floor around them. The wizard dragged the unconscious Raulo over and put him in the middle, next to the detection device.

"What did you do that for?" the gnome asked.

"Blood sacrifice." The wizard grinned and pulled out a curved knife. "All the best rituals have one."

The gnome rolled her eyes. "Fine, but if you get blood on my clothes, you're paying the dry cleaning bill."

The witch joined the circle, and the five of them spread their arms wide. They started chanting, weaving their magic together, combining their power. The Philgard Industries detection device cracked open, and its magic spilled out.

An image began to form in the air between them. A face and a map, too blurry for the route or the person to be seen.

"Needs more power," the wizard said, raising his knife above Raulo. "Time to let the blood flow!"

CHAPTER FORTY-SIX

Fran ran through the doorway down to the basement. She smelled magic in the air and heard voices chanting. Someone shouted about blood. She took the stairs three at a time, lost her footing, tumbled down, and landed on her ass in a shower of dust. She saw a blade held above the prostrate Raulo and didn't stop to take anything else in. There was no time to think, just act.

She opened her mouth, flung her hands wide, and sent a wave of magical sound across the basement. It caught the five magicals standing in the chalk circle and flung them back. The knife spun through the air, hit the floor, and slid under the machines, where every loose thing in the room seemed to end up.

"You!" Fran said as she saw the gnome getting to her feet.

"You," the gnome snarled in reply. "I'm going to mess you up this time."

The two of them advanced on each other, flinging magic as they went. The gnome turned aside a bolt of blinding light from Fran, then flung an ice spell, which Fran shattered with a sonic blast. The air filled with power as spells collided and destroyed one another.

The other magicals advanced, but now Fran's friends were with her, charging into the room.

One of the spirits rushed at Fran, aiming to overwhelm her while she was distracted. Smokey leaped at it, claws outstretched and teeth bared, hissing like a feral beast. His claws tore through its gray rags and to the ghostly body beneath. The spirit shrieked in pain and drew back, raising its clawed hands.

Bart flung himself at the other spirit and went straight through it.

"How did you hurt it?" he called as the spirit grabbed hold of him and flung him into the air.

"Cats," Smokey replied. "Lots of spirits are vulnerable to cats."

Bart landed with a *thud*. His back hurt and his head was spinning. This was worse than falling off his skates.

"I can't turn into a cat," he groaned.

"Then try magic instead."

As the spirit descended on him, Bart filled his hands with power. It grabbed for him, and he rolled aside, then snatched hold of its wrist. Magic crackled and almost gave way, but he had hold of the spirit and pulled it over. He was trapped underneath, but at least he'd started to fight back.

The wizard had drawn another curved knife, the twin of the one he'd tried to sacrifice Raulo with. He advanced on Fran with a look of malevolent glee.

"Oh no, you don't!"

Gruffbar leaped off the stairs straight at the wizard, knocking him to the floor. The two of them rolled in the dirt, the dwarf clinging on tight, the wizard trying to shake him off. The wizard lashed out with the knife, but Gruffbar ducked under it, head-butted his opponent, and twisted the wizard's wrist while he was stunned. The knife fell from his fingers.

"Now it's a fair fight." Gruffbar pulled his fist back. "Or it would be if we were both dwarves."

At the side of the room, the silver-haired witch stood with her wand drawn, evaluating the chaos, deciding where best to intervene. Her brother needed help, but much as she loved him, he wasn't the most useful person there. She should take Fran down, freeing up the gnome. Between them, they would easily overcome these ridiculous civilians with their cheap tricks and their amateur fighting style.

What did that gray-haired gnome think he was doing, pulling the spirit down on top of him where it could strangle him with its freezing hands? No need for her help there. She raised her wand, ready to join in.

"Do they not have fashion where you come from?" Elethin looked the witch up and down. "I know black never goes out of style, but it's very seldom in. You should consider a wardrobe that doesn't scream stagehand or second-rate hood."

The witch narrowed her eyes and turned to face the elf.

"Fashion," she spat. "Who cares about fashion? Power is all that counts."

"Oh, dear." Elethin shook her head. "Do you really think that clothes don't have power? They send a message, and communication is power. For example, your clothes slump to the left, telling me that's your weak side and where my friends should attack."

The witch looked down. Her clothes didn't look any different on the left. When she looked back up, Elethin had closed the gap between them and drawn back her fist. It collided with the witch's face, and she staggered back, clutching her nose.

"You lying bitch!" the witch shrieked.

"Lies, from a public relations officer?" Elethin clasped a hand to her chest in mock shock. "Whoever would've thought it?"

While the others grappled with the magical attackers, Singar ran to the prototype. It had already captured one of their opponents, judging by the elf folded up inside the frame, but it could do much more. This was the smart way to win and to prove what their technology could achieve.

"Keep them busy," Singar shouted. "I've got a plan."

Wishing that she'd brought her tool kit, she pulled the switchblade out from between the folds of her skin and used its tip to start unfastening screws.

"Let me out," the elf said to her. "I'll make it worth your while."

"Yeah, right. Like I've never heard that one before."

She pulled out a fistful of wires and set to work.

Across the room, Smokey had backed the spirit into a corner.

"Good kitty," the spirit hissed, reaching out a hand so thin it was almost skeletal. "We can be friends, yes?"

"I'll give you good kitty." Smokey clawed the hand, and the spirit shrank back, ice crystals running from scratches in what could've been its skin. Then he leaped onto its head and dug in all four claws.

The wizard had finally wriggled out from under Gruffbar. He grabbed the dwarf and slammed him against the wall, feet dangling in the air. Gruffbar tried to kick, but the wizard was tall and kept him at arms' length, too far away to get a good blow in.

"Maybe I'll sacrifice you," the wizard said. "You're so much older than that stupid carpet seller. Your blood will be richer, the power greater, the effect far more impressive. Yes, I think that's what I'll do."

"At least I'll die in a good cause." Gruffbar raised his hands.

"Really?" The wizard tilted his head. "Is that what this world has turned you into, the sort of wretch who would simply die to buy his friends a few more seconds of life?"

"Not if I don't have to." Gruffbar spun his hands around, one hitting the wizard's forearm from below, the other from above. There was a *crunch* as the bone snapped.

The wizard howled and dropped Gruffbar, who landed firmly on his feet.

"You think that hurts?" Gruffbar said as the wizard clutched his broken arm. "Try this."

Gruffbar head-butted the wizard in the crotch.

At the side of the room, the silver-haired witch had brought her wand up and was flinging spells at Elethin. The elf's hands darted from side to side, sketching wards in the air, deflecting spells harmlessly against the walls and floor.

"How are you doing this?" the witch demanded. "You're not this powerful. I can tell."

"I told you, fashion matters. On this occasion, that fashion is an Okorafor and LeGuin spell-silk blouse woven to enhance my defensive magic. When elves select clothes, we select them for style and for more than that."

Elethin caught a spell between her fingers and flicked it back at the witch.

"Help!" Bart shouted from his corner of the room. The spirit he'd tried to grapple with had him in an arm lock up against the wall. Its free hand was on his shoulder, sucking the heat and the magic out of him.

He felt a terrible cold closing in, his arm too numb to use, the other one heading toward uselessness. He tried to kick the spirit, but it was hard to kick backward, and there was no magic in his feet. Suddenly, being young and adventurous didn't feel so appealing. As the threat of death closed in, he longed for the sweet tedium of retirement.

"Why are you doing this?" Fran asked as she exchanged spell attacks with the two-fingered gnome. "Why do you want my mirror so badly?"

"I don't know," the gnome said. "I don't care. My employer is the one with an agenda. I'm just in it for the pay."

"You'd kill people for pay?"

"Everyone has their price."

"That's not true."

"Spend long enough in business, and you'll see."

One of the gnome's spells seemed to go wide, but as Fran raised her hands to cast magic of her own, the spell came back around, hitting her from behind. She was knocked to the floor, light and sound fizzling from around her hands. The gnome stood over her, booted foot raised and pulsing with magical power.

"I'm going to stamp you out," the gnome said. "Then I'm taking your stupid mirror, and I'm selling it to someone rich enough to set me up for years. Isn't capitalism great?"

"Who hired you?" Fran asked. "Why is any of this happening?"

The gnome laughed. "Why would I ever tell you that?"

"Got it!" Singar shouted so loud that everyone looked up. The Willen stood next to the containment unit with a bundle of wires in her hand, each one with a crystal on the end. She spread them between her fingers so that each crystal pointed at one of the intruders and flicked a switch.

There was a flash of magical light. For a moment, the whole room seemed to be full of mirrors, ones that only reflected the intruders. Then the light vanished.

Fran blinked. The gnome wasn't standing over her anymore. In fact, none of the intruders seemed to be in the room. But the containment unit had grown, and now that she looked at it, she saw a tangle of magical bodies and ghostly spirits. The gnome glared out at her from one corner with her face pressed to the frame as if against invisible glass.

"It worked!" Fran said excitedly.

"It did." Singar looked worriedly at the controls. "But it's not going to last." Sparks burst from the corner of the containment unit. "We have to get them into something bigger, fast."

"I've got the control software." Smokey pulled a tablet from his harness and started typing rapidly. "I can adjust it to use the wall mirror. How fast can you rig the hardware?"

"Let's hope it's fast enough."

Singar and Fran started frantically attaching crystals and pieces of circuit board to the mirror, while Elethin and Gruffbar scratched runes along its edges, imitating those on the overcrowded prototype.

"It's going to burst." Bart watched as rods buckled, and electrics sparked.

"Then hold it together!" Singar shouted. "Use your magic. We need more time."

Bart pressed his hands against the rods and let his magic flow. If he could hold this up a little longer, maybe they would be all right. Maybe...

Singar grabbed a cable and ran it from the containment unit to a jack that Fran had screwed onto the mirror. She slammed the end of the cable in, magical sparks flying as the connection was made.

"Ready?" Singar called.

"Ready." Smokey plugged his tablet into the tangle of wires.

"Go!"

The frame of the prototype bulged and buckled, about to overwhelm Bart's hold.

Smokey tapped the screen.

A surge of magic sucked the trapped intruders from the containment unit, down the cables, and into the mirror. They appeared, two-dimensional figures hammering against the glass, silently screaming to be released.

"We did it!" Fran exclaimed. "The prototype worked!"

"It did." Bart held up a handful of buckled and broken rods. "But it's not going to work anymore."

CHAPTER FORTY-SEVEN

Fran climbed onto a chair at the front of the room and cupped her hands around her mouth. Behind her, balloons bounced in front of a banner reading "CONGRATULATIONS ON YOUR NEW BUSINESS!" She'd found the banner in Silicon Valley, possibly the only place on all of Earth and Oriceran where people regularly needed a thing like that. Behind her, a sheet hung over the wall-length mirror.

"Hey, everyone!" she shouted.

Hardly anyone looked around. Between her coworkers, their friends, and some family members, the people Raulo and Gail had invited, and of course, Vaudrek from Smokey's support group, the basement of Worn Threads was jumping. They were all talking, someone was singing, and the music playing in the background added to the noise.

Fran put some Evermore magic into her hands to amplify the sound waves, then tried again. "Hey, everyone!" she shouted. "Over here!"

This time they turned to look. Singar switched the music off, and silence fell.

"First of all, thanks for coming," Fran said. "It's great to see so many of you here. Thank you for your contributions to the cocktail bar. We couldn't have done that without you."

She pointed at a table on the side of the room piled with assorted spirits and mixers. The crowd cheered again, and most of them drank.

"Before I go any further, I'd like to thank Gail and Raulo for having us here," Fran continued. "Not only this evening, but on a more long-term basis. It was incredibly kind of them to offer, but then they're incredibly kind people. This might not look like much of an office and workshop yet, but we'll get there. Hey, we've already moved in some of our stuff."

She gestured at a corner where they'd piled prototypes and spare parts. There was Singar's sign language machine, Fran's rebuilt flying carpet, and several of their attempts to rebuild the mirror containment unit, none of which ever seemed to work right.

"Obviously, we'll be sad to leave the Blazing Bean behind—" She winked at Cam. "—but it's safe to say that we'll be back there when we need caffeine, which is about every twenty minutes.

"Most of my life I've dreamed of running my own business, and thanks to some of the fabulous people here, I now have a chance. Sure, it's a weird business, one with spells and sorcery books, where we have to trap evil spirits to clear up our workspace, but I wouldn't have it any other way. Dealing with crazy things together is part of what makes us who we are and what makes us a team. We're going to achieve great things, and I hope you're all here to help us celebrate every one of them. Here's to Mana Wave Industries!"

"Mana Wave Industries!" everyone cheered.

Fran jumped down from the chair, and the music restarted.

"I'm so proud of you." Josie hugged her friend. "Who would've believed when we were in college that this is where you'd end up?"

"This isn't where I end up. It's a step along the way, but thank you for believing in me. I couldn't have gotten here without you."

"Aw, that's sweet. More importantly, now that you're out of the coffee shop, are you going to ask barista guy out?"

Fran blushed. "I couldn't. How would I cope if he said no and I could never go get my favorite cakes again?"

"He's here, isn't he? He's not going to say no."

"He might, and I'm not risking it."

Josie groaned. "Fine. But when you finally get together, and you wish you hadn't wasted all this time, don't come grumbling to me about it."

"Not even a little bit?"

They both laughed. "Not even a little bit."

Fran went over to the improvised cocktail bar and mixed herself a drink. Bart was there with a shaker in his hand, carefully reading through a recipe book.

"I thought I might take up cocktail making," he said. "It looks quite fun."

"You know you aren't retired anymore, right?" Fran

asked. "You don't have to keep hunting for hobbies to fill your time."

"I suppose." Bart poured gin. "You only live once. Better to try these things while I still have the energy."

"Can I ask you something about the finances?"

"Tonight?"

"Yeah." Fran glanced around to make sure no one overheard. "How badly off are we?"

"About where I'd expect a startup to be, which is to say that we're barely scraping by." Bart set down the cocktail shaker. "Most of the development money from the FBI has gone into building the containment unit, the rest on parts for building prototypes. I know how much of your savings you've spent on equipment and our coffee bills. Even sharing the costs of tonight, things are tough."

"So we need a product we can sell?" Fran asked. "Something easy and cheap to make money quick?"

"No. Then you'd be wasting your time on something derivative, which won't help in the long term. We need investors, people who recognize the value of your designs and who will give us money in return for a share of the profits later. Finding them is the next big step."

"Oh!" Fran smiled. "You've thought this through."

"It's my job." Bart picked up the shaker again. "Being broke is rubbish, but we'll get past this, and in years to come we'll laugh about when we worked in the basement of a carpet shop."

A rush of movement made Fran look up. To her surprise, she saw her mother coming down the stairs.

"Mom?" Fran turned to Irene, a glass in her hand. "You made it! I thought you said you were busy."

"I need you to come with me," Irene said breathlessly, grabbing her daughter by the wrist.

"Mom, let go. You're hurting me."

"Please, Francesca, now isn't the time to be stubborn. Come along."

"I'm not going anywhere. This is my party for my new business. You remember? I sent you an invite?"

"Your party?" Irene looked around. "Of course, yes, but this is urgent. Now come."

"Why should I? What's going on?"

Irene pressed her hand to her forehead, fingers with chewed nails pressing against the wrinkles of her brow.

"I should have talked about this with you more," she said. "Prepared you. But I didn't want it to come to this, and I'm sorry, but your little party isn't so important next to any of it."

"My little party? This is my business! It's the proudest moment in my life. All my friends are here. Why would I go when you won't even tell me what's wrong?"

"Fine. Something's loose on the other side, something powerful and dangerous and connected to the kemanas, connected to all of our power. Now some people are coming, and they're going to seem like the sort of people you should work with, but—"

A shimmering circle of magic appeared in the air next to Irene and Fran. Some of the nearby party-goers cheered, thinking that this was part of the entertainment.

"Oh." Irene sagged. "They're here."

The shimmer turned into a portal. It wasn't like most portals that Fran had seen, but the magic glow reminded her of her power. It was Evermore magic.

Three people stepped out of the portal. In the lead was a man who appeared to be middle-aged, with gray dotted through his dark brown hair and a few wrinkles around his eyes. He held himself with the relaxed confidence Fran had seen in the best business leaders, the conviction of someone used to being listened to.

Next to him and slightly behind was a younger man with blond hair and a serious expression. He wore a tight t-shirt that showed off his muscles and had a row of potion bottles attached to his belt. Last was a dark-haired woman with a hiking stick, which she carried more like a weapon than a mobility aid. She stood back respectfully as if she was only there to observe and defend.

"Good evening, Irene," the older man said. "And this must be Francesca?"

"Fran." She held out her hand. "Welcome to my party. Grab a drink. Have a dance. One quick question first. Who on Oriceran are you?"

The man chuckled. It was a warm, reassuring sound. Behind him, the portal disappeared, and the rest of the party-goers turned away, deciding that there was better entertainment to elsewhere.

"My name is Winslow. I'm an Evermore. Do you know what that means?"

"Ancient witches and wizards protecting the world, and I'm one of you."

"Not really witches and wizards, but close enough."

"Cool. Well, you're all welcome. It's a big day for us. This is our new office."

"So I hear." Winslow looked around. His eyes settled on

the flying carpet in the corner. "You broke your word, Irene."

"Be glad I did," Irene snapped.

Winslow looked at her, and Fran expected an angry response. Instead, he gave a placid smile. It was like watching a Buddhist monk in a martial arts movie, the kind of guy who was perfectly still, but you could sense his power beneath the surface.

"I hear that you've created a containment device," he said to Fran. "Something that can trap powerful magicals."

"Totally," Fran said. "Oh, except I'm not supposed to tell people that!"

"Don't worry. I have a friend at the FBI. He told me all about it, and I think it could be what we need. You see, Fran, a monster has broken loose on Earth, and if we don't contain it, then it could destroy all the magic we've preserved there. We have to recapture it to save the kemanas and protect the magicals on Earth until the gates open again in thousands of years."

"Wow, that sounds like a really big deal."

"It is. It's such a big deal that it has to be dealt with quietly to keep people from panicking. Do you understand that?"

"Sure." Fran nodded. "This is, like, another of those need-to-know situations. You're going to ask me to sign an NDA."

Winslow laughed. "No need to sign anything. I'll trust you on your word as an Evermore." He flicked Irene a pointed look, then brought his attention back to Fran. "But I do need to use your containment unit right now."

"Sorry, but you can't." Fran shrugged apologetically.

"Even if we hadn't promised it the FBI first, we got into a fight with some guys who were trying to steal, like, this other magical mirror. It's a whole thing, but the short version is, the prototype unit doesn't work anymore."

"Well then," Winslow said, "it's time we got to work rebuilding it."

Get sneak peeks, exclusive giveaways, behind the scenes content, and more. PLUS you'll be notified of special **one day only fan pricing** on new releases.

Sign up today to get free stories.

Visit: https://marthacarr.com/read-free-stories/

AUTHOR NOTES - MARTHA CARR

NOVEMBER 6, 2021

There are a billion different people in the world. Maybe we think a lot of us are the same, but there is so much tweaking with our likes and dislikes and views of the world and things that are happening to us – we all end up being kind of different. That's good news. Keeps things interesting.

My tweaking has me always looking for a solution – and then letting it go if there's no more to do at least for now. I've done my share of belly aching in years past and frankly, nothing I liked happened. So why keep doing that one?

Then I tripped over the idea of fitting myself to life instead of constantly insisting life fit me. That last idea never worked anyway. No rewards and I wore myself out always staring at the problem. My constant thought was, if it's not fixed then there must be more to do. It never occurred to me to let go, move on and if something more pops up that I can do, circle back.

This new philosophy of the last fifteen years still leaves

room for some choices where I look up and think, "Well, I won't be doing this again." Like the time I was supposed to be buying a couch and got excited over a very expensive bench. That bench didn't last long, and I won't be doing that again. Another one is I don't do well in high rises where no one wants to talk to you in the elevators. I'm better off in a neighborhood where we have each other's phone numbers. I've learned how to let go more easily and see the very big positive in knowing what I don't like. Those answers inform the next choices – refine them.

That old philosophy of trying to figure things out all the time also had the side woe of making me afraid to take big challenges. What if I'm wrong? What if it doesn't work out? What if I don't like it? What if others don't like me? You get the idea. I can almost feel the spinning in a circle.

This past year I've been undergoing chemo at MD Anderson. The side effects have left me tired among other things. I've been constantly tweaking trying to find ways to get things done. Early in the morning? Space it out over a day? Get help with some of the more laborious stuff? There has to be a way to at least make it better.

How about trying to write at a really nice cabin in the woods? Bonus – it's a new place called Wild Rice Retreat in northern Wisconsin on the edge of Lake Superior. Turns out, wherever I go the side effects go with me. I caught on pretty quickly and did what I could and let the rest go. That made it possible to notice I was lucky enough to arrive just as the color of the leaves peaked. I spent hours walking the trail by the lake listening to the sound of the wind in the top of the trees. Amazing.

And there was yoga, and a sound bath, and a sauna, and

essential oils and a bio walk around the grounds. Plus some of the nicest people. The placc is brand, spanking new and there were a couple of days I was the only guest and it felt more like I was visiting family than staying at a retreat.

If I had ground down on trying to fix being tired and pushed through with writing till I fell asleep at the computer (which I've done a couple of times lately), I might have missed a wonderful, healing experience.

I let myself fit life and trusted, things will work out, one way or the other. They always do even if some parts of the journey are hard and take others walking alongside me to get through them. Big Thank You to all the fans, other authors, neighbors and the Offspring and Jackie who have been walking through this with me. I carry your love with me everywhere now. More adventures to follow

AUTHOR NOTES - MICHAEL ANDERLE

NOVEMBER 6, 2021

Thank you for not only reading this story, but these author notes as well!

For those who know who I am - I'll give you a short update. For those who do not know who I am, I'll add a bit 'about me' to the bottom of these notes.

Presently I am in the UAE for the Sharjah Book Fair. I spoke to a couple of classes of High School Students about self-publishing and was on a small panel that discussed technology and how it affects the future of humanity.

I was honored to be invited.

I'm lying in the hotel bed, typing these notes before we get up at 4:00 AM in the morning (here - about 5:00 PM local time back in Las Vegas the night before), and my eyes are starting to droop.

I can't let them. I desperately need to make it to the airport and get on the airplane for the 14-hour flight before I fall asleep. Otherwise, jet lag is going to be a right <redacted>.

It's five hours before take-off. I'm in Sharjah, and we

have to go to the Dubai airport. It isn't necessarily very far - but if you wait too long, you WILL get into the traffic between the two cities. I would say 'and?' But yesterday I was stuck IN the traffic, and we went nowhere. Like...Not even slowly. It was very crawl-level speed.

In short - I don't want to chance the traffic on a trip to the airport. Therefore, we leave at 4:30 AM for an 8:30 AM flight.

I hope you enjoyed this story and will check out the next one that continues the series. I'll have more author notes in these books (and basically almost all of the books I am a part of. It's a blessing and a curse that I started these author notes back in 2015 and have hundreds... getting close to a thousand... finished!

AND NOW - A LITTLE ABOUT ME

I wrote my first book *Death Becomes Her* (*The Kurtherian Gambit*) in September/October of 2015 and released it November 2, 2015. I wrote and released the next two books that same month and had three released by the end of November 2015.

So, just under six years ago.

Since then, I've written, collaborated, concepted, and/or created hundreds more in all sorts of genres.

My most successful genre is still my first, Paranormal Sci-Fi, followed quickly by Urban Fantasy. I have multiple pen names I produce under.

Some because I can be a bit crude in my humor at times or raw in my cynicism (Michael Todd). I have one I share with Martha Carr (Judith Berens, and another (not disclosed) that we use as a marketing test pen name.

In general, I just love to tell stories, and with success comes the opportunity to mix two things I love in my life.

Business and stories.

I've wanted to be an entrepreneur since I was a teenager. I was a very *unsuccessful* entrepreneur (I tried many times) until my publishing company LMBPN signed one author in 2015.

Me.

I was the president of the company, and I was the first author published. Funny how it worked out that way.

It was late 2016 before we had additional authors join me for publishing. Now we have a few dozen authors, a few hundred audiobooks by LMBPN published, a few hundred more licensed by six audio companies, and about a thousand titles in our company.

It's been a busy five plus years.

Ad Aeternitatem,

Michael Anderle

BOOKS BY MARTHA CARR

Other Series in the Oriceran Universe:

THE LEIRA CHRONICLES
CASE FILES OF AN URBAN WITCH
SOUL STONE MAGE
THE KACY CHRONICLES
MIDWEST MAGIC CHRONICLES
THE FAIRHAVEN CHRONICLES
I FEAR NO EVIL
THE DANIEL CODEX SERIES
SCHOOL OF NECESSARY MAGIC
SCHOOL OF NECESSARY MAGIC: RAINE CAMPBELL
ALISON BROWNSTONE
FEDERAL AGENTS OF MAGIC
SCIONS OF MAGIC
THE UNBELIEVABLE MR. BROWNSTONE
DWARF BOUNTY HUNTER
ACADEMY OF NECESSARY MAGIC
MAGIC CITY CHRONICLES
ROGUE AGENTS OF MAGIC

OTHER BOOKS BY JUDITH BERENS

OTHER BOOKS BY MARTHA CARR

JOIN THE ORICERAN UNIVERSE FAN GROUP ON FACEBOOK!

BOOKS BY MICHAEL ANDERLE

Sign up for the LMBPN email list to be notified of new releases and special deals!

https://lmbpn.com/email/

For a complete list of books by Michael Anderle, please visit:

www.lmbpn.com/ma-books/

CONNECT WITH THE AUTHORS

Martha Carr Social

Website: http://www.marthacarr.com

Facebook: https://www.facebook.com/groups/MarthaCarrFans/

Michael Anderle Social

Website: http://lmbpn.com

Email List: http://lmbpn.com/email/

https://www.facebook.com/LMBPNPublishing

https://twitter.com/MichaelAnderle

https://www.instagram.com/lmbpn_publishing/

https://www.bookbub.com/authors/michael-anderle

Made in the USA
Las Vegas, NV
14 December 2022